DEM♦ON'S
HEART

"Bates has created a world rich in history and originality—a perfect backdrop for an epic romance."
—R. C. HANCOCK, author of *An Uncommon Blue*

"A talented writer can convince a reader that fantasy is real; a gifted author makes it look easy from the opening scene. This was Emily Hall Bates's novel *Demon's Heart*! It's a creative story that simply doesn't stop. Intense action sequences, along with a brave and selfless hero, make this book highly addictive. Every reader who loves original, powerful fantasy will be absorbed in this compelling read."
—RACHEL MCCLELLAN, Amazon best-selling author of the Fractured Light series and *Confessions of a Cereal Mother*

"*Demon's Heart* takes the reader on a colorful adventure through lands of peasants and kings, soldiers and demons. Rustav's tragic past and his solemn destiny make his journey one of poignant self-discovery."
—ADRIENNE QUINTANA, author of *Eruption*

"Bates's style is striking and sophisticated. Her mastery of story-telling grabbed me from the beginning and still hasn't let go! *Demon's Heart* is a fantastic new fantasy that will appeal to fans of author R. K. Ryals and Rothfuss's very popular King Killer Chronicles."
—HANNAH CLARK, author of *Uncovering Cobbogoth*

EMILY H. BATES

DEMON'S HEART

SWEETWATER
BOOKS

AN IMPRINT OF CEDAR FORT, INC.
SPRINGVILLE, UTAH

ISBN 13: 978-1-4621-1515-0

Published by Sweetwater Books, an imprint of Cedar Fort, Inc.
2373 W. 700 S., Springville, UT 84663
Distributed by Cedar Fort, Inc., www.cedarfort.com

LIBRARY OF CONGRESS CATALOGING-IN-PUBLICATION DATA

Bates, Emily, 1990- author.
Demon's heart / Emily Bates.
    pages cm
Summary: When Rustav overhears that his home peninsula is to become a place of human sacrifice, he escapes only to be ensnared by the legendary tuatha who cause Rustav to realize that he, though unwilling, is the savior of the peninsula.
ISBN 978-1-4621-1515-0 (pbk. : alk. paper)
[1. Fantasy. 2. Youths' writings.] I. Title.
PZ7.B29458De 2014
[Fic]--dc23
                                2014020634

Cover design by Kristen Reeves
Cover design © 2014 by Lyle Mortimer
Edited and typeset by Melissa J. Caldwell

Printed in the United States of America

10 9 8 7 6 5 4 3 2 1

For Nathan,
my muse from St. Martinstag on

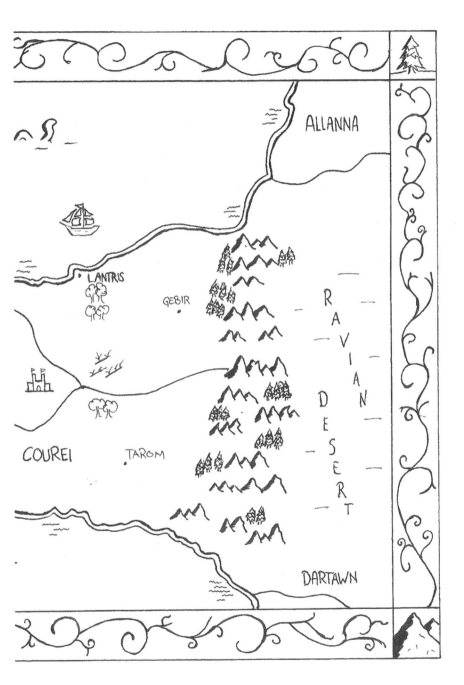

ALLANNA

LANTRIS

GEBIR

COUREI

TAROM

RAVIAN DESERT

DARTAWN

CHAPTER ONE

THE DISTANT FOREST HELD RUSTAV'S GAZE AS forcefully as the hypnotic yellow eyes of a sea serpent. Quiet as the trees might be, the sailors insisted that the mountain forest was every bit as deadly as a sea serpent's iron coils. In spite of Rustav's best efforts as a skeptic, the sailors' tales seemed to hover in the air above the ancient trees, growing more insistent with every long, pounding stride Rustav took.

His legs gave out from underneath him, sending him sprawling into the tall grass at the foot of the mountain. Time for a break. Rustav crawled away from where he had fallen, making sure he was well hidden in the grass before lying flat on his stomach with his face in the dirt. As much as it hurt to lie on his bruised ribs, it was worse to lie on his back. Three days of hard travel had done little to help it heal; as soon as anything began to scab over, the motion of running or falling or hiding cracked the wounds open, and more blood seeped into the back of his shirt. If Karstafel could see the state of his clothes . . . but Karstafel wouldn't ever see him again.

Hovering between sleep and waking, Rustav's mind

drifted back to the taverns at the port of Markuum. The rau-
cous shouts of drunken, land-starved sailors had surrounded
him, each voice telling a different tale. Alluring sea serpents,
ferocious mermaids, rabid pirates—and those were the tamer
stories. The tales that stayed with Rustav, that inspired night-
mares and set his skin crawling, were the tales of the demons.

The island demons were the loudest, the sailors said, and
Rustav was inclined to believe them. His uncle, Karstafel, had
dragged him along to the island of Burrihim on the king's
business when Rustav was only nine. All night, Rustav had
huddled on the floor of the inn, each distant shriek notching
his nerves a little higher. The next day he had nearly ended
up being sacrificed to the demons for being too curious. No,
Rustav had no doubt that the island demons were a threat.

But while the island demons had a shape, a sound, and
a violent disposition, the forest demons were nothing more
than a bodiless whisper, a shadow with nothing to cast it, a
branch moving without wind. Sure, the sailors still told stories of men disappearing into the forest and never returning,
but even the most practiced exaggerators couldn't make the
tales as gruesome as the island sacrifices. The simple truth,
Rustav suspected, was that the mountain people had been
telling tall tales of demons for ages to scare their children into
behaving, and the stories had simply been taken up by the rest
of the Courei peninsula as a way to ward off any mainland
countries that might try to attack through the mountains.

He'd find out one way or the other soon enough. He
had no doubt that Karstafel was already watching every
port and scouring the valley for him. The mountains were
his only remaining chance of escape. Dragging himself once
more to his feet, Rustav rested his eyes on a small village just

outside the forest's edge. He'd stop there and see what he could scrounge; then he would see what awaited him in the trees. *Even if there is something in there*, Rustav thought as he forced his unwilling feet into a pounding run, *it can't be any worse than the island demons.* He had eluded them; he could slip past any forest demons just as well.

He hoped.

DANTZEL ABSENTMINDEDLY BRUSHED THROUGH her long chestnut hair, staring out the window at the small garden plot next to the small mud-brick house in which she and her mother had lived for thirteen years. The tomatoes, in spite of all her attentions, were still pale and small. Even the carrots were coming up slower than usual. Dantzel sighed. The thin mountain soil was offering less and less strength to their little garden, leaving them with either less to eat or less to sell on market day—or a little of both.

If she had only had time to learn the basics of stoneworking from her father, they wouldn't have to depend so heavily on pale vegetables and puny fruits. But she had been only three when the king's Guards had come calling, taking her father to carve stone in the great castle in the valley. Dantzel closed her eyes, remembering that awful night through the blurry eyes of a toddler, the confusion and the crying and the swirling red cloaks swallowing up her father as the Guards dragged him out the door.

The garden had become her relief as well as her nemesis. Though she had inherited her mother's slight frame, years of digging, weeding, watering, and harvesting had made her strong—strong enough to hold her own against the Guards, who still came rolling through the village, eager for any opportunity to torment those who had been left behind after the great purge of the mountain village's artisans.

Withdrawing her eyes from the garden, Dantzel turned away from the window and started as she saw her mother, Anna, smiling down at her. Embarrassed, Dantzel quickly set down the hairbrush and picked up a ribbon, tying her hair back deftly.

"You know, Jeffer likes it better when your hair is down," Anna said slyly. Dantzel rolled her eyes.

"Please, Mother. I'd rather not have to think about dealing with Jeffer until absolutely necessary."

Anna's smile faded slightly. "He's a nice boy, Dantzel. He just wants to catch your eye. Can you at least be civil with him today?"

For a moment, Dantzel examined her mother's face. She had always thought her mother beautiful, and today was no exception, but Dantzel was becoming more aware of the toll that twelve years of hard work and limited means had taken. Creases lined Anna's eyes and forehead, and there was a tired slump to her shoulders, even if she tried to hide it. With a sigh, Dantzel put an arm around her mother. "If you insist," the girl said with a wry smile, squeezing her mother's shoulders. "But just because I love you."

"You're such a good daughter," Anna said, planting an exaggerated kiss on Dantzel's forehead. "Come on, now, quit dawdling. You're going to make us late for the market."

"We wouldn't want that," Dantzel said dryly. "Jeffer might miss his chance to drop a box of potatoes on his foot."

IT WAS A FORTY-MINUTE WALK TO THE MARKET-place with their cart loaded down with produce—longer than it had once taken. Their old donkey, Bella, had a harder time pulling the boxes of vegetables and berries each passing year. Nevertheless, Anna and Dantzel were among the first to arrive in the market square and begin unloading their wares in the cool of the morning. The fountain bubbling cheer-fully in the center of the square was the heart of the town. The relief surrounding the walls of the fountain, a flowing mixture of fantastical creatures and legendary characters, had been carved when the town was first founded. Dantzel's father had loved that fountain; though she had hardly been old enough to speak at the time, Dantzel could remember her father's callused hand tracing the detailed stone pictures, telling her stories about the playful sprites, charming tuatha, cantankerous kobolds, and other mythical creatures that danced around the fountain. The fountain had been carefully preserved by the village's master stoneworkers for decades, but since they had all been taken to the castle in the valley, the relief was slowly diminishing into dust. *Just like the rest of the town*, Dantzel couldn't help thinking.

Dantzel pulled her eyes away from the fountain as she and her mother took their usual position in the southwest corner, where the buildings would provide some shade for the hottest part of the day, and began setting up their stall. The boxes were heavy, but Dantzel dragged them out of the cart as fast as she could lift them. Jeffer had developed the unwelcome habit on market morning of "just happening by" and offering to help them unload the cart.

"What's your hurry?"

Dantzel nearly dropped the box of carrots she had been

hauling over to the stall. Steadying her load, she set it down carefully and turned to find a twelve-year-old boy with light brown hair watching her. He was small for his age, and his eyes crinkled in a perpetual mischievous smile. "Cabel," she said, sighing and reaching out to ruffle his hair. "You startled me. Why don't you make yourself useful?"

The boy hopped over to the cart and grunted as he lifted a bag of potatoes nearly as big as he was. "Pa sent me to find you before you started selling. He's got a new bolt of green fabric in, one like your ma wanted for your dress, and he wants to be the first to trade today."

Dantzel paused in her work and turned to eye her mother suspiciously. Anna hastily took Cabel by the shoulders and turned him back in the direction of his father's shop. "You tell your father I'll be right over, and thank him for thinking of us."

Cabel was off running in an instant—the boy never did anything at half-speed—and Dantzel folded her arms expectantly. Anna sighed.

"I meant it to be a surprise," she said, raising her hands with a shrug. Dantzel shook her head, pursing her lips stubbornly.

"I don't need a new dress, Mother. This one is fine."

"Oh, for the everyday, it is. But Julie and Robert are getting married this summer, and I thought you ought to have something for the celebration."

Dantzel lowered her eyebrows. "You just want me to get into the spirit of the occasion."

Anna's smile was only proof of what Dantzel accused. "It will be absolutely lovely, dear. I'm going to take over some berries to trade with Bryson for the fabric. He's been asking all summer when our blackberries are going to ripen. Watch the stand while I'm gone!"

As Anna disappeared into the growing marketplace crowd, Dantzel leaned on the stack of boxes beside her with a huff. Ever since Dantzel turned fifteen in the spring, her mother had become a veritable nuisance when it came to boys in the village. Sure, Julie had been engaged to Robert at fifteen, but everyone had known that Julie and Robert would marry from the time they were children. There was no one in the village that Dantzel had the remotest interest in courting, least of all Jeffer, who unfortunately seemed to be the most determined. Besides, what would her mother do without her if she ran off and got married?

The sun was well into the sky now, and the market square was getting crowded. Dantzel watched the people filling the town's center, chattering happily or bartering sternly. The familiarity of the scene settled into her heart, simultaneously reassuring and threatening that nothing would ever change.

Until she saw the boy hovering uncertainly on the edge of the square.

He seemed just older than she, and wore a shirt and trousers that had once been nice, but were now torn and caked with dirt. The back was darkly stained, as if he had slept in a mud puddle. His valley-blond hair was tousled, and one of his valley-blue eyes was ringed with swollen purple flesh. A scowl crossed his face as he surveyed the busy market with the eye of a practiced thief, and Dantzel felt her own expression harden. Whatever a ragged valley runaway wanted with their village, it would only bring trouble.

And trouble there was. Across the square, four uniformed men plowed their way through the crowd, red capes streaming from their shoulders and swords hanging from their waists. *Guards!* Hastily, Dantzel ducked under the counter, blood blazing as it always did at the appearance of the king's men. From the corner of her eye, as she dropped out of sight, Dantzel saw one of the young men nudge his companion and look in her direction. Hidden safely behind her stall, Dantzel closed her eyes for a moment before collecting an apronful of potatoes, praying that they would leave her alone. She wished desperately that her mother had not left just then; things always got out of hand when Anna wasn't around.

When Dantzel reappeared, she saw with a sinking feeling that the Guards were pushing their way through the crowds to get to her stall. Anger spread through Dantzel's veins like wildfire. They wouldn't get the better of her today, not with all their pomp and authority. She wouldn't let them.

"Good afternoon, miss," said one of the red-cloaked Guards, winking at her in what he obviously thought was a winning manner. He must have been assigned to the area recently; Dantzel hadn't yet had occasion to be harassed by him.

"Good afternoon," Dantzel replied curtly. "What can I offer you today?"

The Guard leaned across the counter, his sleazy smile broadening. He reached out to touch her arm. Dantzel jerked away just as he moved to tighten his grasp around her wrist.

"Not for sale," she said coldly, dropping all pretense of civility. "Maybe you should try another village." Her voice held a hint of a threat, causing the young Guard to raise an eyebrow at his snickering comrades. Dantzel's blood was racing, and she fought to keep the fear off her face. They weren't usually so openly forward with her. Usually, it was a few taunts about seeing her father cleaning the stables in the king's court or a snide comment about the dirt on her worn-out dress. But this one seemed to be fresh from train-ing, trying to prove his manhood to his new friends.

Turning back to her with a confident smirk, the Guard picked up a handful of berries and popped a few into his mouth. He chewed slowly and deliberately, apparently enjoy-ing the outraged look on Dantzel's face. As angry as she was, Dantzel didn't dare say anything. Two-syllable peasants had been arrested for less, and her mother needed her help in the garden. She clenched her teeth, stepped back, and looked at the ground. Harsh, crass laughter surrounded her; she saw several hands dip into her boxes of produce, and crude com-ments echoed in her ears no matter how desperately she tried to block them out.

"Can I help you, gentlemen?"

The dry, raspy voice sounded right beside Dantzel's ear, and she gasped and flinched away. The ragged stranger stood next to her, a wry half-smile now gracing his bruised face. The laughter from the Guards doubled.

"What are you going to do?" The young Guard smirked as he gave the stranger a once-over. "It looks like you already lost one fight today, beggar."

"Beggar? I'm not the one stealing food," the stranger said coolly, his words sliding perfectly into the arrogant rhythm of the valley. Dantzel curled her hands into fists and opened her mouth to intervene, but the valley boy pressed one hand against her wrist under the stall. She jerked away but remained quiet. "What do you think the earl of Feaul will do when he finds out you've been brawling with his oldest son?"

Earl of Feaul? Dantzel glanced warily at the battered but fine clothing; she wasn't convinced, but the Guard stepped down a little. "Why would the earl's son be wandering around this backward mountain village?" he demanded, his eyes betraying his doubt.

"Does it matter?" The boy definitely had the arrogant stance of nobility. "I doubt you've been out of the academy long enough to keep them from yanking your uniform at a moment's notice. All I have to do is tell them you've been abusing your privileges. The earl will have a syllable cut from your name by sundown, and you'll be out working the fields with the rest of those two-syllable dirt farmers."

The Guard was starting to look like he wanted to give the boy another black eye, but his friends were beginning to mutter among themselves.

"Come on," one of them said. "It's not worth the trouble."

The Guard didn't move for a moment; then he gave Dantzel a spiteful glance and tipped a basket of blackberries onto the ground. "Ugly mountain weasel, anyway," he muttered, stepping purposefully in the pile of spilled berries as the Guards retreated. Dantzel's teeth ground as the Guards disappeared into the crowd, pausing briefly to harass the baker's wife. As soon as they were a safe distance away, she turned to the valley boy, who hadn't moved.

"You're welcome," he said, leaning on the side of her stand and looking over the display of produce as if deciding what to demand as a reward. The last of Dantzel's restraint snapped. He was no earl's son. He was nothing more than a common thief, and he wasn't going to lose her any more of her precious produce.

"Who asked you to stick your big nose in? I was doing just fine before you showed up! Thanks to you, I just lost three pounds of berries, and—are you even listening to me?"

The valley boy's eyes were glazed, and his expression

showed no reaction to her tirade. Unnerved, Dantzel hesitated, watching with increasing concern as his eyes rolled back into his head and he tipped over backward. As he hit the ground with a dull thud, Dantzel let out a stifled shriek.

"Dantzel!"

Dantzel looked up wildly, relief rushing over her at hearing Anton's voice. Anton would make sense of this mess she had landed in. He always did. The gray-haired man was hobbling through the market square toward her, leaning heavily on his cane. Unfortunately, Jeffer was closer and faster. "Are you okay?" he asked, nearly tripping over his gangly limbs as he pushed his curly hair out of his eyes. "Was he bothering you?"

"Yes—no—I'm fine," Dantzel said impatiently as Anton reached them, his veined and knobby hands gripping his cane tightly.

"I heard you shouting, but I couldn't get here fast enough," he said, eyes jumping from Dantzel to the horizontal stranger. "What happened?"

"It was the Guards," Dantzel said, frozen in place as Anton bent over the still body. "Then this valley boy just . . . just jumped into it all."

"And you naturally rebuffed him," Anton said, raising an eyebrow at Dantzel. She shrugged helplessly.

"I was doing fine. He didn't have to come barging in," she said defensively. "But I didn't do anything to him! I mean, I did shout a little. I figured he was just a troublemaker trying to get some free fruit. But then he just sort of—fell over."

"Sure looks like a troublemaker to me," Jeffer offered importantly, with a not-so-surreptitious glance at Dantzel. She fought not to roll her eyes as she remembered her promise to her mother.

"Thank you," Anton said quickly, shooting Dantzel a warning glance. "But whoever he is, he's not well. Would you help me carry him back to my home, Jeffer? I can't take him with my bad leg."

"Are you sure?" Dantzel said anxiously. "What if he turns violent when he wakes up?"

Anton turned a skeptical eye on her. "In the shape he's in? Besides, Dantzel, whether you like it or not, he did stand between you and the Guards. He deserves some thanks for that. Come on, Jeffer."

As Jeffer gathered the stranger's limp body into his arms, something slid out from under the boy's shirt—a wooden pendant, a little smaller than Dantzel's palm, hanging from a string of cheap leather. She'd have thought nothing of it had it not been for Anton's reaction. The color drained from the old man's face in an instant, and he grabbed at Jeffer's arm. Curious, Dantzel tried to lean in for a closer look, but Anton had removed the pendant in a flash and was stuffing it into his pocket. "Go on, boy. Hurry up," he said, a new note of urgency in his voice. Dantzel watched them leave the market square, anxiety knotting in her stomach as she stood uselessly at her stall.

CHAPTER TWO

RUSTAV BECAME CONSCIOUS OF SOUNDS FIRST—shuffling and tapping and some crackling. Then came the smells—most overpoweringly that of a stew that made his stomach cramp with hunger, but also the underlying scent of wood. Finally, he opened his eyes, remaining perfectly still as he stared up at the unfamiliar ceiling above him. It was thatched; he couldn't recall ever having been inside a thatched-roof house before, though he had seen plenty on his trek across the valley. Had one of the field hands taken him in?

No, no, he could recall the sense of relief when he had made it out of the valley and onto the steep slopes that turned into mountains. The relief hadn't lasted long, not after fighting through thorny brambles and waking to find a spiky creature the size of a watermelon pawing at his face in the middle of the night. But the forest was so close. Uphill, uphill, uphill, and then there was the girl, and the Guards . . .

"Awake, are you?"

A face entered his view, old, wrinkled, and topped with bright gray hair. Eyes pierced him, blue eyes like his own.

Only valley people had blue eyes. Had he hallucinated his journey into the mountains?

"It's all right. You're safe here," said the old man, disappearing from Rustav's view. Rustav turned his head, taking in the rest of the one-room house. The mat where he lay was tucked in a corner; on the opposite side, a pot hung over a crackling fire, the source of the heavenly stew smell. A table stood in the middle of the room, and a few sparse shelves stood against the rough clay brick of the back wall. The old man took a bowl from one of the shelves and limped over to the fireplace as he continued speaking. "My name is Anton, and you're in the mountain village of Gebir. You slept all of yesterday and right through the night. I've no doubt you needed it, but I think you'd also enjoy a hot meal, am I right?"

At the suggestion of a hot meal, Rustav jerked up into a sitting position. Immediately, his ribs and back exploded with pain. Suppressing a groan, Rustav refused to collapse back onto the mat. Instead, he propped himself against the wall and watched the old man limping closer with the bowl of stew. As soon as the bowl was within reach, Rustav grabbed it.

"Slowly," the man cautioned, but Rustav was already halfway through, tipping the contents of the bowl down his throat as fast as he could swallow. When the bottom of the bowl appeared, he held the bowl out silently. The old man took the bowl and set it back on the table.

"Let that digest," he said, pulling a chair over from the table and sitting down next to the bed. "Can you hold it down?"

Rustav almost answered with a scoffing yes; then his stomach lurched, and he closed his eyes. He took a deep breath, swallowed hard, and nodded. His stomach was churning ferociously now, having nearly forgotten what to do with this thing called food. Knobby hands grasped his shoulders, pushing him firmly but gently back onto the mat. Too exhausted to protest, Rustav drifted away into unconsciousness once more.

THE NEXT TIME RUSTAV WOKE, THE ROOM WAS dark, and Anton was snoring softly on a mat several feet away. Enough moonlight streamed in through the small windows that he could see around the room fairly well. His head was clear, clearer than it had been for days. The stew had done wonders for his energy; he hadn't had that much sustenance since fleeing his uncle. He sat up carefully, accepting and ignoring the fiery pain throughout his chest.

Even that much movement required a moment's recovery. As Rustav sat with his back against the wall, his eyes fell on a small tangle of leather lying beside his sleeping mat. He squinted through the dim light, and then his hand leaped to his neck, confirming the alarming absence of his wooden pendant. Rustav grabbed the leather string and the attached circle of wood, running his fingers over the familiar smooth lines and chips to assure himself that it was actually his.

Slipping the leather string over his head and dropping his pendant under his shirt, Rustav pushed against the wall to lever himself into a standing position. His legs were a little shaky, but they held. Slowly, Rustav let go of the wall and walked stiffly to the table, wincing with every step. The sleep had no doubt done him good, but his muscles had seized up tighter than a seaman's knots during the long period of disuse. Rustav considered climbing back under the blankets and going back to sleep. But then, who knew what might happen the next time he woke?

When he reached the table, Rustav leaned against it, willing his aching muscles to loosen enough that he could make it up the slope to the forest's edge. A beam of bright moonlight illuminated the table, and Rustav examined it more closely, running his fingers over the surface. It was wood, and not the cheap, flimsy wood scraps poor people sometimes managed to scrape together for the odd piece of furniture. No, the table was solidly built with a flowing pattern adorning the border, and the chairs were of a similar quality. How could a poor mountain man afford such a luxury? In Courei, a small country where the expansive mountain forests were thought to be bewitched, wood was a difficult commodity to come by. Clusters of "domestic" trees could be found in the valley, but that supplied only limited wood to work with, most of which was hauled off to decorate the castle. Most wood had to be shipped in from other countries, making it far too expensive for even many three-syllable merchants to use in their homes.

Beside the table was a metal chest that Rustav hadn't noticed at first. Casting a quick glance to make sure Anton was still sleeping, Rustav knelt by the chest and undid the latch. The lid lifted easily, and Rustav shifted slightly to allow the moonlight to fall on the chest's contents. Cold fear flooded through him, freezing his bones and trapping his breath.

Blades of all shapes and sizes filled the chest, knives and chisels and gouges, the sharp metal gleaming menacingly in the moonlight. Rustav shut the chest as quietly as his shaking hands would allow, reeling back with his pulse racing. He had always been fast enough to get away when knives like that had been pulled in the alleys of Markuum, but he had seen what they could do to the poor fools who weren't so ۱۱د of foot. Rustav shuddered to think what might happen even with the smallest of the knives if he remained. He had to get out of there before Anton awoke.

Stumbling over his own feet in his haste, Rustav leaped to the shelves of food. Fumbling through the darkness, he found a cloth napkin and began loading it with nuts, a chunk of bread, and a couple of apples.

"You'll find some dried fruit on the shelf to your right."

Rustav dropped the apple he was holding as he started around, staring at the bent figure standing between him and the front door. He hadn't heard Anton move. Angry that he had been caught off guard, Rustav turned back to the shelf and dug out a handful of dried apricots.

"Where are you going to go?"

"What does it matter?" Rustav snapped, tying the napkin together with a vicious yank and turning back to face Anton.

"I wish you'd stay, at least until your injuries have healed."

Rustav picked up the packet of food and adopted a fighting stance, ready to bowl the old man over if need be. His voice trembled only slightly as he said, "I'm not staying. I saw your knives."

Anton didn't seem to grasp what Rustav meant at first, staring blankly across the moonlit room. Understanding dawned, and he let out a sigh. "I'm a carpenter, lad. I carve wood for a living. Those are my tools. How else do you think I could have a table like this?"

For a moment, relief trickled down Rustav's spine: of course that was what the knives were for. *But still,* he thought, nerves fraying, *Karstafel's cane had been used for walking, and that hadn't precluded any more creative uses.*

"What have you lived through?" Anton asked softly, almost as if he were talking to himself.

"What do you care?" Rustav's voice rose almost to a shout. Why wouldn't the old man just get out of his way? "I'm nobody, okay? Just let me go and I'll be out of your life. You'll never see me again. Just—just let me go!"

Rustav could feel his legs starting to shake. He was more drained than he was willing to admit. Karstafel had been well on his way to beating Rustav to a lifeless pulp before Rustav had managed to wrench the cane away, and the days and nights of full-out sprinting hadn't done much to help him heal. For an instant, Rustav's resolve trembled.

"Please," the old man said. Rustav thought for a moment that he saw a tear on the man's cheek, but it was certainly only a trick of the dim light, or maybe the fact that Rustav's vision was swimming. "You've been terribly wronged. I don't know what's happened to you, but I want to help you. Give me a chance to show you a different side of the world."

The dark room was starting to get darker, and Rustav swayed unsteadily. He clutched at the shelves to steady himself. In an instant, Anton was at his side, holding his elbow. Rustav pulled away, nearly falling to the floor in the process. Giving in, Rustav sank into a sitting position, head between his knees, drawing in deep breaths and willing himself not to pass out again. Demons or no, he wouldn't make it through the forest in this condition.

"Fine," he said finally. "Fine. I'll stay until I'm better. But then I'm gone, and you won't stop me."

"Good," said Anton, his voice far away. "Come on. You need to be in bed."

Rustav dreamed that he was running through the forest, dodging trees and glancing over his shoulder, always hearing the tromp of boots or the whinny of horses just behind him. He was almost through to the other side, he was sure of it; he'd be free and clear in minutes. But then the trees began swaying ominously, branches reaching down to swipe his face and catch his clothes. A root flung itself up out of the ground, and Rustav tripped hard, skidding along the dead leaves and dirt. In an instant, roots were growing over him, trapping him against the ground. He twisted and pulled with all his might, but to no avail. A root snaked its way around his neck, tightening, unresponsive to Rustav's mad scrabbling for breath—

"Rustav!"

Bolting straight up, Rustav found himself in an unfamiliar room with clay walls and a wood table. He looked around wildly for a few seconds before fixing his eyes on the old man standing beside him. Memory returned in a flood, and Rustav fell back onto his sleeping mat, heart racing.

"Are you all right?" Anton asked, his eyes concerned. Rustav stared at him, trying to blink the blurriness from his swollen right eye.

"How do you know my name?"

"You've been muttering to yourself all night," Anton said, his careful lightness obviously meant to offset Rustav's aggression. All it really did was set Rustav more on edge, especially as he considered what else he might have said.

"What do you want?"

Unperturbed by Rustav's hostile growl, Anton answered, "Breakfast is ready. I can bring it to you, if you'd like."

"No," Rustav said obstinately, throwing his blanket back

and ignoring the throbbing in his head. As he stood, Anton took his elbow; Rustav swallowed his objection as his knees trembled, unsure if he would make it to the table without the old man's help.

AFTER BREAKFAST, ANTON INDICATED A TUB OF water near the fire and a pile of clean clothes, and then he disappeared with the vague excuse of "running some errands." Once he was sure that Anton was gone, Rustav fell gladly into the clean water, scrubbing gingerly at his wounds. Layers of dried blood and dirt fell away into the water. When he dressed in the rough tunic and trousers sitting nearby, Rustav thought he had never felt so good before. The loose neck of the tunic didn't force his head erect like his old collars, and the trousers bagged comfortably at his ankles. By the time Anton returned, Rustav discovered, rather unwillingly, that his suspicions had lessened ever so slightly.

"I'm hungry," he said, his tone falling halfway between aggressive and apologetic. Such a comment in Karstafel's household was a sure request for a beating, but Rustav was beginning to suspect that Anton was of a different breed altogether. Besides, his stomach, having rediscovered food, was becoming very demanding.

"Here." Anton set a pear on the table and gestured for Rustav to sit. Before Rustav could get through the pear, Anton had set bread and cheese before him as well. Rustav paused only long enough to throw the old man a suspicious glance before the presence of the bread and cheese overcame any inhibitions he might have had.

"I'd like you to come with me to see a friend," Anton said.

"No," Rustav replied flatly, taking another mouthful of bread.

"He's a doctor. He'll help you get back on your feet more quickly."

Rustav made his way through a few more bites before he answered, unable to keep his bewilderment from cutting into his defensiveness. "Why are you doing this for me?"

"You remind me of someone I knew once."

"Right," said Rustav, defraying Anton's unnerving earnestness with mockery. "Someone who was very dear to you, someone you lost long ago."

Anton took the empty plate from Rustav and pulled Rustav to his feet, speaking mildly but firmly. "The cart is waiting outside. Get in."

Shrugging off Anton's hand, Rustav threw him a dirty look but obeyed. As he left the small house, Rustav found himself in the middle of several mountain shacks built close together, no more than a mile from the tree line. Excitement and fear twisted in Rustav's stomach as he looked into the forest, searching for any sign of demonic inhabitants and finding none. He could make a run for it now; instead, he climbed reluctantly into a rickety old cart, followed by Anton. With a cluck, the old mare began to move. Each jolt on the dirt road set Rustav's aches on fire. He grumbled under his breath, burying his head in his hands.

"I know it's not comfortable, but I thought it would be better than walking," said Anton apologetically. "It will be worth it, I promise. Father Lute is the best doctor we've known in these parts for some time."

Rustav's head jerked up, his regret at not running for the trees suddenly tripling. "Father? As in . . . priest?"

Anton pointed up the hill to what was apparently the grandest building in the mountain town: a one-story rectangle with several windows. "That's our village church. It has the largest windows in the town to encourage us to look out at what we have and be grateful."

"Grateful for what?" Rustav asked acidly, shrinking back into the seat of the cart. "For dirt-floor homes and lean winters?"

Rustav could feel Anton's eyes on him, but he kept his glare on the church ahead of them, willing the mud bricks to melt into the dirt they stood on.

"What is it?" Anton asked.

Rustav ignored him, staring stonily ahead. The first—and last—time he had entered the church in Markuum was at the age of nine. The younger Rustav had become inexplicably fascinated by the people who came out of the city church every Sunday afternoon, dressed in their fanciest, most expensive clothes. The church was enormous, a magnificently ornate mountain of gray stone, with the only windows being at the very top of the walls. Rustav had tried to climb up and peek in, but that made him a prime target for a group of boys armed with rocks. So, instead, Rustav decided to sneak in and see for himself what drew such a large crowd each week.

The following Sunday, dressed in the best clothes he owned, Rustav joined the flow of people going into the church. As he entered, the people around him began casting suspicious glances in his direction. He retreated to the back corner, shrinking into his seat and doing his best to become invisible. What followed was unlike anything he had expected: two hours of a shouting rage that exceeded even some of Karstafel's ravings, all about hellfire and damnation and "you're all going straight to the devil himself."

When the horrible censure had finally ceased, Rustav had tried desperately to get out as fast as he could. To his horror, the preacher was standing at the door, smiling and shaking hands with the people in a cheerful way that contrasted incomprehensibly with his sermon. The current of the crowd swept Rustav ever closer to the preacher, with Rustav painfully conscious of the burning glances that surrounded him on all sides. When Rustav arrived in front of the preacher, feeling as though he had been unceremoniously dumped on the front step of the church, the preacher's genial smile faded into a stern frown. Rustav could still hear the distaste in the man's voice.

"Your soul is beyond saving, boy. Thank your disgraceful mother for bringing a cursed spirit into this life."

That had been enough for him to swear off religion. If heaven was filled with people like that, he'd gladly take hell.

"Are you coming?"

The cart had come to a stop in front of the old church, which stood unaffected by Rustav's best efforts to destroy it through sheer will. Jaw tightening, Rustav folded his arms and shook his head. Anton opened his mouth, perhaps to insist that Rustav accompany him, but another voice interrupted.

"Brother Anton! What can I do for you this fine day?"

The cheery, melodic voice belonged to a small, rotund man standing just in front of the church's front door. His worn gray robe was rather plain for a clerical man, Rustav thought sourly, and his thin, brown hair was singularly unimpressive.

"A good morning to you, Father!" Anton called, tying the mare securely to the fence. "I've come to ask a favor of you."

"By all means, come in, come in!" The preacher gestured into the church, his eyes flicking curiously to Rustav, who hadn't moved. "Please, young man, join us. It's much cooler in here. I'd hate for you to wait for two old men out in the hot sun."

Rustav looked at Anton, who jerked his head ever so slightly toward the church. Grumbling inwardly, Rustav climbed carefully out of the cart. As he drew nearer to where Anton and the preacher were standing, his shoulders hunched even more under Father Lute's gaze.

"Dear boy!" the preacher breathed, his eyes traveling over Rustav's black eye and scratched limbs. "Come in, please. Come and sit down."

Self-consciously, Rustav followed the two men into the church. It wasn't dark and gloomy like the one in Markuum, nor was it packed with strange, elaborate paintings and decorations; the large windows filled the building with the morning sun, and the interior was painted a plain white. The wooden lectern was the only decorative piece of the building—no doubt Anton's contribution—but even that was carved in a simple design. Rustav couldn't help but stare at the simple mountain church, a thought burning dimly at the back of his mind: if a church could be so different in this place, then what about the people?

"Take a seat," the preacher called, hurrying through a doorway on the side of the room. Following Anton's lead, Rustav sat on one of the cool stone benches near the front, unable to resist rubbing his fingers against the highly polished surface. A moment later, the preacher returned, carrying a large bag. "Is this the favor you wished to ask?" he asked Anton, rummaging through the bag.

"Yes, if you please, Father," Anton said. Looking at Rustav, he explained, "Father Lute has studied medicine as well as theology, and he's as good a doctor as any we've ever had."

Rustav jumped as Lute touched a long scratch sustained from a prickly bush at the base of the mountain. "I don't need a doctor," Rustav insisted, pulling his arm away. "I can't pay for one, anyway."

"I don't require payment, brother," the preacher said patiently, reaching for Rustav's arm again. "And you do need a doctor. Take that scratch, for instance. Judging by the inflammation, I'd say you got it from a yellow thorn about half an inch long about two days ago, and it has festered without ceasing ever since."

Rustav stared, and the preacher smiled. "We have different dangers here in the mountains than there are on the coast, though you seem to have run into plenty there as well. From the way you move, I'd say you have at least one cracked rib, a sprained shoulder, and a wounded back. At least."

Without further ado, Lute pulled Rustav's arm toward him and began swabbing at the scratch. When Rustav found his voice again, he asked, "How did you know I was from the coast?"

Lute laughed. "Not by your features, that's for sure. Your accent gave you away. I thought for certain that you were another runaway from the valley, like Anton here, until you spoke."

Rustav glanced at Anton, then sucked in a breath as Lute smeared a brownish paste onto the wound. The preacher looked up apologetically. "I know it stings, but it's the only way to counteract the thorn's venom. I'm going to need you to take off your shirt so I can better assess your injuries."

Instantly, Rustav's jaw set, and he shook his head. He wasn't going to be gawked at like a caged animal. Patiently, the preacher said, "We can go into my study if you would feel more comfortable, but you must work with me if I'm to be of any help."

"Rustav, please," Anton said quietly. "You'll heal so much more quickly if you do what he says. Trust him."

For a long minute, Rustav looked from one man to the other, gauging the truth in their eyes. He had promised Anton that he would stay until he was healed; the sooner he was well again, the sooner he could pick up and leave. "I want to go into your study," he said, still eyeing the preacher suspiciously. The man nodded pleasantly, evidently immune to Rustav's glare. He led the way through the doorway he had previously disappeared into. Following, Rustav found a small room packed with shelves and shelves of books and a cot tucked away into a corner. In another corner, scrolls and bits of parchment covered a desk, which Lute was now clearing off. There was hardly enough space for all three of them to squeeze in, and Anton stayed in the doorway. The preacher lit a lamp—the small window in this room didn't let in nearly as much light as the great windows in the main church—and turned to Rustav.

"Now," he said matter-of-factly. Rustav stood grinding his teeth for a moment before turning his back to them. *Fine. Let them see. Let them see it all.* After a short struggle with the homespun shirt, he stood still, exposed, and listened to the utter silence.

He could only imagine what it looked like. Years of scars crossed and crossed again over his chest and back, marks from Karstafel's belt and cane. The signs of

Karstafel's latest rage were starting to crust over, but they were still cracking and bleeding. Then there were the signs of hard travel, bruises from the rocky sleeping quarters and close scrapes with the Guards. In short, it was a ghastly summary of his life.

The first sound of movement was heavy footsteps. Out of the corner of his eye, Rustav saw Anton striding out of the room, leathery face pale. Lute's cold hand touched Rustav's back, and Rustav flinched. "Who did this to you?" Lute breathed, his voice heavy with shock. Ears burning with humiliation, Rustav set his jaw and held his head high.

"My uncle, mostly," he said with a casualness that sounded forced even to him. "He didn't like me much."

"Your parents would leave you with such a man?"

"My mother was a vagrant who left me on her brother's porch when I was a baby. I can only guess at who my father was. Probably a lonely Guard out on patrol." That would do it, he was certain. No self-respecting priest would be caught helping a boy without a proper father. The priest in Markuum had made it quite clear that his mother's actions had forever tainted his soul.

But Lute didn't say anything. Bottles clinked softly, and then a cold, wet cloth sponged across Rustav's back. It stung terribly, but Rustav set his teeth and refused to make a sound. When Lute finally finished cleaning and bandaging the wounds on Rustav's back, he inspected his shoulder and the bruises around his torso. Sometime during the process, Anton slipped back into the room, looking older than ever as he stood hunched and pallid in a corner.

"A few cracked ribs, it looks like," Lute said, shaking his head gravely. "Get your shirt back on, and I'll tie you a sling.

I want you to take it easy for the next few weeks. Keep your arm in the sling as much as humanly possible, and refrain from any strenuous activities."

Rustav stood there for a moment, staring from the preacher to the sling and back again. He was overwhelmed with—what? It was a feeling unlike any he had ever before experienced. At a loss for words, Rustav turned to look at Anton, who smiled wanly and mouthed the words *thank you*.

"Thank you," Rustav said, sincerely meaning the words for the first time in his life. Numbly, he followed Anton back outside the church. What was going on? Who were these people?

They said good-bye to Father Lute, climbed back in the cart, and started slowly down the road. Rustav was so caught up in his own thoughts that he failed to notice that they had left the town behind until they were well on the way down a narrow dirt lane. "Where are we going now?" he asked.

"To visit Anna and Dantzel."

CHAPTER THREE

THE SUN WAS HIGH AND HOT, EVEN THOUGH IT WAS not yet noon, but Dantzel was too wrapped in her thoughts to notice the heat beating down as she tugged hardy weeds from the rocky soil. Ever since the encounter at market two days before, she hadn't been able to tear her thoughts away from the mysterious stranger who had collapsed at her stand after fending off four Guards with nothing more than words.

She couldn't help but wonder what a valley boy, of all people, was doing facing off against the Guards in a mountain village. Was he one of the farm workers? a bitter dropout from the Guards' training? When she grew tired of imagining possible scenarios, she puzzled over the strange pendant he wore. Why had Anton looked so surprised? What had been carved on it? She had only gotten a brief glance, and the carving had been so small and fine that she couldn't make out what was depicted.

A familiar rattle interrupted her musings, and Dantzel lifted her head above the tomato vines to see Anton coming toward her in his old cart. The blond, bruised boy sat stiffly at his side, his face set in a brooding mask. In an instant, all of Dantzel's misgivings returned. What had possessed Anton to take such a ruffian into his home? Anxious to appear nonchalant, Dantzel dropped back down and returned to digging up a particularly stubborn weed.

Her mother had heard the cart as well; she came out of the front door as the old mare stopped in front of their gate. "Anton, I'm so glad to see you!" she called, wiping her hands on her apron. "And this must be the gallant young gentleman who came to Dantzel's aid yesterday. Pleased to make your acquaintance."

Startled out of his stony glare, the boy looked from Anna to Anton with wide, uncertain eyes. He eventually settled for nodding his head and mumbling something incoherent. Dantzel watched his flustered face curiously, recalling the boldness with which he had faced four Guards only moments before collapsing. Anna, however, didn't draw any attention to the odd response, gesturing graciously into the house. "Won't you both please stay to dinner? We would be glad of the company."

"Of course, of course. Thank you, my dear," Anton said, smiling his wide smile that creased all his wrinkles together around his bright eyes. His blue eyes had fascinated Dantzel as a little girl; they were so strange, set against a backdrop of dark-eyed mountain folk, and they seemed deeper, more expressive somehow. Now, they were tinged with pain even as he spoke cheerfully to the boy at his side. "Why don't you stay to visit with Dantzel while she finishes in the garden? I'm sure you have no interest in the rambling conversation of older folk."

The boy glanced warily at Anton even as Anna laughed.

"Speak for yourself, old one," she chided humorously. "I'm young yet. Still, I'm certain that Dantzel would be better company for you, Master . . ."

Again, the boy shifted uncomfortably as Anna spoke kindly to him, and he didn't seem to know where to land his gaze. "Rustav," he mumbled, following Anton through the gate and stopping several feet away from Dantzel. Anton hesitated, as if he were going to speak, but then followed Anna wordlessly through the door.

The valley boy remained motionless even after Anna and Anton had disappeared, staring silently down at the plants near his feet. Dantzel watched him for a moment, intrigued and a little frightened by his expression. Though the boy's eyes were every bit as blue as Anton's, they had none of Anton's warmth and friendliness. So flat and lifeless were they that Dantzel could nearly believe that they were black.

Growing self-conscious, Dantzel busied herself once more with the weeds, unsure of how to break the stiff silence. She was relieved—and a little startled—when Rustav asked, "Why are you digging up plants?"

Dantzel looked up, so surprised by his speech that she hardly registered the question. Instead of the valley drawl he had used in the marketplace, his words came out with the sharp staccato of the port cities. "You're not from the valley at all!" she exclaimed, sitting back on her heels with a laugh. "Earl of Feaul indeed! Not with that coastal brogue!"

"What are you laughing at?" he growled, looking her directly in the eye for the first time. "Had you fooled, didn't I?"

"That's why I'm laughing," Dantzel said, checking herself in the face of his annoyance and adopting a more sober composure. "You had me almost believing that a four-syllable noble could turn out a half-decent son. Guess I should've known better. I thought only valley folk had light hair and blue eyes. Was one of your parents from the valley?"

Rustav shrugged and took a step closer. "Anton's got blue eyes, and he's a mountain man."

"Came from the valley years ago," Dantzel corrected him. "He lost all his family and came here when I was little. Mama took him in, sort of, and we take care of each other. It's just the two of us here, and it's good to have Anton around."

"Bum father?"

Dantzel's eyes flashed indignantly at the offhand comment. "My father was the master stoneworker of the village," she snapped. "He was taken by the Guards to ornament King Elanokiev's gaudy monstrosity of a castle."

She ripped up a stubborn weed, spraying the tomatoes with dirt, and shook it fiercely to loosen the clumps of dirt from between the roots. Rustav inched a little closer, watching silently for a bit before he spoke again.

"You didn't answer my question."

Still irritated by his casual slight against her father, Dantzel answered shortly without looking up. "They're not plants. They're weeds, and they'll choke the plants if I don't get them out. Haven't you ever seen a garden before?"

"No. Well, yes, sort of. I've gone by the farms in the valley, but I only saw them from a distance."

Dantzel couldn't help pausing to stare up at him. Imagine, never seeing a garden! Dantzel sometimes thought that she never saw anything else. "Where did you get your food from, then?"

A slight smirk twisted Rustav's lips upward. "A port city

is the center of trade. There was never any shortage of food moving through the coast. We did eat an awful lot of fish, though."

"We catch fish from the stream now and again," Dantzel said, pleased to have finally found some sort of common ground. A brief spark illuminated Rustav's face before he tried to quench it again.

"Is there a stream nearby?" he asked, unable to keep all the hope from his voice. Dantzel furrowed her brow questioningly.

"Sure, just a quarter mile south of here. Want to see it?"

"Yeah, I guess." Rustav looked away, affecting a careless attitude that didn't quite erase his longing expression from Dantzel's memory. Dantzel jumped to her feet, eager to move out from under his intense stare.

"You don't have to be so stoic all the time," she said, pulling a few berries from the nearby bushes and tossing him one. Rustav remained silent, eyeing the berry he had caught before popping it in his mouth and following Dantzel out of the gate and through the meadow.

Even though Rustav was slouching, Dantzel was conscious of how tall he was. Granted, she was on the shorter end of the village, but her head came a few inches short of his shoulder, and she took nearly two whole steps to his long stride. As they walked, he stole several furtive glances up the hill at the tree line, only half a mile from Dantzel's home, before he spoke again.

"Have you ever been in the forest?"

The thought of approaching the old trees made Dantzel shiver, and she shook her head nervously. "It's best to stay away from the forest."

A strange light flickered in Rustav's eyes, and he looked down at her. "Why?"

Suddenly, Dantzel felt uncharacteristically unsure of herself. What if he was only looking for a reason to mock her mountain superstitions? Only they weren't really superstitions. Were they? She struggled for a way to word her reasoning without making it sound absurd. "The trees can be . . . dangerous. Especially for strangers."

"How so?"

Dantzel grew increasingly flustered. "They say that people don't come out of there."

"Who's 'they'? And what's to say something bad happened to the people that went in? Maybe they just went out the other side. Maybe they were looking for a way out of this sordid little country."

Taken aback by the sudden ferocity of Rustav's tone, Dantzel slowed briefly to look up at him. A scowl lined his face, making his vivid bruise all the more prominent. "Is that what you're looking for?"

Rustav kicked at a dandelion, scattering white fluff into the breeze and ignoring the question completely. His refusal to respond irked Dantzel, and she quickened her step, striving to outpace him. He hardly seemed to notice; his long stride and hasty pace already proved a formidable match for Dantzel's short legs. So absorbed was she in this new competition that she nearly half-ran into the stream before she realized they had arrived at their destination.

It was lucky Rustav was so focused on the stream; Dantzel didn't think he had seen her stumble to a stop, nearly sliding down into the water. In fact, once she had regained her balance and soothed her ruffled dignity, she was surprised by how intently he stared at the chattering stream. Slowly, he sank down to sit on the grassy bank, never blinking as his eyes darted over the ever-changing surface of the flowing water. Dantzel joined him, watching curiously.

"Is it anything like the ocean?"

Rustav laughed—a hard, bitter sound. "No. But it's probably the closest thing I'm likely to get in this forsaken wilderness."

Huffing, Dantzel folded her arms. "Are you always so charming?"

With a jerky gesture, Rustav indicated his black eye. "Do I look like much of a charmer?"

"Looks have proved deceiving in the past. After all, you're not from the valley."

A long silence followed, during which Rustav flicked stone after stone into the water. "Why do people here pretend like they like me?" he asked abruptly, throwing one stone with particular force. Dantzel wrinkled her forehead.

"Well . . . I don't know that anyone has found a reason yet to dislike you," she said cautiously, and Rustav turned a piercing eye on her.

"Even you? I did lose you three pounds of berries," he shot back. Dantzel flushed.

"I didn't think you heard that. I was upset with the Guards, that's all. Besides, how was I to know that you weren't just as bad as they were?"

"Who's to say I'm not?"

Oddly enough, more than anything Anton had said or Rustav had done up to that point, that muttered question began to assuage Dantzel's suspicions. She reached out to touch Rustav's shoulder but withdrew when he flinched away.

Suddenly, she understood. The guarded eyes, the defensive hunch of the shoulders, the shying away—she had seen it before, in the son of a trader with a violent temper. Dantzel examined Rustav's battered face with new perspective. The roguish scar cutting through his left eyebrow was now a mark of a dark past; his black eye no longer branded him as a troublemaker, but as a victim.

"You know," she said softly, "whoever you're running away from—not everyone is like that. I think Anton has shown you that already."

Rustav sat silently for a moment, blue eyes drinking in the flow of the clear stream. Without a word, he stood and began making his way back toward the cottage, Dantzel trailing along behind.

RUSTAV SLEPT DEEPLY THAT NIGHT, FOR THE FIRST time in a long time. When he awoke, he was perplexed at the sensation that engulfed him. He stared motionlessly at the ceiling for a while, struggling to determine what it was that was so different this morning.

At last, it came to him. The knot that held his chest constricted and his heart safely hidden—it had loosened considerably, enough that he could draw in a deeper breath than he ever could before. Suspicion instantly descended on the open feeling, closing it off once more, but Rustav, somewhat ashamedly, clutched at the last strands of the freed emotion. It wasn't right to let your insides get exposed like that. It was too dangerous. But . . . it was also pleasant.

Shaking off the foolish thoughts, Rustav tossed back his blanket and got to his feet, taking stock of his injuries. His arm had stopped festering; his back, though sore, was no longer oozing blood; even his shoulder, still bound in a sling, felt better than it had in days. That feeling crept back again, a strange feeling that he could only compare to the way he felt when he was able to escape Karstafel for a day or two and savor the relative freedom.

Anton had already risen, and Rustav could hear him rustling around just outside the door. Anxious to get away from his own thoughts, confusing and mysterious as they were, Rustav walked outside to see what Anton was doing. He stopped in the doorway, a cold hand squeezing away the air in his lungs.

Anton was sitting on a chair in front of the house, whittling a chunk of wood with a small knife and leaving shavings on the ground. Swallowing hard, Rustav tried to pull his eyes away from the sharp blade and couldn't. Before he could retreat, Anton noticed him and smiled broadly.

"Glad to see you up and about! Anna stopped by this morning and dropped off some bread for you, so you won't have to suffer through my coarse loaves."

Rustav nodded, hardly hearing the words. Anton followed his eyes and grew somber, lowering the knife and wood. "Carving helps me think, and I have a great deal to think about at the moment. I apologize if I've made you uncomfortable."

Embarrassed and unsure, Rustav stood silently in the doorway. Anton set the knife slowly on the ground, then stood and took his cane in hand. "You must be hungry," Anton said. "You hardly ate any of Anna's dinner yesterday. Go on in and sit down."

Rustav retreated back inside and took a seat at the table.

Anton followed him in and unwrapped a loaf of bread from the food shelves. Rustav took the proffered bread to satisfy the gnawing in his stomach.

"Where did you get that pendant around your neck?" Anton asked, sitting down across from him. Involuntarily, Rustav clutched at the leather string and then slowly pulled out his wooden pendant, rubbing the intricate designs with his thumb. Leaves and branches wove around the edge, encircling two vague human figures and a background of trees, towers, and crowns. He had spent hours as a young boy poring over the delicate woodwork. It had a chip or two in it now, the result of more than a few hard falls on rocky ground, but Rustav had treated it with careful respect for its delicate carving.

"My mother gave it to me. At least, that's what Karstafel told me."

"Karstafel?"

Rustav took another bite before he answered. "My uncle. He said I had it when his sister dumped me on his doorstep."

"Your uncle, hm? With a three-syllable name—one of the coastal merchants?"

"That's right. He came from a family of two-syllable sailors, but he stepped on as many people as he needed to get into a respectable business. Eventually, he tacked an extra syllable onto his name and ousted the owner. Now, nobody would dare mention that he used to be just plain Karstaf. Course, I was lucky he didn't cut me down to one syllable. He would've had me treated no better than the servants, except that he couldn't stand the thought of being related to anyone of such low status."

Foul memories pressed against Rustav's conscience, and

he had to suppress the urge to begin running again. Instead, he picked up the unfinished carving Anton had set on the table and fiddled with it. As he stared at the incomplete form, a half-formed thought came shooting out of his mouth without stopping to ask permission.

"Teach me how to carve."

Anton blinked once, twice, and looked at Rustav a little harder. Rustav stared back, his resolve quailing but his stubbornness prevailing. A pressing need to explain himself surfaced, and he spat out the first reason that occurred to him for making such a ridiculous request. "I've only ever seen knives used in fights and fish markets. I never thought they could make something like . . ." He fingered his wooden emblem, then held it out for Anton to see. "Like this."

"I—very well," Anton said, his voice betraying his astonishment. "As soon as your shoulder heals, I'll begin teaching you the basics."

Rustav pulled his arm free and undid the sling from around his neck, his shoulder complaining only with a slight twinge. Anton began to protest, but Rustav tossed the sling aside with firm finality.

"All right," Anton conceded, a wry smile folding his wrinkles. "I'll teach you how to carve."

IT WAS SLOW GOING AT FIRST. THE MOMENT ANTON opened his tool chest, Rustav's muscles clenched, refusing to allow him to approach the set of blades. Backing away slowly, he said, "Get the one you were using. I'll start with that one."

Understandingly, Anton retrieved the small whittling knife and pressed it into Rustav's hand. Rustav flinched at the touch of the cold handle, but he gritted his teeth and took the scrap of wood that Anton handed him. His hands gripped the knife awkwardly, and, more than once, Anton had to stop him before he accidentally cut himself. However, he went on doggedly, practicing on the scrap until there was hardly anything left of it. The next day he practiced on a new scrap, and the next day and the next, each day bringing improvements to Rustav's carving, injuries, and mood.

It was on the fourth day of this new obsession that Rustav dared to broach a topic that had been on his mind ever since he had first taken up the whittling knife. He and Anton sat together in front of the house, wood in hand, when Rustav broke the silence.

"Where do you get your wood?" he asked. With a crooked smile, Anton gestured uphill.

"We have a rather large stock of wood in our backyards."

"Dantzel said it wasn't safe to go into the forest. Aren't there demons in there?" Rustav tried to ask nonchalantly, as if he were mocking the tales, but his tone came off a little too earnest. He hoped Anton would laugh at the question; instead, the old carpenter fixed a somber gaze on him.

"As a woodworker, I've spent more time than most on the edge of the trees. We've reached a mutual understanding, I suppose you could say. You see, we have stands of domestic trees here—not nearly as big as those in the valley, of course—but the forest is where I go when I want to make really fine ornaments. I've promised never to touch the trees themselves, nor to go in too deep among them; in return, they allow me to collect the wood that they drop."

"You talk like they understand you," said Rustav.

"Do I, now?"

An uneasy curiosity settled over Rustav, mixing with a renewed urge to start running again. "Would they understand me too? Would they let me through if all I wanted to do was travel to the other side?"

Anton set down the wooden horse he had been carving and looked at Rustav, who remained focused solely on his carving. "Why would you want to pass through the trees?"

"It's my last way out of this wasted country. Karstafel will have all the ports watching for me, and it's only a matter of time before every Guard in the country is on my tail. If I can make it to the other side of these mountains, I'll be in the clear."

"What did you do to make him so angry?"

"Beside breathing? I spied on him when he was plotting with the king."

"Elanokiev?" Anton gasped. "Did the king see you?"

"Nah," Rustav said, setting his carving on the bench. "But Karstafel did, and boy, did I catch it. I think he would've killed me that time if I hadn't gotten the cane out of his hands and broken it over his head. He'll be after me for revenge, mostly, but I'm sure he's convinced the king that I'm carrying their dangerous secrets to the people."

"What dangerous secrets?" Anton asked, leaning in urgently and grabbing Rustav's wrist. Rustav flinched away, yanking his arm free, and jumped up. Anton's sudden movement startled him, and for a moment, Rustav braced himself for a beating. A wave of embarrassment broke over him as he realized that he was overreacting, but it wasn't enough to dispel the years of knowing that a wrist-grab like that would be followed by blows. Rustav took a stumbling step backward, then turned and fled.

CHAPTER FOUR

DANTZEL WAS TIRED OF WORKING IN THE GARDEN. She was tired of sweeping out the packed-dirt floor of their small cottage. She was tired of picking berries and tomatoes, and she was tired of collecting miniature eggs from their scraggly, mean old hens.

At least, that was what she told herself.

She knew better, and she was reasonably certain that her mother did too. It had been four days since her conversation with Rustav, and her curiosity grew each day that passed without news. Dantzel wished for some excuse to visit Anton and at least catch a glimpse of the mysterious boy, but there was too much to do in the garden with the end of summer coming fast. Dantzel was grateful when Anna put two buckets into her restless hands and told her to go fetch some water from the stream. Relieved to have some task that would at least take her away from the confines of their small bit of land, Dantzel set out for the stream with a will.

Whistling in an effort to distract her thoughts from their four-day rut, Dantzel took her time meandering up the mountainside to the stream, looking up to appreciate the beautiful white clouds breaking up the blue sky. When the sounds of gurgling water began to whisper over her music, she finally tore her eyes away from the wide canvas above her—and stared dumbfounded at the lanky figure on the bank of the river, knees folded up to his chest. Her ribs constricted; at the same time, her heart leaped, creating a curious conflict. Chiding herself for her childish excitement, she crept forward, unsure of the best way to approach him. She froze when he spoke, voice heavy with despondency.

"What am I even doing here?"

Dantzel glanced around quickly to ensure that no one else was present, and then she looked back to make sure he hadn't seen her. She remained rooted in place, waiting to see what would happen next.

"Any day, the king could make his move, and the only thing between me and the safety of the mainland is a bunch of trees and the sailors' talk of fairies," Rustav said, disgust evident in his voice. "So the priest gave me a sling. So the girl treated me like a human being. So the old man taught me how to carve." His voice faded on the last few words; after a brief silence, Rustav pulled something out from under his shirt. The pendant! Holding her breath, Dantzel leaned forward, hoping to catch a glimpse. She had nearly forgotten it, but now the memory returned of Anton's strange reaction to its appearance.

As the silence stretched on, Dantzel realized that this was likely the best opportunity she would have to approach without him knowing that she had been eavesdropping. Silently, she shrank back a few paces, then began whistling once more and swinging her buckets as she walked forward. Rustav started and turned to look at her. Dantzel smiled widely and tried to look innocent.

"I didn't expect to see you here!" she said, truthfully enough. "What are you up to on this fine summer day?"

Rustav regarded her with a tight half-smile for a moment before looking back at the stream, his eyes reflecting its clear blue. "Talking to the water."

Caught off guard by the frank answer, Dantzel had to think for a moment before she came up with an acceptable response. "You know, the village may be small, but there are still plenty of people here. You don't have to talk to the stream." She took a seat next to him, peeking curiously at the pendant he still held in his hands. It didn't look like anything out of the ordinary—fine carving, to be sure, but nothing shocking. Perhaps she had read too much into Anton's reaction. Pulling her eyes away from the pendant, Dantzel pushed a little harder for a response. "What brought you to talk to this particular stream?"

"I miss the ocean." For a moment, Rustav's eyes drank in the stream with such painful longing that Dantzel ached. She was certain, in that instant, that he had forgotten she was there, and he was speaking to the stream once more. "I had my own little cave in the rocks, my safe place where no one could ever find me. The waves would crash against the foot of the cliffs, a hundred feet below me, and I got it into my head that they could hear me. I'd tell them everything, the names of everyone who hurt me, wild plans for escape, all the things I'd do once I got away."

"Wasn't there anyone in the city you could talk to?"

Her words broke the spell of the stream; but though Rustav's expression hardened defensively, Dantzel thought that it wasn't quite so impenetrable as it had once been. "There was, once," Rustav said, a bitter bite to his voice even as he waved his hand carelessly. "Ollie the bookseller felt sorry for me. When I was three or four, old enough to start running away from Karstafel, I would hide out in his shop. He taught me to read, told me all kinds of tales. Life was looking up. And then Karstafel realized I could read. He didn't like that someone was being nice to me, and he beat me until I told him who taught me."

Dantzel couldn't withhold a horrified gasp, and she covered her mouth. "When you were four?"

Shrugging, Rustav said, "I might've been five by then. Anyway, a couple days later, the Guards dragged Ollie out of town and burned his shop. They claimed he was guilty of treason, one of the old king's men, but the whole city knew Karstafel had sent for them. After that, no one wanted Karstafel thinking they were on my side, and they made their loyalties painfully obvious to me."

A sharp twisting knifed through Dantzel's stomach as she took in the angles of Rustav's face. Dantzel wished she dared give him a hug, but his hardened exterior extended several inches around him, holding her at bay. "Couldn't you fight back?"

Rustav laughed briefly, a rusty and unused sound. "I tried a couple of times. The governor's Guards tossed me in the city jail overnight for brawling."

"Then how did you make it through all those years?"

"I'm fast." Self-derision weighed heavily in his words. "No one can turn tail and run like I can."

They were silent for a few minutes, Rustav still staring out at the stream, Dantzel struggling to comprehend the grim picture Rustav had painted. She was startled out of her deep thoughts when Rustav spoke again.

"Have you ever thought about leaving Courei?"

His question turned Dantzel's thoughts upside-down, redirecting them sharply inward. She plucked up a thick blade of grass and began shredding it as she stumbled over her answer. "No. I mean, at least not for a long time. I did once, but . . . this is my home."

"Home," Rustav scoffed. "This place has been dying since you and I were kids. King Elanokiev has taxed his people into starvation, fed his Guards into complacency, and spent his way into a debt bigger than the coffers ever were. It's a miracle he's stayed on the throne this long. Why would you want to stay here? Why would anyone stay here?"

"Maybe because we have hope for better days." Now Dantzel was the one staring out at the running water. "I asked Mama once why we didn't just leave behind all the Guards and all our troubles to live on the mainland." Dantzel smiled slightly. "She asked me how the grass could possibly look greener in the Ravian Desert. Then she told me that if all who suffered went away, there would be no one to fight oppression and pain with goodness and light. Besides, she believes the legends that a true king will come someday, bearing the past over his heart with the wrongs of the people written in his flesh."

"Is that what you've heard?" Rustav said harshly, digging a rock out of the dirt and tossing it into the stream. "People all over the country talk about this great king, this miracle man who will overthrow Elanokiev, and nobody can agree on who or even what he is. He would have to come from the valley, the coast, and the mountains all at once to fill everyone's expectations. The valley folk think he'll spring out of the ground to take the throne. The people of the coast claim he has the strength of the ocean waves. And—this one's my favorite—there are sailors who are convinced he'll be able to fly. Is that the man you're waiting on to save this wretched country?"

He had finally turned his eyes away from the stream, their clear blue now stormy. Dantzel drew back, startled and a little hurt by the sudden intensity of his rebuttal. "Isn't there anything that you believe in?"

"Yeah. I believe that I'm on my own. Nobody's looking to help me out, which is fine with me."

"You're wrong on that count," Dantzel contradicted quickly. "Anton's done everything he could to make you happy here. Father Lute practically brought you back to life. Mama's been sending bread so that you don't have to eat Anton's attempts at baking. Cabel thinks you're a hero for standing up to the Guards, and he's already tried to pick a fight with Orik for calling you a drifter."

"Who's Cabel?" Rustav asked, wrinkling his forehead.

"His father owns the general store. He's the errand boy, usually drops off a package of goods for Anton every few days."

"You mean the short kid with more bounce than a jackrabbit? Does he realize that 'drifter' is practically a compliment compared to what I'm used to hearing?"

Dantzel gave an impatient *mmmnh*. "That's not the point. What I'm trying to say is, there are people looking out for you now. You're not alone anymore. And if you're wrong about that," she said, unable to repress a triumphant tone, "then you could just as easily be wrong about the true king."

There was a long pause as Rustav stared at her. Dantzel

held his gaze, determined to defend the legend that, some days, was the only thing that kept her hoping. Finally, Rustav laughed again. This time, it didn't sound quite so hard. "You know, the ocean never told me I was wrong."

Relieved that her words had made some headway, Dantzel grinned. "The ocean never told you anything. See, I told you it was more fun to talk to people."

"I'm not convinced yet."

Getting to her feet and brushing the grass off her dress, Dantzel picked up her buckets and bent over to fill them at the stream. "I'll be here whenever you want to try again."

As she straightened, the weight of the full buckets was lifted from her hands. Startled, she turned to see Rustav standing beside her, holding the buckets. Dantzel tilted her head back, uncharacteristically intimidated by his towering height. His mouth twitched upward in an unpracticed smile. "I think I might take you up on that."

Dantzel nodded, doing her best to ignore the unfamiliar jumping feeling in her stomach. "I'd like that."

AN UNEASY SILENCE PERVADED ANTON'S HOUSE when Rustav returned that evening, and Rustav rose the next morning with the full expectation of its continuance. Anton, however, prepared breakfast with as much chatter as if nothing had passed between them the day before. Rustav followed his lead with relief. Persisting awkwardness would have made it too difficult to remain, and Rustav's growing curiosity about this strange mountain village made the thought of leaving as unwelcome as staying had once been.

As the days flowed by, Rustav found himself falling into a sort of routine in the rustic mountain village. Each morning, as he sat with Anton whittling on the porch, Rustav glanced up at the trees and decided he could afford to stay another day. After all, he'd not yet heard any rumors of upheaval and destruction from the valley. Each afternoon, he considered visiting Dantzel and decided it was too soon. Once a week, he bent to Anton's nagging and visited the village church, where Father Lute would check the progress of his healing wounds with patient acceptance of Rustav's wariness. Twice a week, he accompanied Anton to the general store, bearing Anton's wooden ornaments for Bryson to sell. Each time, the shopkeeper's son, Cabel, would swarm Rustav with questions about the ocean. When Rustav mentioned offhand that he had visited both the castle and the mainland, so many questions came pouring out that Rustav sincerely worried about the boy passing out from lack of oxygen.

While sitting through Cabel's extensive interrogations, Rustav noticed an unexpected side effect: the longer he spent describing the places he had visited to Cabel, the more crowded the shop became. Accustomed as he was to keeping an eye on his surroundings, Rustav was uncomfortably aware of the crowd of young ladies who seemed to be increasingly drawn to the store at the same time he was there. Most of them were content to giggle among themselves and pretend (badly) not to stare; but one, a brazen girl with long black curls, wasn't content to sit as an observer.

"Did you ever meet a desert girl on the mainland?" she asked the fourth time Rustav visited the store, stepping forward confrontationally. Rustav looked up at her coolly, using his peripheral vision to examine the other visitors now watching him closely. There was a crowd of boys on the edge of the crowd, feigning disinterest. He'd have to play carefully here, or he was likely to get a refresher on his nearly faded black eye.

"A few. Mainly slave girls in trading caravans."

"Is it true that their skin is burnt black by the sun?"

"Tessa!" the girl's friend gasped, but Tessa stood firm in her boldness. Rustav felt in his pocket for a scrap of walnut wood that Anton had given him that morning and pulled it out.

"Closer to this color," he said, holding it up. "They could withstand the sun for hours, even in the heat of the day when all I wanted to do was hide in the shade of the tent."

Tessa took the wood from Rustav's hand, her fingers brushing his and lingering longer than was needful. She held it up to the light. "They must have been very beautiful. I daresay you've met many beautiful women in your adventures."

Some adventures, Rustav thought. He had fared no better among Karstafel's trading company than the slaves in the desert did. "You could say that."

Tessa advanced, a coy smile appearing. "And how do the mountains measure up?"

The boys were no longer pretending to look away, and even Anton was watching from the storekeeper's counter to see what would happen next. Though he'd never show it, Rustav's mouth was dry. How did he land himself in these scrapes? Last time a girl had come on to Rustav like this, her father had bloodied Rustav's nose.

As Rustav weighed his options, the store's front door opened, admitting the answer to Rustav's dilemma. With a smile, he stood, took the wood back from Tessa, and made his way to Artha, the baker's wife, who had just entered. He peeled the towel back from the platter she held in her hand, revealing a pile of freshly baked pastries. "What greater beauty can a man ask for?"

As the store erupted in roars of laughter—the loudest coming from the cluster of boys—Tessa's face flushed angrily. Rustav knew well from years of experience when it was time to bow out, and he backed through the shop door while all the attention was on the flustered and bewildered Artha.

Ducking under the window, Rustav skirted around the building and began running, reveling in the ease with which his healing body sped through the streets. He had a lot of practice running through pain, and he could always outpace anyone who had ever chased him; but with his injuries on the mend and nobody coming after him, running was as good as flying. Two minutes took him out of the town, and he sprinted through dirt roads and meadows, breathing in so much joy from the freedom of running that he doubted whether he would ever stop.

But stop he did when a familiar cottage came into view. Almost involuntarily, Rustav slowed his step, coming to a full stop at the edge of a garden where a girl worked, her hair pulled back in a long chestnut braid.

"What are you doing?" he called, energized recklessness from his run pushing him to do what he had feared to do for the past two weeks. Dantzel straightened from her work and threw him a disdainful glance that instantly popped his bubble of satisfaction.

"Working. Some of us have more to do than sit around and gossip in the town."

Her cold tone surprised him and hurt more than it should

have. After all, he thought harshly, coolness was the nicest of tones generally used toward him. Still, the memory of that afternoon at the stream tugged at him, and he couldn't resist taking a step forward and trying another approach.

"I'm sorry I haven't come to visit you."

"I'm sure you've been busy. I heard you made quite the splash in town."

Rustav pulled a face. "Trust me, that's not what kept me away. I just survived a shark attack in the middle of Bryson's store. A girl named Tessa."

"Tessa, huh?" Dantzel jabbed moodily at the dirt with the shovel she was holding. "Reeled her in a little more securely than you expected? I'm sure she just loved hearing about your exotic past. That's all the girls in town have talked about the past week or so."

"She doesn't know a thing about my past," Rustav snapped, unexpectedly needled by her words. "All she's done is eavesdrop while I'm telling Cabel about the mainland."

Dantzel dug a little more around the plants at her feet, and Rustav drew nearer, encouraged by her silence. A funny thought was occurring to him, but he didn't dare give it voice in the face of her irritation. Instead, he focused down on the plant she was working around. "The pumpkins look like they're coming along well."

"They're fine, I suppose."

Giving up on conversation for the time being, Rustav knelt down a few feet away from Dantzel and began searching out the small green sprouts that he had seen her pulling last time. They worked in silence for several minutes before Dantzel stuck her shovel into the dirt and leaned on it.

"All right, then, why haven't you come to visit? You said you would, you know."

Rustav continued pulling weeds out of the dirt, wiggling them carefully to get the roots free. With his eyes on the dirt, he admitted, "I was scared."

"Of me?" Dantzel asked, raising an eyebrow. "After you went and faced down all those Guards in the marketplace?"

With a wry grin, Rustav replied, "The Guards I can handle. But that day at the stream, you got inside of me like no one else ever has. You know more about me than I've told anyone."

"Hardly. You've spent the last couple of weeks telling half the town about your life."

"You're not listening." Rustav sighed, rocking back to sit in the dirt. "They think I'm some dashing adventurer, traveling far and wide and bringing back tales of the exotic mainland. You know that I'm nothing more than a kicked dog running away from my own sorry past."

Her attention now fully diverted, Dantzel left her shovel stuck in the dirt and walked over to sit beside Rustav. "Is that what you see in yourself?"

"Well . . . yeah."

Dantzel watched him closely, and Rustav kept his eyes trained self-consciously forward. "I'm sorry for acting like a jerk," she said.

"It's okay," Rustav said with half a smile, chancing a sideways glance at her. "It was a good joke to see someone jealous over me."

"I was not jealous!" Dantzel protested, flicking a bit of dirt at his trousers. "I was merely concerned for your well-being, getting mixed up with the likes of Tessa."

Sticking his hand in his pocket, Rustav hesitated for a moment, then withdrew it and set something on the dirt, keeping it covered with his hand. "I also waited because I wanted to have something for you when I came back. It's not very good, but—well, it's something."

He was at the edge of the garden before Dantzel had time to pick up the small wooden bird sitting beside her, rough but obviously carefully made. It wasn't like any bird she had seen before, no doubt a seabird that lived on the coast. "Wait!" she called, and Rustav paused, looking back apprehensively. Dantzel held the bird delicately and smiled. "You don't have to wait two weeks before you come back again."

A pleased look flashed across Rustav's face, and he nodded once before dashing off at a startling pace. Dantzel watched him go with a warm, albeit somewhat confused, feeling pulsing inside of her at the unexpected gift.

CHAPTER FIVE

FROM THEN ON, IT WAS A RARE DAY THAT DIDN'T find Rustav at Anna and Dantzel's cottage. Rustav spent fewer mornings contemplating the forest that stood on the slopes above him, telling himself that perhaps Karstafel had forgotten about him by now, that he would hear warnings before the worse threat came snapping at his heels. He would have plenty of time to slip away before the mountains were in any danger.

Dantzel began dreading her hours in the garden less; they seemed inexplicably shorter with Rustav there, telling her the tales he'd picked up at coastal taverns and in mainland trading caravans. Anna's kind and gentle manner seemed to puzzle him at first, but once he had grown accustomed to it, he was willing and eager to do anything she asked of him.

After nearly three months, Dantzel couldn't help but marvel over the change that had taken place in this hardened runaway. His blue eyes no longer glowered darkly, and he no longer leaped to the defensive whenever someone looked at him. The transformation wasn't complete; there were still days when Rustav withdrew into a shell of contrariness that made Dantzel crazy. He could be maddening on occasion, but even after the thorny days, Dantzel found herself waiting anxiously for him to finish Anton's chores and join her.

On this particular day, Dantzel was busily sweeping the hard-packed dirt floor, doing her best not to stare out the window in the direction of the town. Her deception, however, was not lost on her mother.

"No Rustav yet?"

Dantzel shrugged, eyes carefully trained on the broom in her hand as she swept. "I'm sure Anton has plenty of chores for him to help with there. And you know how Cabel is trailing after him every free moment, begging to hear more about the mainland and the castle and the island."

"He is an inquisitive little fellow, isn't he?" Anna smiled into the socks she was darning. "He adores Rustav, and I think Rustav is growing quite fond of him, judging by the way the two of them roughhouse in the garden and race to the stream. They're good for each other."

"Mother," Dantzel said impatiently. "You have that smile on."

"What smile?" Anna asked, raising an innocent eyebrow.

"The smile that says you're thinking something far different from what you're saying. What are you thinking about?"

Anna put down the darning, sighing. "You do love to be direct, don't you, dear? Well, plainly put, it seems that Rustav has grown rather fond of you as well, and you haven't exactly been the exacerbating thornbush you always were with the other boys in town."

Now wishing she hadn't been so direct, Dantzel set her broom aside. "I thought you wanted me to fall in love. Not that I am in love," she amended hastily, "but it sounds like you don't like the idea."

"I'm not opposed, dear, just cautious. I know that Rustav has suffered terribly, and I have seen how much good this village has done him, your friendship has done him. But with someone like him—you just never know how quickly things might change."

Heat was rushing into Dantzel's ears and throat, and she had to bite her tongue for a moment before she spoke. "You think he'll change?"

"I think circumstances might change, very suddenly and without warning." Anna stood and walked to her daughter, taking her hand and squeezing it. "Understand me, love. I don't want to discourage you. He's a fine young man, and I think he cares for you. But I have spent twelve years alone. I know what it is to be separated by a trick of circumstance. And I don't want the same thing to happen to you."

Dantzel studied her mother's face: the tired eyes, the worry creases, the weight of toil, the light of deep love. "If you had known, would it ever have changed your mind about Papa?"

Hesitating briefly, Anna shook her head. "Never."

Neither said anything more. Anna returned to her socks; Dantzel leaned on her broom in the doorway, turning her mother's words over in her mind as she watched two figures, one tall and one short, approaching the house in a zigzag, suggesting that Cabel had started a game of Fisherman's Bait on the way over. Her mother's words had raised an unexpected defensiveness inside of her, a determination to prove her wrong, to prove . . .

What, exactly? Dantzel shied away from admitting, even in

her own mind, what her mother had alluded to and what she almost feared must be true. She had affirmed over and over to Anna that she would grow to be an old maid, the cranky spinster of the village, the strange old lady who got away with anything simply because the entire village thought she was a little off her rocker. But now . . . Dantzel couldn't ignore the pinching feeling inside of her at the prospect of no more afternoons working in the garden or sitting by the stream with Rustav. She had grown attached to Rustav; she couldn't deny how pleased she was that his smile had grown more frequent, or that it was often a result of something she said. With an impatient sigh, Dantzel began sweeping off the carved stone in front of the door, raising a cloud of dust with her vigorous efforts.

It took only a few more minutes for the two boys to reach the cottage, Cabel fully winded, Rustav barely breathing hard. Rustav lifted a hand in greeting as he hopped over the gate, not bothering to open it. Cabel tried to do the same, jumping as high as his short legs could muster, but he still ended up in an undignified clamber over the fence.

"Sorry it took me so long," Rustav said. "Anton needed me to carry some of his projects out to the square for him. Half the village is crammed there today."

"How does it look?" Dantzel asked, relieved to have a distraction from her mother's words. Rustav shrugged as Cabel sidled up beside him with a sly grin.

"Full of people. And ribbon. There's ribbon strung over every inch of the place."

Anna's voice called out from inside the cottage. "That was a very manly answer, dear boy. What color has Julie chosen? How are the tables arranged? Have they begun setting out the food yet?"

"Uh, there was a lot of yellow," Rustav answered, his expression so bewildered that Dantzel had to withhold a laugh. "I saw a few platters of bread, and . . . knock it off, Cabel," he muttered, pushing away the boy, who had been digging an elbow into Rustav's ribs. Cabel gave an exaggerated sigh.

"What's eating you?" Dantzel asked. Cabel folded his arms and looked meaningfully at Rustav, who looked as though he sincerely wished he could throw Cabel in the stream.

"It's nothing," Rustav said irritably. "I've already told him I'm not going."

"Not going where?" Dantzel asked. "To the wedding celebration tonight? What makes you think you can get away with that?"

"I'm not one of the villagers," Rustav said, ducking his head and scuffing at the dirt. "Why would they want me there?"

"You've been here three months," Dantzel said, stepping forward to prod him in the chest. "That makes you a villager whether you like it or not. Julie will want you there because I want you there, and it's her wedding, so you don't have a choice. If I don't see you in the square from the very beginning, I will go to Anton's house and drag you out myself."

As Rustav regarded her with a half-amused, half-scared smile, Dantzel reflected that she might have been a little over-zealous in her urging. *But*, she thought, *if I'm going to have one night in a new dress with no dirt on my hands and knees, he had better be there for it.*

"All right," Rustav said. "It sounds like the town square is a safer place than Anton's tonight."

ANNA SHOOED RUSTAV AND CABEL AWAY AFTER
only a couple of hours, insisting that she and Dantzel needed
the time to prepare for the celebration. Rustav raced Cabel
home, slowing enough to make the smaller boy feel like
he was making a decent showing. They parted at the town
square, Cabel scurrying off to his father's store, Rustav turning up the hill toward Anton's. Before he went too far, Rustav
paused, looking back over the busy square with Dantzel's
words running through his mind: *I want you there.*

Rustav had once seen a performer turning backflips in
the streets of Markuum. He wished now that he had learned
to do the same trick. It echoed exactly the feelings bouncing
around inside his chest at that moment.

Anton was sitting on the front porch, holding a block of
wood and a knife, when Rustav returned. Something about
the scene pulled Rustav roughly back to earth, though it took
him a moment to place exactly what it was. There were no
wood shavings lying on the ground around Anton's chair.
Though the old man held a whittling knife, the wood in his
left hand was untouched. Anton could never resist a piece
of wood; the moment the wood was in his hand, chips were
flying. Usually. Rustav took in Anton's faraway gaze and had
to reassure himself that the old carpenter was still breathing.

"Is everything okay?" Rustav asked, following Anton's
blank stare and seeing nothing. Anton blinked, cleared his
throat in a low rumble, and patted the chair beside him.
Rustav sat obediently, casting another curious glance at
the block.

"How are Anna and Dantzel?" Anton asked, apparently
unaware of Rustav's question. Rustav shrugged, trying
unsuccessfully to suppress a smile.

"Good. All they could talk about was the wedding tonight. Dantzel threatened to come after me if I didn't show up."

Anton's somber nod was enough to melt away the remainder of Rustav's excitement. The reason for the anxiety behind Anton's tired blue eyes became painfully clear. Rustav looked down to study a dandelion at his feet, wishing he'd had the sense to keep his mouth shut.

The old carpenter cleared his throat again and looked down at his wood, though the knife remained perfectly still. "I've noticed that you two have been spending a lot of time together."

Rustav kept his eyes on the dandelion, choosing not to answer.

"Rustav, there are a few things that you should know before—starting anything," Anton continued, his voice soft, as if he were trying to ease the blow. Rustav felt trapped. He should've known better than to think he could get involved with Dantzel. If he were honest with himself, he wouldn't trust himself with Dantzel, were he in Anton's place. He should have just gone through the forest weeks ago. Then he wouldn't have had to sit through this humiliating discussion of why Anton didn't want Rustav anywhere near his dear girl.

"It's okay, Anton," Rustav said shortly, desperate to cut off the conversation. "I know Dantzel deserves better. You don't have to worry that I'll do anything stupid."

Anton's mouth hung open for a moment, then he shook his head and said earnestly, "No, no, you don't understand. I wouldn't have any exception—I would be downright pleased if—you see, it's just—" Anton sighed in frustration.

"What?" Rustav asked irritably, certain that Anton was just trying to think of a nice way to confirm Rustav's doubts.

Anton grabbed his cane and gripped the handle tightly, clearing his throat and opening his mouth several times before he finally spoke.

"I knew your father."

The words hung heavy in the thick air. Rustav stared blankly at Anton, repeating the words over and over in his head before he was certain that he understood them. When he was sure there had been no confusion, Rustav couldn't resist kicking violently at the dandelion. "So you knew the jerk that got Karstafel's sister pregnant. No wonder you're wary of me."

"I am not wary of you," Anton said indignantly. "And Karstafel's sister has nothing to do with it. I'm the one who left you on Karstafel's doorstep."

Rustav's head jerked up, his teeth clenching. Was Anton playing some sort of sick joke? Or was the gray on his head starting to spread to his mind? It wasn't possible. Was it? If there was any chance—if Anton had really known Rustav's father—if Rustav really wasn't related to Karstafel . . .

"Why would you do that?" Rustav asked, scenario after bizarre scenario spinning through his mind. Anton had blue eyes too. Was it possible that these two valley folk in the middle of a mountain village were somehow connected by blood? An unreasonable hope sprang up in Rustav's chest, dispelling somewhat his fear that Anton had gone completely crazy. He waited for an answer, hardly breathing as Anton pulled his thoughts together.

"Your father was a dear friend of mine," Anton said, looking more bent and tired than ever. "We were . . . foolish, I suppose, unaware of the dangers that surrounded us. Too absorbed in our own childish games." Anton rubbed his eyes hard with one hand. "He and your mother were killed by Elanokiev."

Just when Rustav thought he couldn't be any more wrong-footed. "The king? Why? Were they rebelling?"

"Elanokiev wasn't the king yet," Anton said sharply, the deep sorrow on his face replaced for a brief instant with anger, startling in its ferocity. "This was during his struggle for power."

It was too hard to believe, but Rustav found himself desperate to hear more. "But why? How did you end up with me?"

"It happened the night before your first birthday," Anton said woodenly. "I had carved you a present—that pendant you still wear around your neck—and I wanted to drop it off as a surprise for your parents to find first thing in the morning. My timing couldn't have been more fortunate—or more tragic." His mouth trembled for a moment, and a tear slipped its way down his grooved cheek. "I arrived just in time to view your parents' death. With some luck, I managed to sneak into your room and grab you before the murderer could get to you too. I broke my leg jumping out the window," Anton said, gesturing to his bad leg, "but I still managed to get you away from there."

Dumbly, Rustav fingered his wooden pendant, tracing the designs he knew so well and trying to reconcile them with the insane story that Anton was telling him. "Then what?"

"I knew I would be on the run for some time, and even if I ever managed to settle down, I wouldn't be able to give you the life you deserved."

Rustav laughed bitterly. "So you dropped me on Karstafel's doorstep."

Pain etched itself into every line on Anton's face. "If I had known . . . you have no idea the horror that I felt when I realized what I had done to you. All I saw was the large house, the prosperous business. I thought that surely such an afflu- ent person would be more than able to care for an orphaned child. I didn't dare try to leave an explanation, so I just left a scrap of paper with your name."

"He didn't even pick me up off the doorstep," Rustav said. His cheeks were burning with—what? Embarrassment? Rage? "He told me over and over that the only reason I made it into his house was that a servant girl hid me in her room after he had gone to the office. The only reason he let me stay was in hopes of free labor and a scapegoat."

Anton sank his face into his hands, and Rustav struggled to keep breathing evenly. So many questions were pushing their way out that they all jammed up in Rustav's throat. Why had Elanokiev wanted his parents dead? Where had Anton gone after leaving Rustav in Markuum? Why didn't he ever go back to check on him?

The longer he thought, the more a weight pulled at Rustav's chest, an anger that he hadn't felt for weeks. "What's it matter?" he asked, scowling down at the dandelion as he crushed it underfoot. "My parents are dead, and Karstafel is miles away. Besides, it's about time that I started moving again."

"Moving?" Anton sat up straight, finally startled out of his reverie. "You can't still be thinking about going through the forest."

"I am, and I will," Rustav snapped. "I'm getting out of this country while I still can."

"Why?" Anton asked. "You have a new life here, with

people who care about you. The rest of the country has all but forgotten about us, now that Elanokiev has taken all of our artisans to his court—at least, all who are still fit to work," he added with a rueful glance at his bent leg. "Why not stay here with us?"

"Who's to say you'll stay forgotten?" Rustav rubbed the wood in his hand with his thumb. He was an idiot to have forgotten why he was running in the first place. Somehow, he had never expected just one more day to turn into three months. "What if everything changes? What if Elanokiev doesn't stay in power?"

"I'd say all the better," Anton said acidly. "Anyone would be better than that foolish traitor. The day he killed his brother, he signed this country over to worse demons than ours."

"Well, he's going to do something worse."

The wrinkles on Anton's forehead deepened as his eyebrows drew together. "Worse how?"

Rustav's heart was starting to beat faster, and he glanced around anxiously. He had grown to appreciate Anton, even to trust him. Anton deserved a fair warning. But if anyone else heard Rustav talking—he still hadn't forgotten the Guards chasing him out of the castle with swords drawn.

"Elanokiev knows he's out of control," he said quietly, keeping an eye out for anyone who might draw too near to the house. "We have nothing but coastline here, and Elanokiev has cut our navy down until they can barely cover our shores. The Guards are a joke clear across the Ravian Desert, and everybody knows our king's been trading on borrowed gold for years. So why hasn't anyone attacked us in the past fourteen years?"

"Well," Anton mused, "we are a small country. The valley is the only fertile part of the country, though the ports are a useful acquisition for sea trade."

"Anton," Rustav interrupted in exasperation. "Why has no one invaded us?"

With a nod, Anton conceded, "Because they all think the forest is inhabited by demons."

"Exactly. The forest demons, though quiet, provide ample deterrence to most of our potential enemies. The only ones we might worry about are those with more vocal demons than our own."

"The island of Burrihim," Anton breathed, and Rustav shushed him, eyeing the boys roughhousing several houses away.

"The Burrihim islanders are starting to talk with the king about a peaceful transfer of power. They say he'll remain as an image, with all the extravagant lifestyle he's ever enjoyed, but they'll take the government and 'rescue' our country from its economic woes. Elanokiev was talking to Karstafel about arranging for a slow stream of islanders to begin coming through Markuum's ports. They'll leak in week by week, month by month, taking control without all the mess of war and conquering."

"How long?" Anton asked. For the first time, Rustav saw something like fear in his face.

"They're moving slowly, talking about years. But who knows if the islanders are really that patient? Why would I want to stick around and see? No, by the time they start leaking in, I plan to be far away from here."

"You can't," Anton said, a hint of panic in his eyes. "You've got to stay. This changes everything. Your place is not in the eastern countries. It's here, defending your people."

"My people?" Rustav scoffed. "Who am I to be charged with defending anyone? I've been to the island, Anton. I've heard their demons screaming. I've seen the people who offer human sacrifice to those demons. And if those people are coming here, I fully intend to make my escape long before they have a chance to reign in terror. The forest is my only way out, and so it's the forest I'll take."

"You don't understand," Anton said pleadingly. "That is precisely why you must stay. You know what's coming. The people are already primed for revolution; together, they would be far more than sufficient to fight an influx of islanders. All they lack is a unified cause, a figure to bring them all together. You could supply that, better than anyone could imagine."

Anton was speaking with feverish excitement that left Rustav searching the old man's visage for a clear sign of madness. Rustav shook his head emphatically, drawing back away from Anton. "No one would want to follow me, and I'm sure not looking to lead any revolutions. Did you miss the part about how I'm ducking out to save my own neck? Your plan sounds like a perfect path to get killed in nasty ways."

Standing, Rustav started walking down the street. "Where are you going?" Anton called, reaching for his cane and struggling to his feet. "Rustav! I have more to tell you! Come back!"

Rustav began running, the methodical thud of his feet against the dirt roads beating away Anton's wild words. He took the shortest route out of the town and then took a sharp turn to head directly uphill. He blew past the church and slowed only as he approached the tree line.

Five feet from the first of the old trees, Rustav stopped. He hadn't yet decided whether he fully intended to plunge recklessly through the forest, spurred on by the absurdity of Anton's declarations. After all, things had been going so well. It had been three months since he ran from the castle. Three months with no Guards and no sign of Karstafel. He could almost believe that he had outrun his problems.

But if he stayed, his problems were bound to catch up. Not even the mountains would avoid the island plague. The sooner he moved on, the better.

But what about the others? Didn't they deserve a warning too, after all they had done for him? Could he really just leave them behind to suffer under the rule of demon-worshippers?

Torn by indecision, Rustav stared into the darkness of the woods, the world where scarcely any sunlight penetrated the thick tangle of boughs. Something within the shadows drew him in, straining at a place deep inside of him, a place he had never before been aware of. Cautiously, he took a step closer, then another, until he could reach out and touch the nearest of the trees, placing his hand lightly on the deeply grooved trunk.

Whispering filled his ears, and Rustav strained to hear. Though he couldn't understand any words, he could feel the spirit of the message—excitement, anticipation, invitation. The whispering pulled at him, urged him onward. *Into the woods to meet my death*, Rustav thought ruefully, trying to shake the mysticism of the moment. Still, he couldn't free himself from the urgency of the whispers. A breeze pushed at his back, and Rustav pressed his hand a little harder against the rough bark of the tree. He'd be able to hear the words, he was sure, if he just had another moment.

And then the whispering stopped.

"You're not really going in there, are you?"

Rustav spun around, half angry and half relieved at the interruption. Cabel stood with his head cocked to the side, inquisitive brown eyes shining brightly. The boy continued, a gleam of adventure in his eye. "It could be dangerous, you know. Might be a good idea to have someone around who's grown up on the edge of the forest."

Released from the intensity of the moment, Rustav felt a little embarrassed at how powerfully the forest had affected him. He shoved Cabel playfully with his elbow as he turned to walk away from the forest. "You don't think I'd be stupid enough to go into the forest, do you?"

"That's what Anton seemed to think you were doing."

Rustav threw Cabel a sharp glance as the boy trotted down the slope beside him. "Anton sent you after me?"

"No." Cabel ducked his head and kicked at a stone partially buried in the dirt. "Do you really think the islanders are going to invade?"

Halting, Rustav grabbed Cabel by the shoulder. "How long were you listening?"

Cabel shrugged, now digging a hole in the moist ground with his toe. "A while. Pa asked me to deliver a vest that Anton ordered for you, for tonight. I heard Anton asking you about the forest, so I just sort of hung back. Neither of you noticed me."

How had Rustav missed him standing there? What if it hadn't been Cabel, but a Guard? Cursing himself for being so careless, Rustav searched for a way to lighten the words he had spoken but couldn't remember exactly what he had said. In the midst of his struggle, Cabel spoke again, voice small and not nearly as cocky as it generally was. "I don't want the islanders to get me. If you go . . . I want to go with you."

Once again, Rustav became aware of a place deep inside of him, the same part that the trees had pulled at so strongly—only now, it was filled with regret and sorrow at the poorly hidden fear on the boy's round young face. Rustav had to stay, just long enough to spread the warning. One more day wouldn't be enough for the islanders to take over. And besides—Dantzel had threatened him pretty thoroughly if he didn't show up at the wedding celebration.

Reaching out to ruffle Cabel's curly brown hair, Rustav affected a carefree tone. "Listen, nobody's going to get you. Come on, we've only got a couple more hours before the party begins."

CHAPTER SIX

AFTER THE SUN HAD DISAPPEARED BEYOND THE horizon, Rustav trudged behind Anton toward the already crowded town square. A wave of claustrophobia hit him as they squeezed into the square along with the rest of the village. Strange faces pressed in from all sides, and the screeches of musicians tuning their instruments tore at his ears. Rustav was beginning to seriously doubt his foolhardy decision to stay for the celebration. What was he expecting to do the entire time? stand around awkwardly, watching the crowds of unfamiliar faces? And they had dancing. Rustav didn't dance. In his first moment of sanity all day, Rustav tugged at the old carpenter's sleeve.

"Anton, I don't think this was such a good idea," he said. Just then, the people around him erupted in cheers, drowning out his words. Jumping, Rustav looked around wildly and saw a man and a woman, dressed in their finest clothes (which were still plain by valley standards), holding hands and running through the square. As they reached the fountain in the middle, they jumped up together to stand on the broad stone sides of the fountain. A large basket was handed up to the woman—the bride, Rustav realized. She took the basket and faced away from the crowd. After a moment of suspense, the bride brought the basket up over her head, emptying its contents—yellow flowers, large and small and every shape imaginable—onto the crowd behind her, which, Rustav now saw, was made up entirely of girls from ages five to seventeen. The girls jumped and grabbed at the flowers, tucking them into their hair and dresses. As he watched, Rustav saw Dantzel in the midst of the girls, leaning down to help a small girl fasten her flowers securely. All at once, all thoughts of turning back fled.

"Just in time," Anton shouted over the noise of the crowd, a broad grin on his face. A band began playing, and he had to shout a little louder. "They've just been married in a small and solemn ceremony, and now we welcome them as a couple with celebration. Enjoy yourself, lad. There's nothing better than a wedding celebration in the mountains."

With that, Anton disappeared into the crowd before Rustav could say a word. Feeling abandoned, Rustav edged his way over to a table laden with food and drink and watched the people uncertainly. There didn't seem to be any price on the ample amounts of food; people simply ate and drank as they pleased. The lively music of the band had inspired the villagers to clear a space in the square, and couples were beginning to fill the space, moving in rhythm, ducking in and out of each other, forming circles and squares and lines and somehow never colliding. Rustav looked on in bewilderment, wondering how they knew what to do next.

"Feeling a bit shy, lad?" asked a voice with a heavy mountain accent. Rustav turned to see a jolly, rather plump woman standing behind the table, smiling at him. She held out a mug to him, and Rustav took it tentatively. "Drink up! There's a good lad. It'd be a shame to see a nice young newcomer like yourself not enjoying his first celebration here."

Nodding his thanks with an uncertain smile, Rustav turned back to the celebrations and took a hesitant sip from the mug. To his surprise, it was a warm, nutty brew, nothing like the vile grog he had sampled in the taverns of Markuum. He drank a little deeper, feeling some of his apprehensions start to melt away.

"Rustav!"

Heart leaping into his throat, Rustav turned to find Dantzel fighting her way toward him, eyes bright and cheeks pink with excitement, several flowers tucked into her braid. Losing interest in his mug, Rustav set it on the table and turned to greet Dantzel. However, before Dantzel could make it to him, someone caught her by the hand—a tall, gangly fellow with impossibly curly brown hair—and pulled her to the middle of the dancing. Rustav leaned back heavily against the table and returned to brood over his mug.

"That's young Master Jeffer," the woman behind the table said, loudly enough to be heard over the noise. Rustav glanced over his shoulder, distracted.

"What?"

"Jeffer. The young buck who ain't quite learned to manage his hooves yet. He's been sweet on Dantzel since he were a kid."

"Has he," Rustav said sourly, then checked himself. What did it matter who was sweet on who? He was only here to give fair warning, then he was on his way out for good. Another day and he'd never see this town again.

"You ask me, though, he should've given it up long ago. She's a special one, she is. She's just needed the right one to come along."

Rustav didn't answer; he didn't like that this woman he had never met before guessed so much about what he was thinking. He took a long drink and stared moodily at the dancers, trying not to pick out any curly-headed, clumsy boys.

"Why are you drinking alone like a crotchety old man?"

Dantzel appeared at Rustav's shoulder out of nowhere, and Rustav's spirits lifted in spite of himself. "Everyone is too taken in with the dancing to drink with a stranger," he said with half a smile. "Solve my problem?"

"Of course!" Dantzel said, beaming. "Come on!" She took Rustav by the elbow and began to pull him forward, but Rustav dug in his heels in alarm.

"What? I meant drink with me!"

With a smile that told Rustav clearly that she had known exactly what he meant, Dantzel replied, "I thought you meant dance with me!"

Heart racing, Rustav shook his head. "I don't dance."

"Sure you do," Dantzel said, releasing her hold on his elbow. "You just need to drink more."

Rustav lifted his mug with a grin. "I'll drink to that," he said.

Dantzel allowed Rustav only a few minutes of reprieve before she began prodding him once again toward the whirling dancers. Rustav shook his head, refusing persistently. Finally, Dantzel took him by the hand, and Rustav forgot for a moment why he had been so stalwart in refusing. Shaking his head to clear it and thinking that the country brew must have been stronger than he realized, Rustav said, "I don't know how."

"Laddie, half the dancers down there are so drunk that they only remember every other step," said the woman behind the table, who had plainly been taking Dantzel's side. "You've only drunk enough to limber up your feet a little."

Dantzel laughed, pulling a little harder on Rustav's hand. "It's true," she said, cocking her head and looking up at him with an extra brightness in her eyes. Rustav felt his reserves falling away one by one. "Come on, I'll help you."

Later, all Rustav could remember was a whirl of faces, Dantzel's standing out above the rest. He couldn't recall much of the dancing, except for the triumph of not stepping on Dantzel's feet once. Occasionally, another young—or not-so-young—man or woman would cut in to steal one or the other of them away, but they always returned for just one more dance. It was very late when the band began to pack up their instruments and the crowds began to disperse, leaving behind a few who had consumed a little too much ale. Rustav was tired but also oddly exhilarated. He didn't want the night to end, and his mind—moving somewhat slower than usual—searched desperately for a way to make it last. At last, he settled on a temporary solution, one that fell back on the social training Anton had been trying to get across to him.

"Dantzel," he said, his stomach suddenly twisting with nerves, "may I walk you home?"

Dantzel's expression was surprised but pleased. "Of course," she said, blushing a little more easily, perhaps, as she had not entirely abstained from the drinking herself. She slipped her arm through Rustav's, and warm blood shot through Rustav's veins. With a heart so light, he would surely float away if Dantzel weren't there to hold him down.

The summer night was warm and peaceful, and words flowed from Rustav so easily that he could hardly believe he was the one talking. The sky was clear and the stars bright; he pointed out several constellations and told Dantzel the sailors' stories about the different formations. She, in turn, told him about the plants they passed—what they were used for, their significance to the mountain people, legends attached to them. All too soon, they were standing in front of her small home, and she laid a hand on the gate.

"Dantzel," Rustav said abruptly. Little warning bells started clanging in the back of his mind, telling him to turn and run, but it was hard to hear them through all the fuzziness. She turned to look at him quizzically, and he swallowed before plunging in. "I think—I think I'm falling in love with you."

Time froze. The warning bells were suddenly a lot louder, only now they were oh-boy-you've-done-it-now bells. Rustav's breath stayed trapped in his chest while Dantzel stood and stared at him for much longer than was comfortable.

"I think you drank a bit much tonight," she finally said, and he nodded obediently. Then she put a hand to her forehead and muttered, "I think I drank a bit much tonight."

Rustav didn't trust himself to say anything else. The light-headed happiness had given way, and he was starting to realize the enormity of his mistake. Dantzel took a few steps back and opened the gate.

"Good . . . good night, Rustav," Dantzel said, her voice uneven. "Thank you for walking me home."

With that, she fled up the walkway and into the house, leaving Rustav very much alone on the dirt path. He stared at the dark windows of the house for a long time before turning and beginning the slow, long walk back to Anton's.

DANTZEL PRESSED HER BACK AGAINST THE FRONT door as if to barricade herself. Closing her eyes, she sank down to the floor, unable to shut out the image of those wide, earnest blue eyes, the sound of Rustav's uncertain tone. Dantzel put her arms around her knees and propped her forehead on her arms. The most unnerving part of the entire scene was not what Rustav had said, though his words had certainly startled her; no, the most frightening part was how much she felt it back.

CHAPTER SEVEN

RUSTLING AND TAPPING NOISES PRESSED AGAINST Rustav's ears, grinding into the headache that he could feel even before opening his eyes. The sun was already up; a red light shone through his eyelids, but flickered slightly. Anton must be up and moving. Rustav turned his head away to block out the light, listening to the sound of movement as he tried to get back to sleep. In his semiconscious state, he knew that something unpleasant had happened the night before, and he didn't want to wake up enough to remember it fully. Unfortunately, Anton was making enough noise for a small elephant, keeping Rustav from sinking back into blissful unconsciousness. Awareness began to surface, and Rustav remembered the dancing, the drinking, the walk to Dantzel's—and the ensuing fiasco.

Groaning, Rustav threw an arm over his eyes. What in all the skies and seas had ever possessed him to be such a fool? Spouting about love and foolishness, the stuff of children's tales, no more real than kobolds.

The sounds around him were changing, and Rustav

stiffened. Noises were coming from all over the room—far too much area for one old man to cover. Slowly, he squinted his right eye open a slit.

Red cloaks surrounded him on all sides.

Without even taking the time to open his eyes all the way, Rustav flipped off the mat, plowing into several legs as four pairs of hands grabbed at him. One Guard went flying into his buddies, giving Rustav time to spring to his feet. Across the room, two Guards were dragging Anton out of bed, pinning his arms tightly behind him. Rustav launched himself at them, but a Guard caught him around the throat, strangling him. With the help of his elbows and a number of well-placed kicks, Rustav managed to free himself, only to come up against another Guard—the same one he had encountered on his very first day in Gebir. The Guard bared his teeth in a vicious grin, and Rustav barely dodged his fist. Somewhere amid the chaos, he heard Anton shouting. "Run, Rustav! Run!"

"Leave him alone!" Rustav yelled, still fighting his way across the room. Anton met his eyes for a brief second, transmitting in that moment all the urgency backing his words.

"Get out of here!" Anton shouted as one of the Guards shoved him to the floor. "You're the one they're after! Go now!"

Hands were grasping at Rustav's arms and legs on all sides; if he didn't get out of there soon, he would never free himself. Tearing himself away and decking the Guard nearest the door, Rustav fled.

With terror driving his limbs, Rustav was out of the town in less than a minute, flying through the streets so quickly that faces starting to peek out of windows were nothing more than a blur. He was on a direct course for the trees when the thought occurred to him: if the Guards had known just where to find him, who was to say they wouldn't know where he spent his days? A brief glance over his shoulder assured him that he had left all the Guards far behind, and Rustav darted off to the south, not bothering to try and hide. Speed was his only ally, with the sun shining brightly down to pinpoint his exact movement across the slope. Soil churned under his feet, flying up behind him as he left the town far behind.

The windows were still dark at Dantzel's cottage. Rustav glanced anxiously behind him at the crowd of red pouring out of the town and following at half his speed. He had ten, maybe fifteen minutes to get Dantzel and Anna out before they arrived. Banging hard on the door, he shouted, "Wake up! You've got to get out of here! Come on, let me in!"

Anna opened the door in her nightgown, her hair loose and her face pale. With one more glance to gauge the arrival of the Guards, Rustav slipped into the room without waiting to be invited. "The Guards are on their way. You have to leave before they get here. You have maybe ten minutes left. Don't grab much, just get dressed and take a little food. They won't stay long once they realize I'm gone."

"Gone where?" Dantzel demanded, appearing from the back room hastily dressed and not looking terribly pleased to be awake. Her tight mouth transformed into an O and she stopped cold in the doorway. As Rustav met her wide eyes, he realized what she was looking at and shrank back against the door, folding his arms in front of him and looking away from the shock in her face.

The early waking from the Guards hadn't allowed him time to grab a shirt, a fact that had, until now, been out-ranked by numerous others in his mind. Unfortunately, now that Dantzel and Anna were both watching him with open pity, Rustav was terribly conscious of the scars encircling his torso, many of them still purple and vivid. Biting down the humiliation rising along with the blood into his face, Rustav tried to remember what he had planned to say next.

"Rustav, what happened?" Dantzel breathed, her knuckles white as she gripped the doorjamb. Rustav shook his head, fighting hard not to think about whether the night before might have ended differently if she had known, if she had felt—

Disgust filled Rustav's throat. He didn't need her pity, didn't want her pity. She had already dismissed him. He was a fool to ever have hoped.

"There's no time for that now. Get your things together and get out of the house. The Guards will be here any moment!"

"Where are you going to go?" Dantzel asked as Anna disappeared into the back room. Rustav shrugged, and she narrowed her eyes. "You're going into the forest."

"So what?" Rustav snapped, throwing his arms out. "Get some food. I don't know how much the Guards will leave in an empty house."

"Where do you think we're going to go?" In spite of her stubborn tone, Dantzel began gathering some fruit and bread into a bag. Rustav peered out the window.

"The ditch that runs behind your house. The grass is tall enough that the Guards won't see you, and you can get out of their line of sight. Once you're far enough, get out and find a place to hide until they've moved on."

"When will you come back?"

The strain of the morning mixed with the pain of the previous night finally broke Rustav's temper, and words fell hard and cutting from his mouth. "What would I have to come back for?"

Dantzel's hand tightened around the apple she held, and guilt tainted vicious pleasure as Rustav saw the hurt that he felt spread across her face. Anna reemerged from the back room, now dressed and holding a large homespun shirt. Without speaking, she held out the shirt to Rustav.

"Thanks," Rustav said, accepting the shirt with a twinge of shame, knowing that Anna had heard him speak harshly. It smelled musty as he pulled it over his head, and it hung loose on his lean frame; more guilt enveloped him as he realized Anna had given him one of her husband's shirts, saved for over a decade. Regretting his snap of temper, Rustav tried to offer Dantzel an apologetic glance, but Dantzel had turned her back on him solidly and had her head bent over the bag of food. He turned to Anna and found her watching him somberly. Fine. Good. He had managed to make this town hate him as well. It was well past time he was on his way.

"I'll try to draw them off," he said gruffly. "Maybe if I can run them around, tire them out, they'll leave your house alone. But get out of here as soon as I have them looking the other way."

He took two quick steps and was out the door, never pausing, even when Dantzel called, "Rustav, wait!"

As the front door slammed shut, Dantzel flew to the window and peered out as Rustav ran with inhuman swiftness toward the onslaught of Guards. Her ribs constricted, cutting off her breath as two of the Guards fired arrows, but Rustav somehow managed to dodge them both.

He cut wide of the group, now well spread over the slope as the faster ones tried in vain to catch their prey and the slower ones plugged along behind. Fighting back tears, Dantzel turned back to her mother.

"Is this what you meant, with all that 'things may change'?" she demanded, gesturing violently at the window. "Did you know this would happen? Did he? If he was just going to pack up and leave, why didn't he do it ages ago?"

Anna shook her head, taking up the bag that Dantzel had prepared with shaking hands that belied her calm tone. "I didn't know what would happen. And I still don't. No one could have predicted how this day would start, and no one can know how it will end. But if we don't leave soon, it won't end happily."

Dantzel snatched up a cloak and wrapped it around her, then led the way to the door. They slid around the corner, out of sight of the Guards, but Dantzel paused to peer back at the chaos on the slope. Rustav was dangerously close to a cluster of Guards, but he leaped swiftly away, bounding uphill toward the trees. Dantzel looked over at the line of trees on her left, an absurd determination taking hold of her. She shrank back against the wall, fear freezing her limbs. Anna was already halfway to the ditch, looking back. "Dantzel, hurry!"

Dantzel took a step, then glanced back at the trees. She was significantly closer than Rustav, but he was much, much faster. They would get there at about the same time. With one apologetic glance at her mother, Dantzel turned and began running, running with all her soul toward the trees that had terrified her since she was a child. She closed her eyes against the fear, then stumbled and forced them open again. She could hear the shouts drawing nearer, nearer. A few more yards. Lungs bursting, legs burning, Dantzel pushed for an extra spurt of speed. Just before she plunged into the undergrowth, Rustav's light, quick steps caught up with her, and he grabbed her arm as they broke into the tree line. He kept a firm hold on her until they were far enough in that they could no longer see the outside—an unnervingly short distance. When he released her, Dantzel bent over, heaving in as much air as she could.

"What are you doing?" Rustav hissed. "You shouldn't be here!"

"I have as much right to be here as you do," Dantzel whispered back, glancing anxiously at the perfectly still trunks surrounding her. A thrill of terror buzzed through her as she realized that she was inside the forest. Rustav turned away, running a hand through his already-rumpled hair, and Dantzel took in her surroundings, recalling every dark tale she had ever heard. When she was a child, boys used to tell her horror stories about the forest to try and scare her, and she would laugh them off; now, each and every tale came back in gruesome detail. It was dark in there, cold and wet, the dampness clinging to her skin like moss. Rubbing her arms, Dantzel tried to suppress a shiver.

"You can't just leave, Rustav," she whispered, afraid to speak any louder in this close, silent setting. "The Guards will be gone soon. They'll probably think the forest demons got you. We can hide until they leave, then everything can be like it was." *Before we fought*, she added silently. She was bewildered by Rustav's cold sharpness after the previous night's words. Was he regretting what he said? Had he not meant it? Dantzel had hoped he would bring it up with her again, give her a chance to react better now that she had come to terms with her own feelings, but the Guards hadn't given them much chance for communication.

Rustav didn't respond to her suggestion. In fact, he didn't even seem to hear her. He stood with a hand on a nearby tree, facing the heart of the woods with his eyes in shadow and his head tilted as if he were listening to something far away. Hesitantly, Dantzel stepped forward. "Rustav?"

He shushed her, and she bristled, opening her mouth to spell out for him just how much effort and courage it had taken for her to follow him into the forest. But before she could get the words out, he reached back, grabbed her hand, and began pulling her forward into the trees, leaving her too surprised to resist.

Rustav pushed through the thick vegetation, each breath so laden with moisture that it was almost like drinking. His right hand was clamped firmly around Dantzel's wrist; she wasn't going anywhere until he could straighten things out with her. He had been so stunned to see her running toward the forest that he had nearly tripped, and an unreasonable hope had sprung up inside of him; but the whispers had surrounded him the moment he entered the forest, drowning out any chance for conversation.

The whispers propelled him forward, telling him where to go without ever really crossing the line into comprehensibility. Their urgency pulled him farther in, tugging at him more strongly every second. A thrill ran down his spine. This was where he needed to be, he suddenly felt quite certain. Whatever was in here, it wanted him there too. Rustav forged ahead, stepping over roots and dodging around trunks and never pausing to question where exactly he was going.

Until the whispers fell silent.

Rustav stopped in his tracks.

"Rustav?" Dantzel's voice, barely more than a whisper, rang out unnaturally loud in the sudden stillness. "What's going on? Where are we?"

On impulse, Rustav dropped Dantzel's hand to reach out in front of him, laying both palms flat against a tree trunk, digging his fingers into the deep grooves to elicit some hint of a whisper. Nothing. Was he crazy? Had he imagined it all? Rustav remembered the pressure of the wispy voices against his ears; he couldn't have imagined something so vivid, so strange. He left the trunk and turned around in a slow circle, searching the silent trees for any clue. Why had they stopped? In frustration, he called out, "Where are you?"

In response, something dropped from a branch no less than fifteen feet above his head, landing exactly in front of Rustav. He shouted and stumbled backward into Dantzel, who grabbed his arm so tightly that he thought she would squeeze it off. He was too startled at first to realize that it was a person—a young man no older than twenty—that had landed beside them.

The stranger was hardly any taller than Dantzel and looked too delicate to survive such a fall, Rustav thought; but he had landed on his feet without so much as a wince and was now examining them with wide brown eyes that were simultaneously commanding and inviting.

"What are you doing here?"

The man's voice was as piercing as the sound of breaking glass and rang with authority. Rustav considered saying something about the trees whispering, but he was still hardly able to convince himself it had really happened. Instead, he said simply, "We were running from the king's Guards. Who are you?"

"My name is Ayre." The man tilted his head slightly, eyes wary. "Were you sent by the man Antonius?"

Emboldened by the knowledge that this man was nothing more than a one-syllable servant, Rustav answered with more confidence. "Nobody sent us. Who is Antonius?" An absurd thought occurred to him. Laughing at the idea, he asked, "Are you talking about Anton?"

Ayre surveyed them for a painfully long moment; then, disregarding Rustav's question, he asked, "What do you know of the forest?"

Very little, apparently, Rustav thought, bewildered. He was beginning to think (with some relief) that the forest demons were nothing more than runaway slaves. "I've always heard that it was haunted by demons, but you don't look much like a demon."

"You're not," Dantzel piped up, peering around Rustav's shoulder with wide eyes. "You're a tuath, aren't you?"

A tuath? Rustav took a closer look, noting the sharply pointed eyebrows, the feather-light frame, the abnormally long fingers, the earthen-toned skin. Before he could recover from his surprise, the tuath had moved closer, inserting himself between Rustav and Dantzel and taking Dantzel by the hand. His voice was no longer wary but warm and inviting. "You know of us, then?"

"My parents used to tell me tales," she said, her cheeks flushed and her eyes bright. Rustav had to fight the urge to yank her away from Ayre's gentle hand. "Tuatha suthain, the children of eternity. Your lives can last centuries. Anything crafted by a tuath was considered beyond human prices. But your people vanished. No one knew what became of you."

"We were transformed into demons by the short memories and superstitions of your people," Ayre said with an indulgent smile. "But that false perception need no longer stand. Would you like to come see our humble village?"

"Oh, can we?" Dantzel asked, taking an eager step forward. Rustav stepped around Ayre and laid a hand on her shoulder, scanning the trees with growing apprehension.

"I don't think we should," he said shortly, his eyes flicking from branch to branch. At least six other tuatha were perched in the trees, each pointing a bow down at them, their darker skin blending almost perfectly with the tree bark surrounding them. Ayre followed his gaze and then waved his hand. The bows relaxed, and the tuatha melted away into the foliage.

"I apologize," Ayre said graciously. "We have become wary of strangers, and we did not know your intentions. Come. Our home is high in the trees, and we would be glad of an opportunity to show our legendary hospitality."

Dantzel followed him willingly to an enormous pine and allowed him to help her onto the lowest branch. Rustav stood his ground, folding his arms in defiance. If she wanted to go up and get herself killed by bow-wielding mythical creatures, that was her problem. He had come into the forest for a purpose, and he was going to see it through. Now that he had met the forest "demons" face-to-face, there was even less reason for him to fear the trees. He could be free and clear on the other side of the mountains by the next evening.

Dantzel's laugh floated down through the trees, and Rustav's head snapped up. Dantzel and the tuath were already nearly out of view, climbing steadily upward through the thick trees. Shaking his head, Rustav looked away. He wasn't going to go after her. He wasn't.

Not even after she came after you?

Groaning in surrender, Rustav reached out to grip the branch that stretched out just over his head. Instantly, the wood sprang to life. Two small branches sprouted on either side of his hands and clamped themselves over his wrists, trapping him firmly in place. Before Rustav could shout for help, a word came to his mind, felt more than heard, bringing with it a wave of warning and fear.

Remember.

Just as suddenly, the branches straightened into an innocently natural position. Rustav stared at them, frozen in shock. Remember what?

Adrenaline flooded Rustav's veins, and he sprang up into the trees, anxious to get Dantzel away from the danger that was certainly waiting in the branches above. The thick foliage had already obscured Dantzel and Ayre, and Rustav was left with only the faint hints of voices to guide him.

CHAPTER EIGHT

As ANXIOUS AS SHE WAS, DANTZEL COULDN'T help feeling a little breathless at the ease with which Ayre had lifted her into the tree. He had smiled down at her, just briefly, before turning and leaping lithely up through the branches. A tuath! How could she have lived fifteen years on the edge of the forest and never known—never guessed—that there could be such things as tuatha living in the trees? Dantzel had heard the folk tales, of course, but she had never dreamed that they would live so near her or that she would ever get to meet one. He was as perfect as the tales had always said tuatha would be; she had a hard time keeping her eyes off him as they climbed ever higher. As a result, she lost her footing and caught herself with a gasp just in time.

In an instant, Ayre was at her side, laying a hand on her back. "Are you all right, Lady Dantzel? I apologize for moving too quickly. It was inconsiderate."

"Oh, no," Dantzel said, her laugh a little breathless from either the quick climb or the grace with which he addressed her as a lady. She wasn't inclined to correct him. "You weren't too quick. It was just clumsy of me."

"Here. Put your arms around my neck." The tuath turned his shoulder, and Dantzel shied away.

"I'll be fine. Don't worry about it. I don't want to burden you."

"You won't," Ayre said with a winning smile, taking her hand and pulling it over his shoulder. With the tuath so close, Dantzel breathed in the scent of pure nature, of green growing things and rich brown earth. The smell made her lightheaded, and she found herself wrapping her arms securely around Ayre's neck, releasing the tree completely without fear of falling. Once she was on his back, the tuath began climbing once more, his speed diminished only enough for her comfort.

Dantzel wasn't certain how high they were the next time Ayre paused; she could no longer see the forest floor through the branches below them. "You'll have to climb off here," Ayre said, not remotely winded by the climb. "The entrance is only big enough for one person at a time. I'll go through and help you up."

"What entrance?" Dantzel asked, perplexed. Ayre smiled knowingly and reached upward. His hand disappeared as if behind a wall. As he pulled himself up, his top half disappeared, then his legs. Dantzel blinked, straining her eyes to understand what she was seeing. Was there some sort of invisible barrier? She cautiously reached up her hand and felt a solid mass of interwoven branches less than a foot above her head. Incredulously, she moved her head from side to side, staring at the ceiling now coming into perspective. Even knowing it was there, Dantzel was a little unnerved to see Ayre poking his head out of the entrance hole. The ceiling of branches was so well disguised that it looked like his head was floating in midair.

"This is incredible!" Dantzel said, enthusiasm overcoming her fear altogether. "It looks like the trees just keeping going upward forever."

Ayre reached down a hand, a pleased spark in his eyes. "Just wait until you see the other side."

Without hesitation, without looking back, Dantzel took his hand and was lifted through the entrance. The ceiling turned into a floor, and Dantzel regained her feet, turning slowly, more amazed each time her eye darted to a new sight.

Trees still surrounded her, but they were like no trees she had ever seen. The centers of many trunks were hollowed out, turning the trees into perfect shelters from the elements. Each of the thick trunks had multiple holes, some as big as doors, others more like windows. Some had short, thick branches arranged in a stair formation around the trunk, indicating rooms stacked one on top of the other clear to the top of the tree. Branches bent into the strangest of shapes, forming benches and chairs that looked man-made, but were unmistakably connected to living trees. Some branches were wide and flat, curving slightly into a shallow bowl. Dantzel wasn't quite sure what those were for until she saw one tuath reclining on one such branch as if it were a hammock, idly plucking at a stringed instrument.

And the people! Tuatha walked peacefully through the trees, worked placidly at their pastimes, sat serenely on the trees' branches. Some turned curiously in her direction, their ageless faces expressing a mild surprise at her appearance. Each one was flawlessly formed, with skin so clear it glowed and eyebrows carefully sculpted into delicate points. None were more than a few inches taller than she was, and their frames were light and agile.

A blanket of perfect peace lay over the treetop town, and Dantzel could feel it soothing her ruffled senses, suppressing the cares that had been pressing so anxiously on her mind. Her muscles relaxed, releasing all tension. It was, therefore, an unpleasant surprise when an indignant shout rang out from beneath her feet. Annoyed at the disruption of her newly discovered utopia, Dantzel looked down for the source.

A moment later, Rustav's head popped up through the entrance, a red mark on his forehead from where he had apparently bashed it against the barrier. Dantzel was mildly surprised to see him; when he hadn't followed immediately, she had nearly forgotten about him. A twinge of guilt vibrated under her contentedness as Rustav hoisted himself through the hole, obviously disgruntled. When he caught sight of her, he strode over, folding his arms as he glared moodily at Ayre.

"Thanks for waiting," he said shortly. Dantzel's guilt disappeared in the face of her annoyance at his obtuseness. Couldn't he see where they were? Couldn't he feel the incredible peace of their surroundings? Ayre's reply was as courteous as ever. He would never be so rude, she was certain.

"I am pleased that you could join us. I am sorry, I haven't heard your name."

Rustav tilted his head and eyed Ayre narrowly. "Rustav."

Ayre inclined his head briefly and offered his arm to Dantzel, who took it gladly, all disquiet disappearing with his touch. "Come along, then. Let me show you the beauties of our magnificent city."

FROM THE MOMENT RUSTAV LOOKED UP THROUGH the hole in the camouflaged ceiling, a strange sensation fell over him, one that was somehow similar to the peace he had felt in Gebir, but not quite the same. It slowed his racing heart, calmed his hurried breathing, and for a moment, Rustav let it wash over him, sweeping away the pain and the fear in both body and heart.

Then he turned and saw Dantzel standing there, and he remembered that they weren't simply guests, that they had been kidnapped at the point of a dozen arrows, that the tuath had deliberately separated him from Dantzel. The memory made him angry enough to shake off the haze moving over his senses, to haul himself up through the hole and stride over to where Dantzel and Ayre stood. Not angry enough, however, to miss the irritable glance Dantzel threw him or the constant calculations spinning behind Ayre's genial manner. Nor was he unconscious of the tuatha milling about the town, peaceful for now, but overwhelming in numbers and, if the folk tales held true, strength. Grinding his teeth, Rustav resigned himself temporarily to the situation. He would find a way out. He always did. Running away was what he did best.

As Ayre began to lead them through the town, Rustav's focus was dominated by Dantzel walking arm-in-arm with their tuath captor, chatting gaily about nothing and staring bright-eyed with wonder at the town around them. Rustav tried to catch Dantzel's eye, tried to communicate with her silently, but her eyes were too busy with the trees and with Ayre to see him.

The trees were entrancing, Rustav was forced to admit. As he took in the living wood that formed everything from tables to clotheslines, Rustav became intrigued against his will. He stopped in his tracks when he saw one tuath kneeling next to a low branch, whispering to it. The branch grew longer and thicker, winding back and forth in a most unusual way, taking a very specific shape, though Rustav couldn't tell what exactly it was going to form.

The tuatha could speak to the trees! The realization took his breath away, and for a moment, Rustav forgot that he was angry. If they knew the language of the trees, they probably could have understood the urgent whispers that had led him into the heart of the forest. And maybe—maybe they could teach him. Maybe next time, he would know what the trees were trying to tell him.

Neither Ayre nor Dantzel had paused with him, and they were drawing farther away. With one wistful glance at the tuath and the weaving branch, Rustav hurried after them, catching up just as they paused on the edge of a wide-open, tree-free space, no less than two hundred feet wide and three hundred feet long. Targets were lined along the far side, with tuatha shooting from various distances and exhibiting absolutely no anxiety that a fellow archer might ever hit them. Rustav winced when one tuath darted forward, retrieving her arrows and spinning out of the way an instant before her friend's arrow struck the center of the target. The two of them laughed together, conversing in a quick, fluid tongue that Rustav enjoyed hearing despite not understanding a word of it.

Shaking his head, Rustav turned his gaze to two tuatha nearer to them, swinging swords with quick, effortless movements. They leaped and thrust and danced all over the place, moving with tireless grace until one of the tuatha touched his flashing blade to the center of his opponent's chest, ending the rapid match instantly. The two tuatha stepped back and bowed to each other.

"These are our practice fields," Ayre said, indicating the open space with a sweeping gesture. Pride emanated from every aspect of his figure. "The dance of the sword, the precision of the bow—they are art forms as beautiful as our living woodwork. Of course, we practice only for sport, never for battle. We tuatha have not used our weapons in aggression for many a century."

"Except, of course, when humans come wandering too near," Rustav said caustically.

"Rustav!" Dantzel hissed, meeting his eye for the first time in over an hour to glare at him. Rustav tried to use that instant of her attention to communicate some sort of warning, but she turned away with a huff.

"You have every right to be upset," Ayre said placatingly. "But we are forced to defend our home from loggers. Surely you can understand the power of intimidation. One moment, please. I wish to have a word with Pak, our swordmaster."

Ayre stepped a few feet away from them to speak to the tuath who had won the duel, using the same flowing language Rustav had heard from the archers. The tuath bowed respectfully, but signs of hesitation were written in his wide eyes as Ayre punctuated his words with sharp gestures. Rustav took advantage of Ayre's distraction to lean in and talk to Dantzel.

"I don't like it here," he muttered. Dantzel cast him an incredulous glance before her eyes returned to Ayre.

"How can you not like it? Have you ever felt a place like this? It's untouched. No violence, no fear, no anger, nothing."

"No?" Rustav raised an eyebrow. "What about the arrows pointing down at us today?"

"They have to protect their home. You can't blame them, not with Guards and thieves and goodness knows who else that come wandering into the forest. Besides, Ayre said they only use bows for sport."

"Right. And what about when Ayre took off with you and tried to leave me behind?" Rustav conveniently forgot that he had intended to go on alone in his determination to make her see his side.

"You can't blame him because you were slow coming up," Dantzel snapped. "Ayre has been a good deal more civil today than you have!"

Rustav's face burned as he remembered the harsh words he had thrown at her that morning. He opened his mouth to defend himself, but Ayre turned back to them, interrupting the heated discussion.

"It is settled," Ayre announced. Dantzel turned away from Rustav with a stubborn set of her lips, leaving Rustav to fume silently at the back of her head. "Rustav, Pak has agreed to introduce you to the sword."

Rustav opened his mouth and closed it again, unsure whether "introduce" meant that he was going to wield the sword or be impaled on it. The second tuath saved him the trouble of asking.

"As much as you can learn as you stay, I teach you," Pak said, his heavy accent and uncertain syntax marking him as noticeably less confident in the Coureian language than Ayre. "Your size, you will be a strong fighter."

"Wait a second," Rustav said as Ayre took Dantzel by the arm and began to lead her away. "I'm not interested. I don't care about sword fighting. I've never touched a sword in my life. I'm not staying here, anyway. And where are you two going?"

"To the archery range," Ayre called over his shoulder. Dantzel followed him willingly, the enchanted expression on her face turning Rustav's stomach. Determined not to let this go any further, Rustav took a step after them, but Pak grabbed his arm. Rustav tried to jerk free, but Pak's grip was immovable. Rustav opened his mouth to shout, but Pak held a finger up to his lips.

"Do not cross Ayre," Pak breathed, his accent so thick that Rustav could hardly understand him. "He wields high power here in the trees."

"He can't have that much power. His name is only one syllable."

Pak shook his head. "We are not like you, human. We are all equal, all short names. Ayre is the adopted child of the Eldest."

"The who?"

"The Eldest. The tuath of greatest age, greatest experience. The leader of our Council, of the tuatha. He is most highly respected. Ayre was taken in by the Eldest after Ayre's parents and the Eldest's daughter perished in battle, and so Ayre shares that respect in the trees. He has asked that I teach you sword; I will teach you the sword."

Striding lithely over to a trunk that grew square and box-like, Pak laid a hand on the bark and spoke inaudibly. The trunk opened in front, the wood shrinking away to reveal a small collection of swords, gleaming brightly.

"How did you do that?" Rustav asked, his insistent rebellion fading slightly in a renewed urgency to learn this strange

tongue the tuatha had mastered. Pak, however, feigned deaf-
ness as he looked Rustav up and down, sizing him up. With
a sigh, Pak lifted out the longest sword and held out the hilt.

"You are far too tall for my swords, but that has to do for
this day."

Gingerly, Rustav took the sword, holding it away from
him and eyeing it suspiciously. Weeks of working with Anton's
knives had mellowed his instinctive aversion to blades, but he
still didn't like the idea of putting himself on the wrong end
of Pak's sword. "Your swords? Did you make all of those?"

"And many more. Swords are my best and favorite work.
Language, you may notice, is not." Pak offered an apologetic
smile as he drew out the sword from the sheath strapped
to his back. "I will teach you the Tuathan tongue with the
sword, and we speak better. Now, you hit me."

Rustav glanced at the sword, then at Pak, raising a reluctant eyebrow. "Is this sharp?"

"Yes, very. But you cannot hurt me, and I will not hurt
you."

"Thanks for the vote of confidence," Rustav muttered.
"Listen, what if I don't want to learn how to sword fight?"

Pak frowned, then glanced over his shoulder. Following
his gaze, Rustav saw Ayre standing behind Dantzel, arms
around her as he helped her with a bow and arrow. Pak
turned back, his expression grim. "You want to learn how to
sword fight."

Rustav watched Dantzel release an arrow, watched the
arrow fly straight and bury itself in the target—not in the
center, but not a bad shot, either. He gripped the sword
tighter, suppressing the foolish urge to run over and pick a
fight with Ayre then and there. But as he watched, Dantzel

turned, her face bright with excitement, smiling and laughing as Ayre leaned in to help her with the bow once more. Shrinking back slightly, Rustav wondered: did he have any right to take Dantzel away from here?

I thought I loved her, but I led the Guards right to her home. She's safe and happy here. Who am I to take her away from that?

The flat of Pak's sword smacked Rustav's shoulder, and Rustav flinched, startled. Unapologetically, Pak raised his sword again. "If you do not guard yourself, you will have a bruise. Now, hit me."

Still trying to keep an eye on Dantzel and Ayre, Rustav gave a half-hearted swing. Pak knocked it away easily and hit Rustav in the thigh. "You cannot afford less than full attention," the tuath admonished.

"I've never held a sword before in my life!" Rustav protested, dropping the point of the sword to touch the ground and glancing once more at the archery range. "I don't know what I'm supposed to be doing."

"Once you give me your full attention, I teach you form, I teach you technique. Until then, I continue to hit you." And so he did, this time striking Rustav on the elbow. Frustration finally overflowed inside of Rustav, and he jerked his sword up with a shout, swinging it at Pak with all his might. The tuath blocked him and stepped back, inviting another attack. Again and again, Rustav hacked away, allowing his anger to pour out into the clashing of the swords.

After a few minutes of blocking and parrying patiently, Pak twisted his blade and sent Rustav's sword soaring into the air, coming down straight into Pak's waiting hand. The tuath handed it back with a satisfied smile. "Now, we work."

CHAPTER NINE

RUSTAV HAD NO IDEA HOW LONG THEY REMAINED there on the practice fields, with Pak drilling him endlessly on both the details of swordplay and the Tuathan vocabulary for it. It was a surprise when Rustav stepped away from an intense round of sparring and found that the treetop town was now lighted by lantern-shaped branches. He wiped his forehead with his sleeve, noting that Pak wasn't so much as breathing hard.

"Do tuatha even sweat?" Rustav asked wryly, taking a seat on a nearby bench and stretching out his tired muscles. Pak laughed, hanging his sword back inside the tree.

"No. That is a human trait. A strange phenomenon, water squeezing out from your skin."

Pak took Rustav's sword and placed it carefully in the tree, speaking and closing the tree so that not a seam remained. Rustav watched the process, something stirring slightly under the blanket of contentment that now covered his mind. When Pak was finished, his eyes flicked away for just a moment, darting to the far corner of the field. Rustav followed his gaze automatically and wondered briefly why Pak was interested in the deserted archery targets.

Ice flooded Rustav's tired limbs, and he rigidly clutched at the bench he sat on. In an instant, Pak stood in front of him, holding up his hands in an attempt to placate him.

"Where is she?" Rustav demanded, nearly choking on his panic. When had he stopped checking on Dantzel? After all he knew, after all he had realized, he had allowed himself to be lulled into a sense of security, getting along wonderfully with Pak while losing all memory of why he was there.

"Keep quiet," Pak said in a low voice. "You cannot draw attention."

Rustav grabbed the front of Pak's tunic. "How long has she been gone?"

"Several hours. You have impressive stamina for a human. I thought you would give in long ago." Pak pried Rustav's fingers open and straightened. "Please, Rustav. You must be calm. Others would not be so kind as I am, would not remind you."

"Take me to her. Now."

"I cannot. Ayre took her to her quarters."

In an attempt to intimidate the tuath, Rustav stood, towering over Pak. "Then take me to her quarters."

Pak shook his head firmly. "Private quarters are for meditation and rest. It is discourteous to disturb a tuath once retired."

"We're not tuatha! She would think it was discourteous if I didn't check on her!" *If she even remembers who I am by now.* Rustav shook the thought from his mind. When Pak continued to shake his head, Rustav softened his stance slightly.

"Please, Pak. At least show me where she's staying. I have to watch out for her." *Even if she doesn't want me to.*

After a long pause, Pak tilted his head slightly. "She means a great deal to you, this girl, does she not?"

Rustav nearly answered with a hearty affirmative; but the words died on his tongue as he remembered Dantzel's stunned look at the gate after the wedding celebration, her anger the next morning, her speedy and intense devotion to Ayre's tuath charms. Turning away, he spoke through clenched teeth. "I have a responsibility to keep her safe. It's for others' sakes that I'm concerned, not hers."

The way Pak looked at him, Rustav was sure that the tuath knew he was lying; but in the end, Pak nodded. "I will show you. But you must not attempt to see her until tomorrow."

Only after Rustav had spoken his promise did Pak start off through the tree town. They weaved through the trees, some reaching over a hundred feet overhead, some barely breaking the top of the barrier, all with limbs that formed something other than branches. Rustav made note of each tree they passed, determined to be able to find his way through the town on his own.

"There," Pak said, pointing to a fir tree several yards away. It rose no higher from the barrier than Dantzel's cottage had stood; a doorway was hidden by vines and moss, and an abnormally straight branch stuck out above the door, blossoming into a lantern. Two lower branches formed chairs; several other branches led upward like stairs to a hammock branch.

Without warning, Rustav darted forward; but before he had gone three steps, Pak had his arm and yanked him back, nearly pulling him off his feet. Rustav resisted, but Pak was already pulling him relentlessly in the other direction.

"I will show you to your quarters now," Pak said, his long fingers holding Rustav's arm in a painfully tight grasp. "You need rest."

No matter how Rustav pulled, he could not get his arm free until Pak had pushed him through the mossy curtain to a small room furnished with a vine hammock and a small wooden table, which was covered with a generous supply of fruit, nuts, and a heavy, cakey sort of bread.

"Do not make them replace me," Pak said in a low voice. "I have great interest in your well-being. Others would as soon see you banished to the wilderness beyond the forest."

"The what?" Rustav asked, but Pak had already disappeared through the doorway. Turning, Rustav surveyed his cramped quarters with a sigh. The room was undoubtedly just as big as Anton's small house, but somehow the thought of being inside of a tree was unspeakably oppressive. By the light of the lantern that seeped through the curtain, Rustav sat on his hammock and helped himself to the spread on the table. *It's not too bad*, he thought grumpily, refusing to admit even in thought that it was the freshest food he had ever tasted. It would suffice until he left to take Dantzel away from these cursed trees.

THE LIGHT OF THE LANTERNS FLICKERED EERILY over the dark stillness of the tuath town; their flickering was the only movement among the trees. Hardly daring to breathe, Rustav slipped out from between the vines covering his door, the first step sounding horrendously loud to his ears.

He paused to glance around anxiously, but not a soul stirred. Letting out his breath, Rustav continued forward, moving as quickly as he could without making a sound.

The walk seemed like an eternity, but Rustav eventually saw the shape of Dantzel's tree melting out of the darkness. He moved more quickly, deciding that if no one had caught him yet, a little more noise couldn't hurt. Holding his breath, he slipped through the curtain of moss and vines covering the doorway, squinting as his eyes adjusted to the even darker interior.

"Dantzel?" he whispered, locating a hammock on the far side of the room. "Wake up. I need to talk to you."

A figure stirred, and Dantzel lifted her head. "Who is it?" she mumbled, and Rustav breathed a little easier. He had feared that Pak had deliberately pointed out the wrong tree.

"It's me. Rustav."

Her head fell back, and her voice came out muffled. "What are you doing here? What time is it?"

"Are you okay?" Rustav asked, unsure of how to proceed.

"I'm tired. It's the middle of the night."

"I know, but—" Rustav blew out a breath in frustration. "I'm worried."

"About what?" Dantzel's voice was full of impatience, and annoyance surged through Rustav's chest. "Nobody can get to us here. The tuatha will keep us safe."

"It's the tuatha I'm worried about," Rustav murmured. Dantzel sat up straight, and Rustav's heart jumped; had he gotten through to her?

"Is this about Ayre?"

Caught off guard, Rustav spluttered for a moment before he answered indignantly, "No! Well, yes, but not—I don't care about your stupid infatuation with his pointed eyebrows." Lie. "I'm just trying to tell you—we could get trapped up here. I want to get out."

"You're obviously not trapped enough, seeing as how you're waking me up in the middle of the night."

The words only fanned Rustav's anger; he took a step forward and pointed a finger at her. "I don't care if you hate me," he growled through clenched teeth. Another lie. "But think about your mother. Think about how she was left to hide from the Guards alone. Think about how much she's crying, with her only daughter lost in the forest tonight."

Though Dantzel's face was hidden by darkness, Rustav could hear the hesitation in her voice. "I—it's only a night or two. Ayre will get us home when it's time. He's taking good care of us."

"Wake up, Dantzel!" Rustav snapped, barely resisting the urge to take her by the shoulders and give her a good shake. "They are not going to let us out of here! Their hospitality is nothing more than a farce, a show to keep us complacent until we've forgotten everything!"

"We're sorry you feel that way," said a smooth voice from the doorway. Someone twisted Rustav's arms painfully behind his back, throwing him effortlessly to the floor and pushing his face against the interwoven branches. By twisting his head as far as he could, Rustav could just see Ayre putting a protective arm around Dantzel. Rustav yelped as his shoulders twisted farther back than they were ever meant to.

"Did he hurt you?" Ayre asked, his voice all concern and compassion.

"No," Dantzel murmured, then gasped as Rustav was

lifted several inches off the ground and slammed back down. "Please don't!" she said. "He was only . . ."

"Only what?" Ayre prompted. Rustav squeezed his eyes shut tight, praying that Dantzel would believe him over Ayre. But he could feel the weight of Ayre's presence in the room, pushing all other thoughts aside and squeezing the very breath from Rustav's lungs. It was hopeless.

"I just wanted to talk," he said, desperate to counteract Ayre's spell somehow. A sharp slap landed on the back of his head, knocking his face into the bark.

"He wanted you to leave," Ayre said grimly. "He wanted to take you away from the safety of our protection."

There was a long pause, and then a soft *yes*.

"No!" Rustav shouted, jerking wildly and fruitlessly against his tuathan captor. "Dantzel, listen to me! You're already forgetting! Remember—"

A blow to the head stunned him and cut off his desperate ranting. Another tuath seized his legs, and the two tuatha dragged him through the town, throwing him roughly into his tree. Rustav remained where he landed, sprawled across the branchy floor, as Ayre spoke and the door grew together, sealing itself and plunging him into complete darkness.

I can't stop now. There has to be a way out. There's always a way out.

Rustav rolled over and pushed himself onto his hands and knees before he became aware of a faint whispering filling the air. The trees! Rustav listened hungrily, desperate for the energy and guidance they had offered before. But instead, the strength drained from his limbs, and he collapsed to the floor, exhausted beyond description. At the same time, new branches sprouted beneath him, snaking through the tangle of the floor—feeding off of his energy. Somewhere deep inside, Rustav felt a vague sense of betrayal, rage that the trees had led him here and were now weakening him, trapping him as the tuatha's prey. "Why?" he demanded angrily, that one word all he had the strength for. For a brief moment, he thought he could catch a word or two . . .

Forgive . . .

. . . but then his eyes closed, and he heard the whispers no more.

RUSTAV STOOD AT THE FOOT OF A HILL, LOOKING up at the cottage sitting at the very top. Warm light poured out of the windows, and warm safety. He began climbing, but the grass grew taller and taller, soon towering well over his head. Clumps of grass twisted together and became trees, growing over him until he was surrounded by forest. Somewhere far away, voices called his name, familiar yet nameless voices. Rustav began running, fighting his way through the trees, slipping and sliding and falling, desperate to find the people calling him. But the voices grew fainter and fainter until, at last, they faded into silence.

CHAPTER TEN

WHEN RUSTAV AWOKE THE NEXT MORNING, A faint headache pulsed in the back of his mind. Rubbing his eyes and striving to push it away, Rustav rolled out of the hammock, wincing at his sore shoulders and arms. A bruise on his cheek ached dully; Pak must have gotten carried away while they were sparring yesterday, though Rustav couldn't remember Pak ever hitting him in the face. He'd have to talk to the tuath about going easy on him until he was trained up a bit.

The table beside him was laden with food, and Rustav quickly lightened its load, starved from the strenuous exercise of the day before. He was surprised for a moment when he found the door of his tree open, though on reflection, he wasn't sure why. Doors were never closed here, up in the trees. Shaking off any unease, Rustav strode out into the town, wandering aimlessly through the trees and pausing now and again to watch one of the tuatha at work. Some acknowledged him with a smile and a *"fen risalba,"* which Rustav repeated back, assuming it was a standard greeting.

Eventually, his wanderings took him to a thick trunk on the edge of the town from which waves of heat and a great clanking noise poured out. Rustav approached curiously, peering through the mossy hangings before the doorway. A blaze of heat scorched his face, and Rustav had to squint to see Pak hammering away at a length of steel before a roaring fire.

"*Fen risalba*!" Rustav called cheerily, proud to show off his new vocabulary. Pak paused mid-swing, frozen in the midst of the furnace. For a moment, Rustav feared that he had somehow managed to distort the greeting into something terribly offensive; it was a relief when Pak turned to answer.

"*Fen risalba*, my friend," Pak said, his tone light but his eyes heavy. "It is too hot here for you. Wait outside, and I will join you soon."

More than happy to escape the burning heat, Rustav stepped away from the door and watched two squirrels chase each other around and around a nearby tree. When Pak joined him, the tuath smelled of smoke and fire, and his face was smudged with ash.

"You must have slept well," Pak said, the offhand comment sounding guarded. "You are in much better spirits today."

Bewildered, Rustav asked, "Was I cross with you yesterday? I apologize. I am grateful for all your help with the sword and with Tuathan. I was hoping you could help me more today, especially with Tuathan. My own language sounds so ungraceful, and I would much rather be able to speak to your fellow tuatha in their tongue. It would sound more respectable, wouldn't it?"

"It would indeed," Pak murmured, looking hard in the direction of the town's center for so long that Rustav feared he had imposed on the tuath.

"If it's too much to ask," Rustav said hesitantly, "I can find someone else to—"

"No!" Pak met Rustav's eyes swiftly and forced a smile. "I am happy to help, my friend. I just find it interesting, this language of yours, this—how do you call it?"

"You know," Rustav said slowly, "I don't recall." He laughed, shaking his head. "Obviously isn't important. You will help me, then?"

"Of course." Pak reached out to grasp Rustav's shoulder, his eyes still a little too pained for Rustav's understanding. "I will always help you, my friend. If you remember nothing else, remember that. I must finish your sword now."

"My sword?" Rustav's eyes lit up. "You're making me a sword?"

Pak smiled and nodded. "You wait in the town, and I will find you when I am finished. We will visit the library tree. I will try to help you with words, then I will help you once more with the sword."

"*Fen risalba!*"

Ayre melted out of the surrounding trees to join them, a warm and gracious smile on his face. There was a rapid exchange of Tuathan between Ayre and Pak, during which Pak's eyes never left the ground. Ayre responded to Pak's mumbled words with loud, clear authority. After a few minutes, Pak shut his mouth and looked meaningfully at Rustav, who stood by watching the exchange with mild interest.

"I apologize, Rustav," Ayre said smoothly. "It was thoughtless of me to leave you out of the conversation. I trust you slept well?"

"Very well, as always, thank you," Rustav said, trying to ignore the itch deep inside of him that had appeared with

Ayre. What it was, he couldn't tell; but he didn't like it and pushed it away in favor of the perfect peace he had enjoyed all morning.

"Why don't I escort you to the library tree?" Ayre suggested. "I understand you wish to learn our language. Perhaps we can find someone to help you there while Pak finishes his project."

It seemed a sound plan, and Rustav agreed. He followed Ayre back into the center of town, into the largest tree Rustav had ever seen. Upon entering the tree, Rustav sucked in a breath, unable to open his eyes wide enough to take it all in.

Every solid inch of wall space inside the tree was packed with books, all the way up to the ceiling five feet above Rustav's head. A ladder grew out of the floor and disappeared into a hole in the center of the ceiling. In wonder, Rustav asked, "Is there another floor?"

"Not just another floor," Ayre chuckled. "Twenty-three other floors."

"Twenty-three," Rustav mouthed, reaching out and running his fingers over the nearest bindings. The covers were wood, perfectly smooth, raised letters flowing artfully across the cover. Rustav pulled one of the books out, breathed in the smell of the wood, rubbed the embossed letters gently. An image flickered briefly in his mind, a knife smoothing away a curl of wood, and Rustav's grip tightened on the book. Knives would never have touched this wood. The tuatha shaped the wood with words, not blades. Unsettled, he placed the book back on the shelf and tried to dismiss the strange image.

Ayre was speaking with another tuath in rapid Tuathan, so Rustav wandered away to examine the shelves more closely, brushing his fingers along rows of fine covers. The script was beautiful; Rustav examined it, struggling to guess at what it might mean, or even where one flowing letter began and ended. Curiosity led him up the ladder to the second floor, which, while not as tall as the first floor, was equally packed with elegantly covered books. Rustav pulled one off the shelf and flipped through it, pausing at the fine illustrations.

"Rustav?"

The rich, high voice belonged to a tuath, small and slight with wavy black hair falling freely down to her hips, standing just to the side of the ladder. A woven bag was slung casually over one shoulder, and her green eyes sparkled with amusement as Rustav stood dumbly with the book in his hands, staring openly.

"My name is Tay," she said, offering her hand in a businesslike way. "Pak told me that you wish to learn Tuathan."

"Yes," Rustav said, becoming uncomfortably aware of how ridiculous he must look. Clearing his throat, he set the book back on the shelf. "Are you—do you know—did Pak send you?"

"He did. He wished to ensure that you were given the help you desire."

Ayre emerged from the hole in the floor; though the tuath kept a tight rein on his expression, Rustav could see that he had not expected to see Tay there. Tay regarded Ayre coolly, her green eyes no longer shining.

"Ayre, Tay is going to help me to learn Tuathan," Rustav said, looking uncertainly from one tuath to the other.

"I do not wish to infringe on your routine," Ayre said to Tay, inclining his head slightly. Tay responded with equal politeness that even Rustav could tell was a thin veil for stubborn opposition.

"It is no trouble. I am eager to make practical use of my knowledge of the Courei language. And besides, I am intrigued by our young visitor. I would like to know him better." Tay allowed herself a brief smile in Rustav's direction, and Rustav was suddenly aware of nothing else in the room.

Ayre surveyed Tay for a long moment, calculations spinning in his eyes. At last, he nodded curtly and disappeared back down the ladder without so much as a farewell, leaving Tay and Rustav alone together. The moment Ayre was out of sight, Tay's face fell into a stern glare, staring down the ladder. She shook her head and turned back to Rustav, lowering her voice.

"I apologize if I seemed forward," she said softly, sitting cross-legged next to a shelf and gesturing for Rustav to sit beside her. "It was my hope that Ayre would be more willing to leave you in my hands if he thought I would serve as a further distraction for you."

"Distraction?"

"Yes. But please do not take offense. I am sure that, were my emotions not already taken, I would be quite disappointed to learn that your affections were engaged elsewhere." Tay smiled mischievously. "Especially after observing your valiant efforts against our swordmaster yesterday."

Rustav missed the dig about his sword lesson in his confusion over Tay's initial comment. "Elsewhere?" he asked blankly. "I think you've been misinformed."

Tay's smile faded, and she reached out to touch Rustav's knee. "There is no one you wish to be close with?"

Briefly, as quick as the striking of a flint, an image illuminated Rustav's mind: a girl with braided brown hair, dirt on her cheeks, and a determined glint in her eyes.

Then it was lost again, and Rustav shook his head haltingly. "No, of course not. You and Ayre and Pak—you're the only ones I know."

An odd glimmer of moisture gleamed in Tay's eye for a moment before she turned away, pulling a large, waxy leaf out of her bag. "We'll use this for practice," she said, setting it on the floor along with a quill, a bottle of ink, and a rag. "The sooner you can get to know the rest of the tuatha, the better."

By the time Pak arrived, Rustav's head was spinning. There were thirty-four letters in the Tuathan alphabet, nearly all of which had different forms at the beginning or end of a word. He had covered the leaf with practice writing, wiped it clean, and covered it again countless times. Tay had drilled vocabulary into him for everything in sight and showed him how to write it. As excited as Rustav had been to learn Tuathan, he was relieved when Pak emerged from the ladder door.

"How is the lesson?" Pak asked.

"He is a fast learner," Tay said before Rustav could answer. Rustav's chest swelled with pride as she gave him an approving smile. Pak nodded.

"Of course he is. Here." Pak held out the sword in his hands, encased in an elegantly wrought sheath and attached to a long leather strap. Rustav took it reverently. He could sense the quality of the workmanship, the toil that had gone into its creation. Carefully, he slid the sword a few inches out of its sheath and turned the blade, admiring its shine.

"Thank you," Rustav said, looking up at Pak and Tay. "Both of you."

Pak stood and wordlessly showed Rustav how to strap the sword to his back. With a nod at Tay, Pak said to Rustav, "Come. We will put to use the sword."

WITH THE NEW SWORD IN HAND, RUSTAV FELT far more confident than he had before. The sword fit in his hand with ease, its balance flawless. It almost seemed to know what to do by itself. Still, it didn't take many of Pak's exercises and drills before Rustav was breathing hard and sweating harder.

After endless drills, Pak and Rustav began a round of sparring. With even just a little more experience behind him, Rustav could see how hopelessly outmatched he was, but Pak was careful never to push too aggressively. Still, Rustav felt his limits closing in. After some time, he made a wild lunge to try to end the round, anxious for a chance to rest. Pak sidestepped, and Rustav overbalanced, falling hard on the branchy floor. Face flaming, Rustav leaped back to his feet and raised his sword, but Pak was standing with the tip of his sword down, staring at Rustav.

"May I see your pendant?" Pak asked. Surprised, Rustav looked down at the circle of wood that had fallen out from inside his shirt. He pulled the leather string off of his neck and handed it to Pak, who held it close to his eyes. "This is beautiful woodworkings," Pak said. "May I borrow it for better inspection?"

For a moment, reluctance tugged at Rustav's stomach, but why should it bother him? Pak had done so much for him already. He could borrow a meaningless chunk of wood for a few days. "Sure, go ahead."

Pak placed it carefully in his pocket. "I think you have worked enough for today. We will return tomorrow. If you have any needs, find me. I will help if I can."

Rustav didn't ask Pak about his pendant the next day, or the next, or the next. As his confidence in speaking Tuathan increased, Rustav went out of his way to meet others in the treetop town, anxious to hear what wisdom came from centuries of experience. It wasn't long before Tuathan came more naturally to him than his native Coureian. He read book after book in the library, soaking in stories of ancient wars, heroic deeds, political unrest, valorous rulers of many creatures and many nations. He spent hours each day swinging a sword at Pak, gradually decreasing the number of bruises he got and increasing the amount of time it took for Pak to win a round. He watched masters at work as they crafted art in every medium imaginable and tried to replicate their techniques on his own simpler projects. The tuatha enjoyed his company, if only for the praise that he gave and the amusement of his fumbling (though increasingly adept) attempts at imitation.

Sometimes the leaves around him turned orange and yellow and red, and sometimes the only branches that were not bare were those of the evergreens. Even then, the branches wove together tightly enough above the town that very little rain or snow made it inside. Rustav was only ever exposed to the full force of the elements when he climbed up to the highest branches and looked out over the endless spread of trees, breathing in the crisp air that somehow seemed more refreshing than the still, quiet air of the tuath town.

Over time, Rustav began to sense a change in the atmosphere of the treetop town. Where there had once been cheerful greetings called from yards away, there were more and more whispers shared in clusters. Rustav caught only hints of the conversations, words like *union*, *broken*, *outside*. Some tuatha gesticulated excitedly; others simply folded their arms and frowned. Whenever Rustav drew too near, the whispered conversation cut off until he had moved on, leaving Rustav with only speculation as to the cause of the quiet unrest.

It was on a hot day that Rustav woke late, having stayed up far too late in the night reading. Noises stirred just outside his tree; Rustav twitched aside his vine curtain just enough to peer out. A group of tuatha huddled not far from his doorway, apparently unaware that Rustav was still inside, speaking just loud enough for Rustav to catch their words.

"That kind of talk could be considered treason."

"How can it be treason to discuss what has already happened? The Union is broken. The heirs are dead."

"But to just stand back and watch them be crushed—"

"What have they done to merit our help? We stood by their side when they called for us. We lost many in that battle, to death and worse. And how did they repay us? By calling us liars? By pouring salt in the wounds we had sustained on their behalf?"

"So we take the side of the traitors over our allies?"

"Former allies. And we're not taking any sides. That's the point. We were forced into this alliance, and now we're free of it."

"What of Ayre's humans? Are they to be turned out to suffer with the rest?"

"Ayre can do as he pleases with his pets," came the disdainful reply. "They are no concern of ours."

Rustav pulled away, letting the vines drop back into place. Though the movement was only a fraction of an inch, it sparked a sudden silence outside his door. Rustav picked up his bag of books to return to the library tree, strapped his sword to his back, and walked outside. As he had expected, not a single tuath remained near his tree.

Humiliation burned in Rustav's stomach as he walked toward the practice fields. Was that all they saw him as? A pet? He had long since stopped thinking of himself as anything different from the tuatha. Taller, maybe, and not as skilled. Human—yes, he was human, though the word had not crossed his mind in recent memory. But a pet?

It wasn't until he reached the fields and began warming up with his sword that he realized—the tuath had said *humans.*

Rustav paused, letting the tip of his blade fall. Were there more like him in the trees? Why had he never seen them? How long had they been there?

How long had he been there?

Pak's voice startled Rustav out of his thoughts. "Rustav? Is everything all right?"

"Yes, fine," Rustav said, nodding automatically. Then he stopped himself and shook his head. "Pak, are there others like me here?"

Tilting his head, Pak asked, "Others? What makes you ask that?"

"There were tuatha talking near my tree this morning," Rustav said, embarrassed at first that he had been eavesdropping, then angry that it had taken eavesdropping to hear even a hint of what was going on in the town. "They said that Ayre's humans were pets."

Pak sighed, rubbing his neck. "Rustav, whatever purpose Ayre had in bringing you to the trees, I can assure you that it was not as a pet."

"Then what was it?"

Pak held up his hands, shushing Rustav and glancing to the side. "I don't know, and this is not the place to discuss it."

"Then take me somewhere we can talk," Rustav said, a surge of defiance welling up in his chest. "I have other questions too. What is the Union? Who is going to be attacked? Why don't the tuatha want to help them?"

"Rustav, please!" Pak's eyes were wide in alarm. "You mustn't speak so loudly. If anyone else heard you—"

"Everyone else is talking about it." Rustav folded his arms. "If I'm anything more than a pet, then why shouldn't I be included in the discussion?"

Something folded in Pak's eyes, buckling under sudden resignation. Pak peered nervously over Rustav's shoulder, then whispered, "I will explain. Come with me."

Rustav nodded. The anger had seared through his mind, giving him the sense of waking from a long sleep, and he was determined to get some answers. Pak motioned for Rustav to sheathe his sword and then led him back toward the forge tree. Just before they reached the forge, Pak veered to the side and entered a wide oak tree.

Rustav knew instantly that he was in Pak's quarters, and a moment of shyness overcame him. He had never entered a tuath's quarters. It simply was not done. The quarters were for privacy. But then Rustav realized that someone was already there.

"What's happened?" Tay asked, looking up from the desk where a quill pen and a square of parchment lay. Pak strode over and squeezed Tay's shoulders, and Rustav realized with a rush of embarrassment that there was a reason the two of them were together so often. Looking back, it seemed so obvious—how had he never realized they were married? Was he truly that blind?

Without saying a word, Pak gestured for them to follow him up the ladder to a second floor. Tay obeyed with a curious glance at Rustav, who followed with a string of foreboding stirring in his stomach.

When Rustav emerged on the second floor, Pak held out an old tome with an ornate cover. The script of the title was old, so old that it took Rustav a moment to decipher it.

"The Book of the Trees," he read slowly. "What is this?"

"One volume of several mysterious histories. No one truly knows where they came from or who wrote them, but the books record of all that the trees have seen and heard through the centuries. Open it."

The pages were brittle with age, and Rustav had to turn them carefully. The old script made it slow going at first, but as Rustav gradually understood the rhythm of the letters, he realized that the first page was something of an introduction.

Many hundreds of years ago, all creatures could hear our voices; but, race by race, they lost their hearing. Kobolds cared only for the ground—soil and rocks—and abandoned us. Men, in their foolishness, saw trees only as objects to be used for their own personal comfort, and we withdrew from them. Tuatha retained their hearing much longer; they were crafty at hiding their true intent. They used their hearing to learn our secrets, how we grew and breathed and changed. When the tuatha began to exercise power over us, we realized that we had been deceived. Though the tuatha's knowledge of our ways forced us into subjection, we took an oath to maintain utter silence toward the tuatha from then on.

The book wasn't about the trees; it was by the trees. A faint memory stirred in Rustav's mind, a faded imprint of a whispering among the trees. Shivering slightly, as if trying to shake off the eerie thought, Rustav turned the page and read a bold title at the top of the next page: "The Union of Man and Tuath."

Our cloaks were golden fire when the leader of the humans entered our shelter. A ring of soft metal sat on his brow, but his heart was softer than the metal, softer even than the cushion of leaves on the forest floor. He sought to resolve the tension with his tuathan brothers and spent many days walking through our branches with his counselors and the Council of the tuatha.

One tuath in particular shared his goals of peace— and his soft heart. She was the daughter of the Eldest; she held a prominent place on the Council and was greatly respected by her fellow tree-dwellers. They spent many hours together outside of political discussions and formed a deep attachment. As a result of the political implications and the feelings of his own heart, the leader of the humans offered marriage to the tuathan woman, who accepted without conferring with the Council, knowing that they would make every effort to discourage the union.

As expected, the tree-dwellers met the decision with thinly veiled anger. They knew, far better than the leader of the humans, the consequences of such a marriage, for the dealings of tuatha diverge greatly from the dealings of humans. The union would extend a portion of tuathan characteristics to the descendants of the man and tuath, characteristics that tuatha were reluctant to share with other races. Perhaps more importantly, it would create a bond of protection for the royal house, an alliance between town-dwellers and tree-dwellers of greater permanence than the human race could imagine. Such a bond would not fade with time; no matter how many generations passed in the human line, one-half of the blood in each heir's veins would remain tuathan.

In spite of the Council's misgivings, the marriage took place after the cold, when our branches were coming to life once more. At that ceremony, the tuatha presented the human king with the Union Crest. The bearer of the Crest was to be honored as a brother in the tuathan society. Any tuath who broke the pact would be subject to expulsion from the brotherhood of the tuatha. This Crest served as a physical marker for the heir of the Union: a mark of protection, but also of danger, for many tuatha resented the Union long after the first king had passed on.

The page ended on that ominous note. Rustav turned another page and found a richly detailed illustration of the Union Crest on the verso. Leaves and branches wove around in a circle, intertwining as thickly as the branches underneath his feet. Trees mingled with towers in the background, crowns hovering over two figures standing in the foreground. Rustav studied the illustration for several minutes, drawn at first by the beauty and harmony of the graceful design, then by an inexplicable sense of familiarity. Eyebrows knit in concentration, he focused on the knotting in his stomach, the quickening of his pulse, every sign that something was fighting its way to the surface of his mind. Rustav ran his hand over the illustration, pausing at a spot that didn't look quite right, where there should be—

A chip in the wood.

Rustav's hand flew to his chest, and for the first time, he remembered that his pendant was no longer there. Rustav looked up with his mouth open to demand that Pak return it, but the tuath was already holding it out. With a shaking hand, Rustav snatched it away and slapped the small wooden pendant down next to the illustration.

Line for line, curve for curve, it matched exactly.

CHAPTER ELEVEN

RUSTAV'S MIND RACED WILDLY, AND HE GASPED for breath in the torrent of memory. Everything he had lost—everything he had forgotten—it was all breaking its bonds, crashing over him, threatening to swirl him away. He knew now that the forest was not endless, that there were houses outside of the forest, that he knew people living outside the forest: Anton, Anna, Cabel, Father Lute, all the people of Gebir. Once, long ago, he had lived outside the forest. How long ago? It had been summer when he had entered; it was summer now. Rustav vaguely recalled a period of cold, of wind and wet weather, but had it been only one? How many winters had passed? It was all so blurry, so muddied with tuath spells that Rustav couldn't remember whether a month had passed or five years.

Tay's voice broke into his thoughts. "How long have you known?"

"Almost from the beginning," Pak said, his eyes on the floor. "I saw this pendant around his neck the day after he arrived. I tried to brush it off as a coincidence, but the longer

I watched, the more I could see that he showed a remarkable affinity for our ways. It wasn't long before I knew that Rustav was more than an average human."

"What?" Rustav looked up from the pendant that had jolted him so violently back to reality. "What do you mean, more?"

Pak tapped the book in Rustav's hands. "A child of the Union. Half tuath, half human. The last living child of the Union, in fact. As a second child, your uncle, the king Elanokiev, didn't inherit that bloodline."

"My uncle?" Rustav's head was spinning too fast to keep up with Pak's words. "You're not saying—you don't think—what do you mean, my uncle?"

Tay, however, was rising to her feet, her cheeks turning scarlet. "All this time, you knew. You knew he was the heir to the throne—to the Union—and you said nothing? Not to the Council, not to Ayre, not to me?"

"I assumed Ayre already knew and had a plan for him in place. Why else would he bring Rustav to our trees? And I was afraid." Pak hung his head. "I did not want to cross Ayre. I feared what he would do if I ruined his plans. I thought I would be blameless if I simply allowed Ayre to have his way."

Rustav didn't envy Pak the blistering glare that Tay had turned on him. In a low, heated voice, she said, "And now that the trees are a hotbed of debate as to whether to end the Union? To watch the humans fall? Before, he would have been hailed as a brother. But now, with so many contending for dissolution . . ." Tay shook her head, her wavy hair bouncing with indignation. "Of course, that may have been Ayre's design all along. I could believe that he started this entire movement against the Union to serve his own pompous purposes."

"Tay," Pak said with a hint of reproof, "assigning blame without evidence is no more admirable than standing aside when action is required."

Tay's mouth tightened. "Fine. I retract my blame. Now you take action."

"She's right," Pak said, turning to Rustav, who had been sifting their words in a desperate attempt to understand what was happening. "The danger for you has risen too far, with more and more tuatha hoping that the Union has been broken. They believe the heirs of the Union to be dead, and use that belief as validation for allowing the inhabitants of Burrihim to oppress and destroy the humans on the peninsula. They may go to great lengths to keep their argument valid. You must leave the forest before those who oppose the Union realize who you really are."

Burrihim. Rustav's palms began to sweat. Of course. That was why he had come to the forest in the first place. The islanders were coming to take the peninsula. "Have the islanders already come?"

"There have been no attacks as yet. But whether there are any islanders on the peninsula, I cannot say for certain."

Tay broke in now, her voice soft and urgent. "Please, Rustav, the Union must be restored. My people must be reminded that they are not cowards, that they cannot stand by and watch our human brothers slaughtered. You must return to your country and show both your people and mine that we need each other, that we will stand stronger together than apart. Under your leadership, we can be reunited."

"You're crazy," Rustav said, shaking his head. "Completely crazy. I'm not a prince!"

Pak threw up his hands in exasperation. "Believe what

you will. You will not be able to deny the truth for long. For now, all I'm asking is that you leave the forest before anyone else realizes who you are."

Rustav was more than willing to leave the forest, if only to get away from the terror of forgetting and from these two delusional tuatha. But a fearful certainty clenched in his stomach, holding him back. "Ayre won't want me to leave."

"Ayre won't be here," Pak said. "He's leaving the forest tonight. He won't be back until morning."

"He's leaving the forest?" Rustav raised his eyebrows. "I didn't think you ever left the forest."

"Some do, on occasion," Pak said. "They bring news of the outside world. But Ayre has been spending many nights out there, more than necessary to satisfy curiosity. What his purpose is, I can only guess, but tonight would be the best opportunity to leave without resistance."

Still, something caught at Rustav's mind, refusing to let him turn and run. Rustav fought the trailing wisps of fog, banishing them as much as he could in the search for the nagging link that held him back.

Dantzel.

Sickened, Rustav slumped back against the wall, staring blankly ahead as her face swam into focus in his mind. He hadn't seen her since the day they came to this cursed forest, however long ago that was. How had he so thoroughly forgotten her? He had never asked about her, never so much as thought about her. What happened? She had followed him into the forest, he remembered that much clearly. It had sparked an irrational hope inside of him when he saw her running toward him with all her might.

But in the trees—everything had changed. She had

turned her back on him. He had tried to talk to her, but she didn't want to talk. Rustav clenched his fists, his muscles rigid as he remembered the night he had tried to escape with her. She had betrayed him, had left him a prisoner of the tuatha.

But she—she had already been a prisoner. Of that, Rustav was slowly becoming certain. Her memory had disappeared; her personality had been completely altered. She was as much a victim as he was.

"I'm not leaving without Dantzel," Rustav announced, his jaw set.

"Listen to me," Pak said, his voice low and urgent. "She is not like you. She will not remember you. She will raise the alarm, you will be caught, and you will awake once more with no memory of who you are."

"If I can remember, so can she," Rustav said stubbornly. "Besides, if her mother saw me coming out of the forest without her, my life wouldn't be worth your spit. I'm not leaving without her."

"Of course you aren't," Tay said, shooting a stern glance at Pak. "But it will be difficult, Rustav. She has been close to Ayre."

A twist wrenched Rustav's stomach. "All the more reason to get her somewhere safe."

Tay nodded, a determined glint in her eye. "We will help bring you both to safety."

"You must stay here until dark," Pak said. "The first tuath to see you will know that you have thrown off the fog. It will create suspicion, and you will never leave unnoticed." Pak hesitated before continuing. "This will not end tonight. Ayre brought you here for a purpose, and I fear he will not let you go easily. And the tuatha who wish to dissolve the Union will not be easily silenced. I did you wrong by keeping you here with us, but I will not fail you again. If you need help, I will come. I believe in the power of the Union."

Rustav couldn't answer. How could he acknowledge Pak's insistence that he was a prince, a half-tuath, a lost heir to a forgotten bloodline? Instead, he sank down into a chair and stared down at the pendant in his hands until Tay and Pak had descended the ladder, leaving him alone.

IT WAS SEVERAL HOURS PAST DARK BEFORE PAK returned, whispering that Tay was keeping watch for wandering tuatha. As they left the tree and crept through the shadows, a cloud pressed in against Rustav so thickly that he had to remind himself to breathe more than shallow breaths. Whether it was his imagination or not, Rustav couldn't wait to get out into the free air once more.

The walk seemed to last an eternity, but Pak finally stopped in front of a tree that Rustav remembered only vaguely. He gestured to the doorway and whispered, "I'll wait out here."

As Rustav entered Dantzel's tree, a wave of déjà vu swept over him, and fear clutched at his stomach. With great effort, he stepped forward, swearing grimly that this night would not end the same way.

"Dantzel," he whispered. His eyes had adjusted well enough to the darkness that he could see her outline as she sat up in her hammock.

"*Wesiran?*" she asked in Tuathan. *Who's there?*

Rustav had been speaking Tuathan for so long that Coureian felt blocky and awkward in his mouth. It took conscious effort to remember the words he had once spoken instinctively, but he pressed forward, hoping that the language would jar something in her mind and startle her out of her trance. "It's me, Dantzel. It's Rustav. I came to talk to you."

Tensed as he was for any unexpected event, Rustav reacted with explosive swiftness when he heard her draw in a deep breath. Launching himself into the hammock, he covered her mouth tightly with one hand and wrapped his other arm around her, suppressing her fight to free herself. "Please don't," he begged, doing his best to keep her quiet without frightening her any more. "I just want to talk. It's been so long since I've seen you. Can we just . . . just talk for a minute?"

She nodded hesitantly. Cautiously, Rustav pulled his hand away, watching her carefully for any sign that she would scream. However, Dantzel just shrank away from him, turning to face him in the darkness. "They said someone might come for me, someone who would want to hurt me."

Her words were halting, but at least they weren't Tuathan. That was encouraging, even if the words themselves weren't. Rustav let go of her and held up his hands to show he wasn't attacking her. "I'm not here to hurt you. I'm your friend, remember? Do you remember me at all?"

She was silent for so long that Rustav began to feel the cold tendrils of despair creeping across his chest. Finally, she responded, "You came into the forest with me."

"Right," Rustav said, doing his best to be patient while still pushing her into action. "I met you in the village just outside of the trees."

"Outside?" She was obviously working hard to follow him. "It's been a long time since I've been outside of the trees. It's safer in here."

Rustav clenched his teeth, forcing back the anger that threatened to sharpen his voice. He couldn't risk her feeling threatened. "Do you remember any of it?"

"No."

Come on, Dantzel, work with me. "Your mother? Anton? Nothing?"

This time, there was hesitation in her voice. "I suppose . . . yes, I lived with my mother." With a touch of impatience, she added, "Why does it matter? We're here now."

"It does matter," Rustav said, his voice shaking with suppressed anxiety. He had to crack that wall, had to release the memories that were bound deep inside of her. "Your mother has no idea where you are or even whether you're alive. You disappeared without a trace months ago. Can you imagine how worried she must be?"

"Months?" Dantzel's voice wasn't as dreamy and light anymore. "It hasn't been months."

"It has," Rustav insisted. "You just said that you haven't been outside the forest for a long time. How long has it been?"

Dantzel rubbed her eyes, impatience coloring her voice. "I don't know. I guess it has been a while. Mama must be wondering what happened. Maybe Ayre would visit her and explain what's happened."

"Do you think a stranger would be able to comfort your mother much? She'll want to see you, to hear your story from your own lips."

He was almost there. Dantzel was teetering on the edge, and Rustav waited to see where she would fall. After a long, tense wait, Dantzel shrank back and shook her head. "I can't do it. Who knows what's out there?"

In a heroic effort to keep from exploding with frustration,

Rustav nearly bit his own tongue off as he counted backward from ten three times. When he had regained his temper, he took her hand. "I'll tell you what's out there. There are friends who need you, friends who have no idea what happened to you. There's a garden out there that you poured your heart and soul into. There's a stream out there, the clearest stream you've ever seen. We used to sit there for hours. Do you remember that?"

Dantzel didn't answer for a moment; then, slowly, she pulled back her blanket and dug her fingers into the weave of the hammock. The object that she extracted was small enough to fit in the palm of her hand as she held it out. Rustav squinted at it through the darkness. When he recognized it, his eyes widened, and his throat swelled until he couldn't speak.

"This was in my pocket when I came here," Dantzel said. "A wooden bird, but not like the tuatha shape wood. It was cut from dead wood. I didn't know why I was saving it, but . . . you cut it. You gave it to me, out there in the village."

Rustav swallowed several times before he was able to speak. "Come with me, Dantzel. I swear I won't let anything happen to you."

Dantzel nodded, curling her fingers protectively around the carved seabird as she stood. She folded her blanket and placed it in a woven bag, then pulled a cloak around her shoulders. After a moment's hesitation, she picked up a bow and quiver of arrows that leaned against the wall, sliding them carefully over her shoulder. Giving the room one final glance, Dantzel turned to Rustav and nodded once more.

Undisturbed in the dark stillness of the night, they rejoined Pak and slipped through the trees to the edge of the town, where Pak opened the trapdoor, inclined his head, and disappeared without a word. Rustav climbed down first to help Dantzel through, concerned that she wouldn't be as steady in her confused state. She climbed mechanically and only with a great deal of prompting; but they made it to the ground with no mishaps—and, more important, no sign of being followed. Rustav let out the breath he felt had been holding ever since he entered Dantzel's tree. After taking a moment to get his bearings, Rustav took her hand once more, whispered, "Let's go," and began walking toward freedom.

CHAPTER TWELVE

As Dantzel approached the edge of the forest, a weight pressed harder and harder against her chest. She couldn't remember the last time she had felt so worried. It was unpleasant, and she briefly resented Rustav for having disturbed her peace of mind. But it was hard to stay angry with him when his firm grip on her hand neutralized her anxiety so well. The farther they traveled, the more she became aware of emotions stirring inside of her, strange, complex emotions that were well beyond the simple contentedness she had enjoyed for so long. As confused as she was, Dantzel couldn't help feeling a little invigorated by the sudden change of pace, the resurgence of emotions long since forgotten.

And then the trees cleared, and Dantzel froze.

She could see her cottage, just as she had left it—how long ago? The slow rise of feeling surged into a flash flood, and Dantzel breathed more and more quickly, terror overwhelming her. All at once, the memory of that terrible day rose up before her eyes: Rustav showing up with nightmarish scars encircling his torso, her mother pulling her away as he ran to face the Guards, leaving her mother standing in the ditch as she pelted toward the forest. She had left her mother alone and never returned. Not once had she worried about what had happened to her mother; not once had she worried about what had happened to Rustav.

Without quite knowing what she was doing, Dantzel tore down the hill, racing back to the home and life she had abandoned. Her mother—what would her mother say? Had she already mourned? Had there been a funeral? Why hadn't any of this occurred to Dantzel before?

When she stood on the stone before the front door and reached for the doorknob, Dantzel stopped once more, fear turning her limbs to stone. What awaited her inside? Her hands refused to obey her, simply would not turn the knob.

Light footsteps sounded behind her, and Rustav's large hand covered hers. Its warmth sent life shooting back into her veins, as did his low voice in her ear. "It's okay. We'll go in together."

Slowly, gently, he turned the doorknob with her and pushed the door open. As the hinges creaked out a long groan, stale air rushed against Dantzel's face and she knew, even before she could see the shattered dishes, the splinters of her mother's wooden rocking chair, the thick layer of dust that covered everything in an ominous sort of funeral shroud. Numbly, Dantzel stepped into the house, taking in the wreckage before her, unable to accept the truth of that terrible scene. She dropped to her knees, staring with dry, agonized eyes. "How long has it been?" she whispered, picking up a shard of a clay bowl and rubbing away the dust that had settled into its flowery design.

"I don't know," Rustav said bleakly from behind her. "I don't know."

Dantzel folded over, hugging herself as she buried her face in her knees, muffling her broken voice until it was barely audible. "Where have I been?"

Rustav knelt beside her and put a hand on her back. After a moment, he spoke, shaking her gently. "Come on, Dantzel. Let's get you out of here. We need to check on Anton."

He led her out, back under the open skies. She followed without protest, looking up and stepping carelessly as they crossed the yard to the path into town. Bumps and holes threatened to trip her as she stumbled along; still, she kept her eyes on the sky, her emotional center overloading and shutting down. She focused on the pinpricks of distant light, blocking out the noise of all other sensations.

"Do you know how long it's been since I've seen the stars?" she asked. Talking felt good; she kept at it, determined to keep herself together. "Of course you don't. I don't either. But I remember when it was. I was with you; we were walking home together from Julie and Robert's wedding. You told me all about the constellations, about the bear who followed the honeybees up a mountain and into the skies, about the ship that was sucked up by a twister and sails through the stars— all of the stories."

She paused, remembering all too clearly what had followed that pleasant starlit walk. Chancing a quick sideways glance, she found Rustav staring straight ahead, his expression as stiff and guarded as it had been when they first met. Dantzel sighed, too full of emotion to know what to do with it. Far too tired to find the right words, Dantzel settled for the first action that crossed her mind: she reached out and took Rustav's hand. Startled, Rustav looked over at her, his iron façade broken by surprise. Dantzel smiled, and then her smile trembled, and finally a tear spilled down her cheek, followed immediately by another and another. Embarrassed, she tried to explain, her voice high and unsteady.

"My—my mother is gone." Her voice failed her before she could force out the thousand other concerns pressing on her mind, and Dantzel bit her lip as more tears escaped her. Rustav let go of her hand and put his arm around her, pulling her in close and pausing to allow her to dry her tears on the front of his shirt. Dantzel pressed against him, fighting to regain control.

"We'll get her back," Rustav said firmly, laying his hand on the back of her head. "In the meantime, I'm here. And I'm not going to let anything happen to you."

Nodding, Dantzel took in a deep, shuddering breath and pulled back, offering a shaky smile. "Let's go find Anton."

Rustav watched Dantzel carefully out of the corner of his eye as they made their way toward the town. He kept her arm pulled firmly through his, worried that she would fall without his support. She walked beside him with a stiff, jerky stride, and her face was as deathly pale as it had turned when she had first seen her ruined cottage. After that single outburst of tears, she had resumed her dry-eyed, wide-eyed expression, teetering on the edge of shock. Had the sudden reawakening been too much for her? What else could he have done? It would have been worse to just leave her there. Wouldn't it?

The closer they drew to the town, the more Rustav had to fight the urge to run with all his might to Anton's house, to see what awaited him there. The urge held until the house actually came into sight. Rustav didn't realize that he had stopped until Dantzel tugged on his arm. He looked over at her, and she managed a wan smile.

"Waiting won't make it any easier."

Nodding, Rustav stepped forward once more, his heart banging mercilessly against his ribs. Releasing Dantzel, he reached out and pushed the door open.

The kitchen was just as he had left it, albeit vacant of Guards. The shelves were neatly stocked with food, the table was dust-free, and a small pile of shavings showed that Anton had been working at the table. Rustav inhaled the sharp scent of wood dust, weak with relief.

"Thank the clouds," Dantzel murmured behind him, and Rustav nodded, moving dreamlike into the center of the room and turning slowly to reassure himself that nothing was out of place. A rustle came from the shadows in the far corner, where Rustav knew the sleeping mats lay. Their noise must have awakened Anton; Rustav watched the movement in the shadows, waiting eagerly for Anton's astonished face.

But the figure that leaped out of the corner was not Anton. A scrawny kid with a mess of curly brown hair brandished a knife at them, scowling as he advanced. Automatically, Rustav grabbed Dantzel and pushed her behind him, reaching for his sword. However, before he could draw it out, the boy's face changed, uncertainty stealing across his narrow features. He lowered the knife and stared.

"Rustav? Dantzel? Is that really you?"

Relaxing his grip on the hilt of his sword, Rustav squinted hard at the boy; Dantzel peeked out from behind him and gasped. "Cabel?"

Dropping the knife, Cabel sprang across the room and grabbed Dantzel in a hug, picking her up off the floor and swinging her around. Rustav stared in wrenching disbelief. Last he remembered, Cabel had been a full head shorter than Dantzel; now, he had at least two inches on her. His face had lost much of its roundness, though his boyishness was preserved in his expressions and actions. When he set Dantzel down, Rustav grabbed him by the shoulders, shoulders that were much higher off the ground than his memory told him they should be. "What are you doing here?" Rustav asked urgently. "Is everyone okay?"

Cabel's smile dimmed, and his gaze dropped to the floor as he shrugged. "Not exactly. A lot has happened since you disappeared."

"Where's my mother?" Dantzel demanded, squeezing Cabel's hand bloodless. Cabel pulled her over to the table and pulled out a chair for her, perching on the table as Rustav stood restlessly behind the second chair.

"The day you left, the Guards roughed up your house and Anton's house a little," Cabel began, his legs swinging and his face somber, "but your ma got away fine. She came back the next day, after the Guards had gone, and we all assumed the two of you would show up eventually as well. But a week went by, we got the houses back in order, and there was still no sign of you. Then, the Guards came back. They brought a merchant with them this time, a rich old cad with a fancy wood-and-gold walking stick."

"Karstafel," Rustav groaned, rubbing his forehead. "He was looking for me?"

Cabel nodded. "He thought that Anna and Anton were hiding you. When they kept telling him they didn't know where you were, he told the Guards to take Anna back to the castle."

Rustav looked at Dantzel. She was white and stiff, but her expression was stoic. "What about Anton?" she asked, not acknowledging Rustav's glance.

"He was too old for a slave," Cabel said, glowering at the floor. "The Guards wouldn't take him, so the merchant used his cane."

It was just getting worse and worse. "How bad was it?" Rustav asked, dreading the answer. He knew all too well what that walking stick could do.

"Not as bad as it could have been. They had dragged Anton into the town square by that point, so I saw what was happening and jumped into the fray before the merchant swine got too far. He got in a few lucky hits and knocked me down, so my pa decked him. The Guards took my pa away." Cabel's face clouded over, his eyes low, and Dantzel put a hand on his knee. "The merchant left with them. He hasn't been back since, or I'd have smashed his head in with his own walking stick."

"I tried that once," Rustav said woodenly, the memory feeling more like a dream than the life-changing event it had been. "His head's as hard as an iron pot. It damaged the stick more than his skull."

Cabel laughed quietly. "I'd believe it. Who is he?"

"My uncle. Sort of. I thought he was, but Anton . . . how is Anton? Did he pull through okay?"

"Mostly," Cable said with a shrug. "His bad leg is worse than ever now, so he can't get around very well. I moved in to help him recover, and I've just sort of stuck around since. I run the store during the day now that Pa's not around, then I come back to help out Anton in the evening. I didn't like leaving him alone at night. He doesn't sleep much anymore, and sometimes he goes wandering. I try to keep an eye out and go after him if he's gone too long."

All my fault, Rustav thought, strangling the back of the chair with his grip and letting his head hang down to stare at the dirt floor. *Thanks to me, Dantzel's mother and Cabel's father are gone. Cabel and Anton took beatings that should have been mine. And Dantzel*—Rustav looked at Dantzel, but quickly diverted his eyes to Cabel when she tried to meet his gaze. He couldn't face the pain in her eyes. "Cabel," Rustav said, dread creeping into the words he feared to ask, "how long has it been?"

"What?"

"Since we left. How long have we been gone?"

Forehead furrowed, Cabel replied, "Two years. Almost exactly."

Dantzel's hand covered her mouth, and Rustav closed his eyes, the anxious pain in his stomach worsening. He had harbored an irrational hope that somehow, they had only been in the trees for a matter of months, a year at most. Two years of their lives—gone, sucked away in the unnatural branches of the tuath town.

From the front door came an odd, strangled sound. Rustav's head snapped up, and he saw Anton mouthing wordlessly in the doorway, gripping the doorjamb until his knuckles were as white as his face. In an instant, Rustav was at his side, holding him steady and leading him over to a chair. Anton never took his eyes off of Rustav's face. After he was safely seated, he reached out a trembling, knobby hand to touch Rustav's arm, as if to assure himself that Rustav wasn't a ghost.

"I thought you were dead," Anton said, his jaw quivering slightly. "I thought—I thought all was lost."

A thousand questions jammed in Rustav's throat, threatening to strangle him before he could get any of them out. If what Pak had told him was true, he would never be able to turn his back on this country. He would never be able to leave it behind. And he would never be able to ignore what he now knew about the forest. Where could he even begin? Which question didn't require a thousand other questions to be answered first? In the end, only one word made it out, a word that Rustav heard only once, two years previously.

"Antonius?"

Dantzel and Cabel exchanged a glance, but Rustav was only conscious of Anton's hand tightening around his arm. "Then you know," said the old carpenter, his sunken blue eyes suddenly flooding with tears. "Please, my lord, forgive me. I've done penance every day for my mistakes. I will serve you just as faithfully, no, more faithfully than I served your father, may his soul be at rest."

Cabel's feet halted mid-swing, one foot extended outward. Rustav felt his face flame and had to force himself not to glance over his shoulder at Dantzel. "No, Anton, don't say that. Don't call me that. You've saved my life twice now, and I've repaid you pretty poorly. And I don't know—all I have are bits and pieces. I need you to tell me who I am."

"But—how did you know my name?"

Impatiently, Rustav brushed the question away with his free hand and replied shortly, "A tuath told me."

Silence reigned in the small kitchen, broken only by Dantzel's stifled giggle. Rustav turned to raise an eyebrow at her, and she broke into a full laugh, shrugging helplessly. For a moment, he feared she had finally broken under the strain, but she quickly regained control and said with a slightly hysterical grin, "They're going to think we've completely lost it."

"Where have you been for the past two years?" Cabel asked, one foot still hanging in the air. Rustav pushed it down, allowing himself a reluctant smile as he acknowledged the absurdity of his simple comment. The smile grew less reluctant when Dantzel caught his eye again, her eyes holding all the familiarity and understanding of a shared joke. He liked that look. They'd shared it a lot . . . two years earlier.

"We were in the forest," Rustav said.

Anton's eyes positively shone, and he leaned forward in his chair. "And who did you meet in the forest?"

Rustav raised an eyebrow, trying to read the avid interest in Anton's eyes. Just how much did the old man know?

"You won't believe this," said Dantzel, shaking her head, "but there are—"

"Tuatha?" Anton interrupted eagerly.

Rustav exchanged a long glance with Dantzel, unnerved by Anton's inexplicable knowledge of the forest people. "Anton," he said finally, "what do you know about the forest that you've never told us?"

"Nothing for certain," Anton said, his hands trembling with excitement on his knees. "But I long suspected that it was a safe haven for beings who wished to be left alone."

"One of them spoke as if he knew you," Rustav said, the memory unnaturally clear in comparison to the haze of the past two years. "The day we arrived, he asked if Antonius had sent us."

Anton didn't seem nearly as concerned as Rustav. "They may have watched me on the edge of the forest. I developed an old man's habit of muttering to myself as I gathered wood, telling the trees the secrets that had weighed me down for years." Waving a hand, Anton leaned forward and said, "But you've lived with them for two years! What was it like?"

Jaw clenching, Rustav replied, "About as good as it can be as prisoners."

"Did they throw you in dungeons?" Cabel asked, looking incredibly envious at their good fortune of being held captive by mythical beings.

"No, not at all," Dantzel said, shaking her head. Her voice was unsteady, as if she was reluctant to admit all that they had done. "They taught us to read and speak Tuathan, to draw, to make music, to do anything that they could teach us. I learned archery"—she touched the bow that now rested against the table—"and Rustav learned the sword."

Cabel's eyes made an owl look squinty. "Can I see your sword?"

Rustav drew the sword out and placed the hilt in Cabel's hand as Anton said dubiously, "That doesn't sound much like you were prisoners."

Dantzel shook her head, her face peaked, and looked to Rustav for help. He answered in a hard voice, masking the terror of how completely he had been erased. "We were separated the first day. After that, we had no memory of who we were or where we had come from. We never marked the passage of time, never thought about the ones we had left behind. We forgot everything."

The glow in Anton's eyes dimmed considerably, and Cabel forgot all about the sword he held. In hushed tones, Anton asked, "How did you remember?"

Rustav slung the bag from his shoulder and dropped it on the table, eyeing it with foreboding. Did he dare tell them about the book? They were sure to laugh him out of the house with what he was suggesting, weren't they? But Anton—Anton knew far more than he should. In truth, he was just as terrified that Anton would confirm Pak's story as he was that it would be proved ridiculous.

"Rustav talked me out of it," Dantzel said when Rustav didn't speak. "But in the end, he still had to pull me out of the trees. It wasn't until I saw the town that I remembered everything." Her eyes bored into Rustav's back, searching him for answers. "How did you do it, Rustav?"

With a sudden decisiveness, Rustav reached into his bag and slid out the Book of the Trees, holding it up briefly for them to see before setting it back on the table and opening it. "One of the tuatha showed me this," he said, searching for the pages he had seen. "There was a story in here about a human king marrying a member of the tuathan Council. It had a detailed illustration accompanying it."

"The Union Crest," Anton said, quietly but clearly. As if in response, the book fell open to the drawing, and Cabel and Dantzel both leaned in to scrutinize it.

"That's yours!" Dantzel exclaimed. Rustav kept his eyes on Anton, who was brushing his gnarled fingers lightly over the delicate ink.

"What do you say, Antonius?" Rustav asked, his voice calm even if his heart was not. "Why did you carve this for me?"

With one hand still resting on the book, Anton looked up to meet Rustav's eyes with a solemn gaze. "Because you are Marustavian, son of the slain Rilotorian, rightful king of Courei."

CHAPTER THIRTEEN

"I WAS ONCE ANTONIUS, FORMER EARL OF VESSEN," Anton said, his slouched posture and callused hands the furthest thing from the picture of an earl. His words were halting at first, but soon poured out with an air of relief at finally being able to speak so freely. "King Rilotorian was a dear friend to me. I practiced the art of woodcarving, and I think the king appreciated having someone in the court who did more than order servants to and fro. I'd often carve little trinkets for him and his wife. I was also something of a scholar—really, just a curious old man with nothing better to do than skulk through rooms full of old books.

"I found a book like that one in the royal library, back in a corner so thick with dust that it might have gone undisturbed for centuries. It was written in Old Coureian, not Tuathan, of course, and I showed it to the king. It became an obsession with us; we pored over it together for hours, dissecting each legend, learning all that we could and guessing at what we couldn't. He was particularly engrossed in the tale of the Union of humans and tuatha. The royal family has long been rumored to possess certain special abilities, things that fit with what we knew of the tuatha. Rilotorian himself was absurdly fleet of foot, and his stamina was unrivaled, whether it were in swordplay or on a long march."

Rustav stared down at his feet, which had outrun enemies in three countries. He thought of how quickly he had learned the sword, how impressed Pak had been during their long rounds. He remembered the tuatha and hated them a little more for making him less than human.

"The idea that he might have tuathan blood resonated with Rilotorian. He never doubted the truthfulness of the book, and his earnest belief was infectious. He enlisted me to help find his lost tuathan brothers. We studied and searched long for any hint of where the tuatha could have gone, as determined as little boys chasing after lightning. Rilotorian's desire bordered on obsession, and he began to spend more time on the search than he did on the affairs of the kingdom. Your birth brought back his sense of responsibility for a time, but then Ayre came."

Rustav's heart jolted. "Who?"

"A boy from the mountains looking for work in the castle. He heard that the king was looking for tuatha and claimed he knew where to find them. Of course, Rilotorian brought him in for questioning immediately. The boy said he had entered the forest one day on a dare and seen tuatha climbing in the trees."

Rustav exchanged a long glance with Dantzel. It couldn't be a coincidence. But what could Ayre have hoped to win by leading Rilotorian to the forest? Had he been trying, even then, to put an end to the Union? "Was there anything out of the ordinary about the boy?" Rustav asked. If the king—Rustav still couldn't call him his father—had been so obsessed with tuatha, wouldn't he have noticed Ayre's pointed eyebrows? Wouldn't he have realized what Ayre was?

Anton wrinkled his forehead in concentration. "It was a long time ago, but . . . I believe his head was bandaged. Yes, he said he had been attacked on the road."

"And it covered his eyebrows," Dantzel said.

"Yes, it did," Anton said. Then, as the significance of her words sank in, his eyes widened. "He was a tuath?"

"That's how he knew your name," Rustav said, still puzzling over Ayre's intentions. "He had seen you while you were still an earl. He must have recognized you when you came to Gebir. What happened then?"

"It was thin evidence, but Rilotorian would leave no corner unchecked. He began preparing an expedition to investigate the forest. It was to depart the day after your first birthday." The rising sun was beginning to illuminate Anton's haggard features. He was staring into the nothingness in front of him, lost in the past. "After you were born, I began carving a replica of the Union Crest, based on the illustration I had found in the book. I wanted it to be perfect, and it took several months and many failed attempts to create an acceptable crest. I finished it the night before your first birthday—the perfect gift, I thought, and perhaps a good omen that the tuatha would be found on your father's expedition."

Anton looked up at Rustav sorrowfully. "I told you what happened when I went to deliver it. There were no Guards by your parents' door, and the door was ajar. I peered in to see what had happen, and there was Elanokiev standing over the bed." Anton's voice trembled, pleading for understanding. "I couldn't do anything. He acted before I could move, before I could cry out, before I even realized there was a knife in his hand."

Rustav closed his eyes briefly against the image that swept in front of him, a knife plunging twice, changing his life forever. "Then what?"

"I ran. I went to your room and snatched you up before Elanokiev could get to you too. I put the crest around your neck, hoping that, somehow, this relic from the past would offer additional protection. I knew that if Elanokiev found me with you, he would brand me as your parents' murderer, so I fled out the window and all the way to Markuum."

"And left me with Karstafel," Rustav said, bringing the strange, foreign story into what he had known all his life. It was hard to accept the fact that they weren't discussing some stranger, some legendary figure—just him. "He assumed from the beginning that his sister had left me with him as retribution for leaving her to fend for herself after their parents died. He never guessed that it was the prince he was kicking around all those years, or he probably would have sold me to Elanokiev."

"If you knew how I've tortured myself over your fate, my lord—"

"Don't!"

Even Rustav was startled at the intensity of his own cry. He hadn't meant to shout quite so loud, but it ripped out of his chest, carrying with it all the fear of what might come if he allowed Anton to call him "my lord." He shook his head and spoke again, pulling his voice back into a normal range. "This is me, Anton. Just me. I'm not a prince, I'm just Rustav."

"You are a prince," Anton said, his firmness laced with a hint of compassion. "You have no choice in the matter."

"Who would follow me?" Rustav demanded, his legs itching to leap up and begin running. "Even if you believe that I'm the old king's son, why should anyone else?"

"When Elanokiev took power, he expelled every one of your father's supporters from the castle and the valley," Anton explained. "I tracked down my trusted friends. I described the Union Crest, the pendant you wear. And as I have said, the royal house is widely known to possess superior strength—due, as your father and I discovered, to the undiminishing qualities of your tuathan heritage. Your bloodline shows itself in your speed and your stamina."

Trapped. Trapped, not by Karstafel or bullies or mythical creatures, but by his own blood, by the very skills he had once thought could make him free. Unable to remain still any longer, Rustav shoved the *Book of the Trees* back into his bag, then took his sword from Cabel and slid it into its sheath. Anton's white eyebrows lowered sternly.

"And where will you run away to now?"

"There's nowhere left for me to run, is there?" Rustav snapped, slinging his bag forcefully over his shoulder. "Listen, I'm not responsible for this country. Even if I was meant to be once, that way closed a long time ago. But I am responsible for the people who were taken from this village on my account, and I'm going to get them back."

This time, Anton actually stood up in alarm. "You can't just walk into the castle! You look far too much like your father. Elanokiev will recognize you and have you beheaded on the spot!"

"I've spent half my life causing trouble on the castle grounds while Karstafel sucked up to the king," Rustav said. "I wasn't beheaded once. Trust me, I know how to get in and out without being seen."

"I'm coming with you," Dantzel said, instantly followed by Cabel.

"Me too!"

"No," Rustav said firmly, shaking his head. "I can travel faster by myself. I'll be back in a few days."

"Rustav, my father might be there," Dantzel pleaded. "You wouldn't know him."

"Your mother would," Rustav answered. "If he's there, she can lead me to him. You're not going."

"Nobody is going!" Anton protested, thumping the ground with his cane. "Of all the foolhardy, suicidal—"

"Please, Rustav," Dantzel persisted, her pale face earnest. "You can't leave me here on the edge of the forest. If Ayre came after us and found me alone . . ."

That arrested Rustav's anxious movements. He ground his teeth, weighing the dangers of the forest with the dangers of the castle. There was really no battle between the two, but Rustav didn't like the only option it left him with. Finally, he conceded. "Fine. You can come along, but you're not going inside the castle."

Dantzel murmured something that sounded like, "We'll see," but Rustav ignored her. Cabel hopped off the table, incensed.

"If she's going, so am I! I want to get my pa out!"

"No. You're twelve—" Rustav caught and corrected himself. "Fourteen years old. You're not coming with us."

"I'm not just a kid anymore!" Cabel insisted, his face reddening with anger. "I'm almost as old as you were when you went into the forest. I'm taller than Dantzel now. If you two are going—"

"You're not coming!" Rustav said, determined to get his

way on this point. "If you try to follow us, I'll tie you to the table."

"Cabel, listen," Dantzel said, placing a hand on the boy's arm. "The fewer there are that go in, the easier we'll get out. If you want to help, stay here and keep Anton's heart from stopping with worry. We'll be back soon, I promise."

Cabel nodded miserably, his hazel eyes brimming with hurt. "Fine. Leave me here again. I'll see you in another two years." Jumping noisily down from the table, Cabel kicked aside an empty chair and stormed over to the corner, falling into the shadows and yanking a blanket up over his head.

"Please, Rustav," Anton said, his soft plea contrasting sharply with Cabel's angry outburst. "Don't do this. There are better ways, easier ways. I can help you, but not like this."

"Come on, Dantzel," Rustav said, stepping around the old man and making his way to the door. "I want to get as far from the trees as possible before anyone starts looking for us."

Dantzel didn't know where Rustav was getting the strength to press on hour after hour. She had at least gotten a few hours' sleep before he had come for her, and she doubted that Rustav had slept at all the previous night. Her exhausted mind could barely keep up with the landscape slipping past—the rough, prickly wilds of the foothills giving way to the neatly organized farmlands and orchards of the valley.

As tired as Dantzel was, a dull sense of curiosity still stirred deep inside of her. For seventeen years, the valley had been nothing more than a vague, distant painting stretched out at the foot of the mountains. Now it was big and real and overwhelming in its strangeness. More than once, they ducked away from the road to hide as a train of merchants or nobles passed. Dantzel couldn't help but stare at the impossible finery they wore—velvets and silks, hats and cloaks, colors as deep and bright as a sunrise. The tuathan dress she wore was the finest she had ever touched, and it was still plain and simple by comparison. Once, she glanced over at Rustav, a startled thought reverberating in her head. One day, maybe one day soon, he could be wearing the finery fitting of a prince. Dantzel turned her eyes to the ground, trying not to imagine her own rough, dirt-covered clothes beside such rich material.

They walked without stopping until late afternoon, avoiding as many fellow travelers as possible. Although she refused to ask for a break, Dantzel couldn't repress a sigh of relief when Rustav announced, "We can stop here for the night." Wearily, Dantzel dropped her bag and sat gladly on the hard ground, her feet throbbing with the repeated pounding against the unforgiving ground.

"Not in the open," Rustav said hurriedly, and Dantzel held back a mutinous glare. "There's a little apple orchard over there."

Dantzel remained where she was, reluctant to stand after finally getting to rest, and even more reluctant to go anywhere near another tree. "What's wrong with the open?" she asked. "It's been two years since you disappeared. No one here will be looking for you anymore. And we're miles away from the forest by now. The tuatha don't travel this far from the trees."

"They do sometimes. Ayre does regularly."

A chill ran through Dantzel at the certainty in Rustav's voice. "How do you know?"

"Pak told me. Ayre was outside of the forest last night. That's why we got out so easily."

For another moment, Dantzel sat, processing Rustav's words; then she stood and followed Rustav into the orchard. Though the sun hadn't yet set, she was so weary that she barely stayed awake long enough to eat a few bites of the leathery dried fruit they had taken from Anton. Her hunger partially satiated, she pulled her blanket over her and was asleep in seconds.

WHEN DANTZEL AWOKE, EARLY-MORNING SUN-shine was casting shadows through the apple leaves. Dantzel shrank away from the trunk near her face. Though the apple trees were tiny in comparison and unmistakably unlike the trees of the old forest, they still made her uneasy. She had dreamed during the night that the trees grew together around them, trapping them in a cage of living wood. Shaking off the ominous remnants of the dream, Dantzel turned over to see if Rustav was awake.

He was gone.

Disbelief battled terror as Dantzel ran her hands across the dirt where she had seen him lie down the night before. It was as if nobody had ever set foot there; the only marks were those she had made. He had left her! Taken her halfway to the castle and left her to fend for herself.

Leaping to her feet, Dantzel stormed to the edge of the trees, shoving aside branches with violent force. She was going after him, and he was going to hurt by the time she was done with him.

As soon as she stepped out of the trees, she leaped back

into their cover, startled by the appearance of a figure heading her way. Slipping back among the trees, she curved around to come out on the other side of the stand.

"Dantzel?" called a low voice, and Dantzel paused. Fear quickly gave way to fury once more, and she ran back to where Rustav was waiting on the edge of the trees.

"What do you think you're doing?" she demanded, shaking a fist at him. "First you wander off without telling me, then you scare me halfway into my grave. Where were you? Why didn't you wake me up?"

Rustav watched her tirade with an amused smile that only irritated Dantzel further. "I thought you could use the sleep." He held up his bag, now bulging with much more than just his book. "And some food."

Immediately, Dantzel reached for the bag, which Rustav relinquished without a fight. Her empty stomach growled with anticipation as she opened it to find fresh bread, dried meat, and several carrots. "Forgiven, then," she said dismissively, reaching into the mouth of the bag only to pause once more.

"There's plenty there," Rustav said, waving his hand. "Go ahead."

Slowly, Dantzel pulled back her hand, unable to tear her eyes away from the enticing food. "Where did you get this?"

Gesturing vaguely toward the north, Rustav said, "We're on the edge of the valley. There are plenty of farms around."

Dantzel hovered over the bag's opening, staring longingly at the food, but held back by her conscience. "Is it stolen?" she asked tentatively, hoping that somehow she could be wrong. Rustav snorted and pulled the bag away from her, handing her a piece of bread.

"We have no money, Dantzel. It's steal or starve. Eat."

Reluctantly, Dantzel bit into the bread, unable to resist the warm, tempting smell any longer. Rustav took some bread for himself, and they munched wordlessly as the sun climbed higher in the sky. It was a long time before Dantzel broke the silence.

"What was it like for you back there?"

Rustav looked over his shoulder to where the trees had faded into a massive green blur across the mountainside. "Probably a lot like it was for you," he said, shrugging and dropping his gaze to his bread once more. "I learned to speak Tuathan, and I tried to learn everything from them. Pak was with me most of the time. He even made me this." Rustav tapped the hilt of his sword.

"He was your jailer, then," Dantzel said, trying to make light of the memories that still made her break out in cold sweat. Rustav paused, reaching back slowly to run his fingers along the sword hilt.

"I don't think so," he said slowly, staring blankly downward. "I've thought of him that way too. But he was different from . . ."

"From Ayre," Dantzel finished when his voice trailed off, trying too hard to sound offhand. She couldn't explain why even his name struck deep inside of her, rattling the weak grip she had only recently regained on reality. Rustav nodded.

"He's the one who told me who I was, in the end. Pak said there was a divide among the tuatha—that some of them wanted to leave the trees and take over the peninsula to rule over the humans, and he wanted to keep me safe. He and Tay helped us get out of the forest. It's hard to trust him, after he kept me from remembering for two years. But sometimes I wonder if he might have been a true friend after all." Pausing for a bite of bread, Rustav chewed slowly and then shrugged. "It could easily just be whatever's left of the spell of the trees. You probably think the same thing of Ayre."

"No," Dantzel said emphatically, the slightest bit jealous that Rustav could still have hope to trust in a tuath friend. "I was an idiot to listen to Ayre. But he was always so attentive, so caring. Everything he said was so logical and so appealing. It wasn't until you came that I realized it was all just . . . empty." Dantzel shivered and folded her arms, shrinking away from the memory of it all. It wasn't just frightening; it was humiliating to think of how infatuated she had been, how Ayre had always been on her mind even when he was gone, how it had all been pure playacting and Ayre had never thought of her as anything more than a problem to be solved.

Dantzel was pulled out of her thoughts when Rustav wrapped a blanket around her shoulders. She looked up into his clear blue eyes, which were watching her somberly. "Do you wish you could have stayed with him?"

"No! He lied to me. Everything he said was designed to make me trust him without ever giving me a reason to. And he took me from you." Dantzel looked down at the bread in her hand, her cheeks uncomfortably warm. "I mean, we never saw each other after that first day. We never had the chance to talk things out. So much happened right before we went into the forest, and there was a lot that I didn't get to say to you."

She didn't dare look Rustav in the face again, but she could hear the careful lightness of his voice. "Like what?"

Like what? Dantzel bit her lip, wishing she had planned

what she was going to say a little further in advance. "Like . . . I enjoyed the wedding celebration. And I was glad that you danced."

Could she sound any more foolish? Even with the events of that night two years behind her, even with the absurd reality of all that had happened since, she couldn't bring herself to talk about what had really happened. Rustav shifted beside her, leaning away.

"Oh."

"And," Dantzel continued, gritting her teeth and plowing forward before she could think better of it, "I shouldn't have run inside the house that night. I should have stayed, and I should have told you that what you said was wonderful, and I should have explained that I was so terrified by the fact that it made me happy that I couldn't think straight."

"Oh," Rustav repeated, his tone significantly lighter. He shifted back closer to her. "Would it—would it still make you happy? And would you still be terrified?"

Dantzel laughed and tucked her chin into her knees, hardly able to believe they were having this conversation. A nervous thrill was running through her stomach, and she couldn't decide whether happiness or terror was winning the battle inside of her. "Yes."

His reaction was not quite what she had hoped. All at once, a dull stillness settled in the air beside her, and Dantzel looked over to see Rustav staring glumly into the flickering flames. Alarmed, she asked, "What did I say?"

Rustav shook his head with a fleeting grin. "Nothing. Sorry. What you said is great. It's just . . ."

Dantzel could see the dream of a repaired relationship slipping away in shreds. "What? What's wrong?"

Rustav turned to face her, his eyebrows drawn in concern. "Why?"

Nonplussed, Dantzel struggled to piece together what he was asking. "Why does it terrify me?"

"No," Rustav said, waving a hand. "I get that. It scares me too. Why does it make you happy? What could you see in me? Why would you even consider connecting yourself to a scrounging, rawboned beggar on the run from the coast? Even if all this madness that Anton told us is true, it's not like I'm actually a prince. I don't exactly have a country and a castle. Why me?"

Dantzel froze in astonishment for a moment before she could answer. "Do you remember telling me about the first time you were thrown into the castle prison?"

Puzzled, Rustav thought back to that long-ago conversation in the garden. "Yeah, I guess. What about it?"

"Why were you arrested?"

"I was harassing the Guards. That's what got me most of my time in the castle prison."

Dantzel shook her head. "You were fighting back for a servant girl they had been bothering. And that's not the only time. You freed a caravan servant who was treated badly. You tried to save your friend Ollie's books even though he was gone and you were beaten for it. You had hardly a single decent soul in your life to show you what kindness was, and yet you were kind to anyone who couldn't help themselves."

"Come on," Rustav scoffed. "I'm not some sort of saving angel. I just liked to cause trouble."

"Right. Well, besides a tendency to inadvertently help suffering people, you can also be funny and charming when you're not trying to be tough. You think about the world around you instead of letting it pass you by. And did I mention that you saved me from the forest?" Dantzel hesitated, then finished her thoughts aloud. "There's no one else who could be a better king than you."

If Rustav had withdrawn before, he now beat a full retreat behind iron walls. He didn't even respond when Dantzel touched his arm. "It's the truth. You've lived among the people. You know what your country is really like, what the people need, how everything functions. And you care. You won't let suffering get swept under the rug. You've been there yourself. Forget the legends—we've got you!"

That earned her a reproachful glance from Rustav, but Dantzel was too wrapped up in what she was saying to notice. Her grip on Rustav's arm tightened, and she laughed as she gave him a little shake. "As a matter of fact, don't forget the legends. Think about it. The valley said you'd come from the valley: you were born there. The coastal legends: you grew up on the coast, so you came from there as well. I don't know about the strength of the ocean waves, but judging by the way you run and the fact that you're half tuath, I'd say that's covered. And the mountains—" Dantzel beamed. "Coming from the forest, bearing the past over your heart. You just came from the forest. Your pendant is a token of days long past. And as for having the wrongs of the people written in your flesh—"

"Stop it," Rustav snapped, shoving himself to his feet and snatching up his bag. Dantzel watched, torn between amazement at her revelation and bewilderment at Rustav's reaction. "Come on. We've got a long way to travel today."

Without waiting for her to follow, Rustav stormed away,

leaving Dantzel to hurriedly gather up her blanket and bag and run after him. *What did I say?* she wondered, running through the conversation in her head. Everything she had said was in his favor. Wasn't it? Why did everything she say only make matters worse?

CHAPTER FOURTEEN

THE NEXT TWO DAYS OF TRAVELING CONSISTED of careful, stilted conversations. More than once, Dantzel tried to return to the conversation they had started in the apple orchard, but Rustav refused to be drawn into any more talk of legends and kingship, much to Dantzel's ever-increasing chagrin. Toward the end, Dantzel finally lapsed into a frustrated silence, leaving Rustav both grateful to have her off his back and annoyed that she was so stubborn about it all. Couldn't she understand what a ridiculous idea it was that he, of all people, should be leading a country?

At long last, the walls of the castle loomed before them, driving away any thought outside of their current mission. The sun had already disappeared over the horizon, leaving behind a darkening twilight. By the time Rustav reached the castle, the only light would be that of the stars.

"Wait in there," Rustav said, pointing to a crop of corn growing about fifty feet to the east without taking his eyes away from the stone walls that he would have to climb. It wouldn't be easy, but if there was one thing he had learned in the past two years, it was how to climb.

"I'm going with you."

The comment was expected, but Rustav still sighed as he turned to face her. He had hoped they wouldn't have to go through this. "I can move faster alone. I'll be in and out before you have time to worry."

"What if something happens to you?"

"Then you'll be safe, and you can get back to the mountains. Stop killing time and go hide in the corn."

Dantzel huffed and folded her arms. "I'm not staying here alone."

"Fine," Rustav said with a touch of impatience. Why did everything have to be a fight with her? "We'll just stand here, right outside the castle, until the Guards come and escort us right on in. Won't that be nice? I'm sure we'll find your parents then."

Muttering under her breath, Dantzel stormed off in the direction of the corn. Relieved, Rustav crept carefully the remaining distance to the eastern walls. He knew well that the lookout on this side of the castle was limited; the only thing east of the castle was the mountains, and traveling through the mountains and the old forest was unthinkable. In his typical shortsighted manner, Elanokiev had ordered the bulk of the Guards to watch the north, west, and south walls, where he expected any enemies to come. It was really a marvel that Elanokiev hadn't been murdered in his sleep yet.

Rustav picked his way up the wall, the cracks and protruding stones of the neglected wall making the climb easier than expected. He slipped his fingers over the top of the wall and pulled himself up until he could just see into the darkened courtyard. His eye quickly picked out three Guards patrolling. One had his back turned and would soon be out of sight, and the other two were far from wary. It would be simple to sneak past them once they were in the right position. Rustav lowered himself again, hanging down from the wall and timing the Guards' progress in his mind.

A noise from below startled him, and Rustav swung to hang from one arm so he could see what was under him. Groaning, he recognized the slim form following his path up the wall. She was impossible, absolutely impossible. For a moment, he was tempted to disappear over the wall and leave her before she could reach him, but at the rate she was climbing, he wouldn't be able to slip past the Guards until she was up there with him.

"I can't believe you," Rustav grunted as she neared, his shoulders aching from the strain of hanging there. Before she could answer, he pulled himself up to peer over the wall again; all was clear for the moment. No time to waste berating her. Hauling himself over and hoping in vain that Dantzel wouldn't follow, Rustav quickly found his way down the other side and dropped to the ground. A moment later, Dantzel landed beside him, and they ran for the hedges, bending low to the ground. The moment they were safely under cover, Rustav turned to face Dantzel's determinedly obstinate expression.

"You're going to get yourself killed," he whispered, running his hands through his hair in exasperation. "Can't you listen to me just once?"

"We're in this together," Dantzel replied, folding her arms stubbornly. "The sooner you accept that, the better. Shouldn't we get going before someone finds us here?"

Together. The word sounded strange in Rustav's ear, but it softened the edge of his irritation. Maybe it would be helpful to have another set of eyes while sneaking through the grounds. In any case, she was there, and he wasn't going to risk getting caught while trying to force her back out. "Come on, then," he grumbled softly. "I'll tell you how crazy you are after we get out of this alive."

They dodged up and down lanes, Rustav leading the way through the botanical labyrinth. This was the part he was least worried about; he had once hidden in the king's hedges for the better part of a week before rejoining Karstafel's caravan on its way out. It was easy to lose the Guards when they couldn't see more than five feet in a straight line. Eventually, the paths would wrap around to the rear of the castle, stopping just shy of the stables. That was where things would get a little dicey. The slave quarters were just on the other side of the stables, but there were always a few Guards watching over the king's prize horses.

Rustav and Dantzel were approaching the edge of the gardens when urgent voices reached their ears. Tugging Dantzel to the ground, Rustav rolled underneath a nearby hedge and held perfectly still, straining his ears to catch the words spoken in low tones. When the sounds began separating into words, Rustav tilted his head, raising an eyebrow. Dantzel looked up at him, her eyes equally puzzled. Rustav motioned for her to stay where she was, and he began to roll out from under the hedge. Dantzel grabbed his arm and shook her head emphatically, but Rustav only pointed to his ear, pulled free, and extricated himself from the grasping twigs. He had to get closer to understand what he was hearing. The language was familiar in an uncomfortable way, almost as if the speakers were speaking Tuathan with all the vowels switched around.

Cautiously, Rustav turned a corner, keeping a row of hedges between him and the speakers. It wasn't just the similarity to Tuathan that bothered him. Something in the words struck inexplicable fear into his bones, chilling him with all the terror of a nightmare. He had heard that language somewhere before.

The speakers were just on the other side of the hedges now, their words clear. Rustav leaned closer to the hedge, and then his memory supplied a scene connected with the language: iron-gray skies, sparse rock lodgings, cries of slaves and demons.

Those were islanders in the king's garden.

Jerking away from the hedge as if it had sprouted snakes, Rustav turned to run back to Dantzel. They had been gone for two years. If the islanders were already in the castle—

Two figures melted out of the shadows in front of Rustav, blocking his way. He couldn't shout and draw attention—the only people running to help wouldn't help him. Reaching for his sword, Rustav tried to calculate the odds that he could beat these two and get moving before anyone came to find what all the ruckus was about.

He never got the chance to try. Before he touched the hilt of his sword, someone leaped on his back from behind, knocking him forward. Before he knew what was happening, no fewer than six islanders swarmed him, the moonlight reflecting off their pasty, feral faces. A gag choked him, and his hands and feet were bound painfully tight. A rope was thrown around his neck and drawn tight, severely limiting his ability to struggle as he was lifted up and borne roughly into the castle, surrounded by snarling laughter. The sound was horrid, as bone-chilling as the demon screams Rustav remembered hearing as a child. The islanders had been worshipping the demons too long; they were beginning to sound like them.

After a wretched, jolting journey, Rustav was thrown into a dark room, kicked at a few more times, and left to struggle helplessly against his bonds. He recognized the room; it was the same place he had seen Karstafel meet with the king. The islanders seemed right at home in the castle. Had they already taken control? What did they want with him? Surely it wasn't common practice to take trespassers into the king's council room. And what about Dantzel? Had they found her as well? Rustav cursed himself for allowing her to ever accompany him in the first place. She should have stayed with Cabel and Anton. *Stupid, bullheaded, stubborn . . .*

A figure melted out of the shadows, and Rustav cringed, expecting another blow from an islander. Instead, the gag in his mouth loosened, and Rustav breathed in a grateful gasp of free air when the cloth was pulled out. He rolled over, anxious to see who was helping him, and stiffened.

"I don't have much time," Ayre said, his Coureian as flawless as his Tuathan. "You will be taken to the island. That is the king's favorite punishment of late, and you are sure to merit the worst he can imagine. I will follow as quickly as I am able. I will free you and bring you back, Prince Marustavian."

"Can't you free me now and save me the trip?" Rustav asked, as alarmed at Ayre's sudden respectful attitude as at the idea of being taken to the island. Ayre offered a strained smile.

"We would be killed before we left the room. I am sorry,

my brother. I have been looking for you since you went missing, trying to find you before your uncle the king did."

"Why should I believe you're going to help me? You trapped me in the forest. You made me forget everything."

Ayre sat back on his heels, his face grim. "Perhaps it was wrong of me to give you no indication of why you were being held in the forest, but I believed you would be safer that way. If you learned the truth, I feared you would do something rash. I wanted only to keep you safe until the danger of Burrihim had passed and a way to the throne was prepared for you. After the tragedy that occurred when I spoke with your father, I thought it better to ensure you could not be killed before my mission was fulfilled."

Then it was true—Ayre had spoken with Rilotorian just before the regicide. Still, Rustav rebelled against the belief that Ayre was truly on his side. Was he supposed to just forgive Ayre for wiping away two years of his life? "Tay thought you just wanted me out of the way so you could break the Union."

Sharp anger flickered through Ayre's face. "I misjudged Pak and Tay. I thought you would be safe in their hands. I didn't think they would send you out to be slaughtered."

The weight of the accusation vibrated in Rustav's bones. "What?"

"They told the islanders," Ayre said, looking down at Rustav sympathetically. "After they discovered your identity and forced you out of the safety of the forest, they followed you. They warned the islanders that you would be entering the castle, told them exactly what to look for."

Ayre's words echoed loudly in Rustav's ears, drowning out all other thoughts. Could it be true? Why else would so many islanders be prowling in the gardens late at night? Was Ayre the one trying to save the Union?

"There is no more time," Ayre said, standing and glancing anxiously at the door. "Please, believe me when I say I will do all in my power to get you home safely. I have retrieved your sword and will safeguard it until you reclaim it. I must go now, before they return."

"Ayre, wait." It was painful for Rustav to force the words out, but if he had truly been betrayed by Pak and Tay, there was no other choice. Ayre was the only one who could help now. "Dantzel is in the garden. She may not know what happened to me. Go find her and get her out of here."

Ayre nodded and disappeared as quickly as he had come, slipping through a tapestry on the western wall. Another voice was becoming clearer as it neared the room, whining in distinct valley Coureian. "Dragged out of bed in the middle of the night, no respect, this is still my castle, you know."

"You would not want to miss this, my lord," an islander said, his accent heavy and his voice thickly smug. The door swung open, admitting Rustav's six island captors bearing several torches. One of them tugged at the rope around Rustav's neck, dragging him into a kneeling position as the final person entered the room.

Hatred blazed up hot and choking in Rustav's chest as he met the surprised eyes of the king of Courei. Though he had caught glimpses of the king during his earlier trips with Karstafel to the castle, Rustav was now able to study the king with full knowledge of who he was and what he had done. Elanokiev was soft and bloated from years of excessive living, his pudgy fingers decorated with so many rings that the swollen flesh was hardly visible. His wide mouth dropped open, his limp blond hair falling in all directions around the puffy cheeks. By the light of the torches, Rustav saw Elanokiev's complexion blanch as pale as the islanders'.

"Rilotorian?" Elanokiev breathed, clutching desperately at his gilded staff and pulling his velvet robe tighter around his huge form. "No—no, it can't be. How foolish of me, of course not. He's gone, long gone."

It was true, then. Anton had said that Rustav resembled his father; the confirmation of that statement made a hot sort of pride start swelling in Rustav's chest, accompanied by a painful streak of rage as the extent of Elanokiev's betrayal finally sank in. The islander holding the rope around Rustav's neck jerked it viciously.

"It's his brat, the one you lost all those years ago," he sneered. "Finally come back to avenge himself on his wicked uncle."

"By all the demons I've ever sold my soul to," Elanokiev breathed, his beady eyes wide with wonder. "You look just like him. I could almost believe . . . but it's ridiculous, absolutely ridiculous. Who are you, boy? An escaped servant? A misguided rebel?"

Losing the last of his restraint, Rustav spat in Elanokiev's face, and the flabbergasted king stumbled backward. Without wasting his breath on shouting, Rustav yanked his arms free, flames of anger licking away his common sense. One good punch, that was all he would need to knock out this flabby joke of a king. But the rope around his neck tightened, cutting off his breath until he stumbled and fell to the ground. His anger turned to panic as his vision began to darken and no air reached his lungs.

"Stop," Elanokiev said, holding up a heavily ringed hand. The rope loosened, leaving Rustav gasping for air on the floor. The king took Rustav's jaw in a weak grip, turning his face from side to side. When Rustav tried to jerk away, the islanders tightened their grip on his limbs, keeping him still for Elanokiev to examine. After a minute, a wide smile spread over Elanokiev's flabby face.

"After all this time," he said, jowls wobbling. "I searched for you for years, you know. I finally decided you had died in a dark alley. I guess one can never be too careful." He released Rustav and waved one puffy hand. "I can't have him wandering about here. Take him to the island."

Dread flooded Rustav, giving him an added spurt of strength for one last attempt to free himself. He managed to launch himself upward enough to head-butt the islander holding the rope, but his bonds had cut the feeling from his hands and feet, leaving them unable to support him. Crashing back to the floor, Rustav hit his head hard against the stone and grimaced as everything in the room doubled. A screech sounded behind him, and Rustav's blood froze solid in his veins. He had heard that noise before, only it was much closer now than he had ever heard it on the island. Fearing what he might see, Rustav rolled over to face whatever had made the sound.

For a moment, he was certain that he must have hit his head harder than he thought. On the other side of the room, a black beast was unfolding its leathery wings, its glinting black eyes towering a full foot above the islanders. Where had it come from? Rustav had been facing the only window in the room; there was no way that creature could have fit through the door or any secret passageways without a noisy struggle. Mangy, patchy fur covered its body, and rotting fangs poked out of its vile snout as it hissed angrily.

Before Rustav was done gaping at the demon, it cocked its head, bloodthirsty eyes zeroing in on him. The islanders parted to allow it a direct shot, cackling and whispering among themselves as they watched the demon with as much glee as a child at a puppet show.

This is it, Rustav thought, watching the ragged wings spread farther and farther. *I'm about to have my throat ripped out by a decaying devil.* He struggled against his bonds, wishing he could at least make some brave stand before his life was unceremoniously snuffed out, but he could hardly even move.

In a flash, the demon swept across the room, wings beating all around Rustav, crooked claws scrabbling at his body. Rustav rolled away as well as he could, but only succeeded in getting his arm and chest gouged before the claws close around his middle, squeezing his ribs painfully but not crushing him. After one failed takeoff that squashed Rustav against the floor, the beast crashed through the window, glass shards scattering. Rustav closed his eyes against the shower of glass, feeling several broken pieces slice against his face as they fell. Wind rushed past his ears, and Rustav opened his eyes to see the ground approaching at an alarming rate. Just when he had resigned himself to a messy death at the foot of the castle, the massive wings flapped harder, straining at the air, gaining altitude slowly at first, then more quickly.

Once he got over the initial shock of not being torn to shreds and not being smashed to a paste on the castle grounds,

Rustav realized that surviving them would mean nothing if his breathing was so severely restricted much longer. He pulled in vain at the decaying claw compressing his lungs, his shallow breathing capacity becoming less and less sufficient the more desperately he fought. At last, as the ground below turned to water, Rustav gave up fighting for breath and went limp in the monster's grasp.

CHAPTER FIFTEEN

IN SPITE OF THE WARM SUMMER NIGHT, DANTZEL shivered as she huddled under the king's hedges. Rustav had disappeared around a corner over half an hour ago, and still she remained, lying with her face in the dirt, growing angrier with every passing minute. A gnawing suspicion told her that Rustav had used the strange voices as a prime opportunity to leave her behind and continue on his own. Why did he so persistently refuse her help? Dantzel knew that she had been a burden back in the trees; she had gotten Rustav trapped there as well when he had tried to free her the first time, and he practically had to drag her away the second time. Even now, her face burned as she remembered how useless she had been. But that was precisely why she had insisted on coming. She had to show him that there was more to her than a stupid mountain girl who fell helpless at the first sight of a fair tuath face.

On the way to the castle, Rustav had sketched out a rough map of the castle grounds in the dirt. Dantzel had a fairly good idea of where the slave quarters were from the gardens, and she was sorely tempted to go find them herself. She'd get past the Guards by herself, and then Rustav would see just how helpless she was.

But then, her ears burst with the memory of that horrible cacophony, the harsh, high-pitched, inhuman screams that had exploded shortly after Rustav had gone. The noise had left Dantzel ice-cold and shaking, images flashing through her mind of some hideous band of barbarians hidden away in the king's gardens. It was possible—

No, it's not. Dantzel knew Rustav's strength. A few measly barbarians would be no match for him, especially with his sword strapped to his back.

Right?

Unable to remain still any longer, Dantzel began wriggling her way out, wincing as her hair caught on the low branches. She paused to try to untangle it, but halted abruptly when two light feet turned the corner and came bouncing toward her, clad in soft boots like Rustav had been wearing. But the stride was all wrong. Dantzel didn't dare move, even to retreat farther under the bushes. She tensed herself, ready to strike, as the feet stopped a few feet away from her.

"Dantzel? It's all right, it's just me."

Even as a whisper, Ayre's voice flowed over Dantzel like heat from a fire on a cold night. A moment later, Ayre knelt and lifted some of the outer branches. Dantzel shrank back as he offered her a hand. Was he here to take her back to the trees? Had he been following them the entire time?

"Rustav has been captured by the king," Ayre said, his voice calm but urgent as he took her wrist and pulled her gently out from under the hedge. "He asked me to get you out safely, and I swore I would. Come on, Dantzel, we have to go now."

Without her consent, Dantzel's ruffled nerves calmed at Ayre's smooth voice. Though suspicion had planted itself firmly in her mind, Dantzel scooted out from under the hedge to join him. As he began walking, Ayre tried to take her hand; but Dantzel pulled away, causing him to turn back to her with a hurt expression in his eyes. She couldn't hold his gaze. Her eyes flicked away, and Dantzel tried in vain to tell herself that there was nothing to feel guilty about.

"You don't trust me anymore."

Dantzel could feel herself wanting to trust Ayre, wanting it more than anything, but she held on to the doubt. "Last time I trusted you, I forgot everything about my life for two years. Including Rustav."

"Ah." Ayre surveyed Dantzel for a moment, a frown making his warm brown eyes large and troubled. "It wasn't my decision, you know. I only wanted to show you our home, perhaps open a way for our two worlds to come together again. There were others, tuatha who feared the outside world, who thought you could only be dangerous. They insisted you be kept from ever returning to your home, lest you reveal our existence to the rest of the world. I did all I could to keep you safe and comfortable until I could see you safely returned home. And as for Rustav—you can't blame me for trying." He offered an apologetic smile that softened Dantzel's heart, no matter how she fought it. "I've lived for centuries, Dantzel, and I've never known anyone with your spirit."

As he reached for her hand once more, Dantzel struggled to pull away—or not to pull away—she wasn't sure which was harder. Before the battle could be decided, an enormous crash exploded high above them. With a gasp, she looked up at the south tower, visible high above the surrounding bushes. A window near the top had burst outward, its shards falling like glittering rain through the dark night. But Dantzel's gaze was fixed on the patch of black, darker than night, that was plummeting downward. It was massive, whatever it was, and had huge black wings that were beating desperately at the air. As it uttered a screech that chilled Dantzel's stomach, it opened its mouth wide enough for her to see yellowed fangs protruding. With a few more steady beats of its wings, the beast stopped falling and began to rise, adjusting its grip on the heavy item it held in its claws. Dantzel looked closer and felt her heart stop.

Rustav.

She took a step forward, mouthing his name, but Ayre was already pulling her in the other direction. She resisted, but Ayre was much stronger. "You'll be no use to him now," Ayre said, and Dantzel's fingers turned icy.

"He's not dead," she said automatically, and Ayre put an arm around her shoulders, guiding her through the maze of hedges.

"I hope not. But the fleyder aren't known for their delicacy."

At that, Dantzel dug in her feet once more and pulled away from Ayre. She only got two steps before Ayre wrapped a hand around her wrist, muttering incomprehensible words under his breath. In an instant, all the energy drained from Dantzel, the grass beneath her feet growing impossibly quickly as if it were sucking away her strength. She began to fall, remaining conscious only long enough to feel Ayre catch her and sling her over his shoulder.

When Dantzel awoke, she could smell familiar breakfast smells of eggs and porridge mixing in with the odor of a cooking fire. She lay on a sleeping mat, wrapped in a blanket, staring up at a thatched roof strangely like those found in the mountains. Vaguely, she remembered being in the castle. Rustav had left her alone to investigate the strange voices. And the horrible beast crashing through the tower window—Dantzel closed her eyes, trying to block out the terrifying memory. She could see Rustav's face, imagined with much greater detail than she had been able to see, as he was borne away by the decaying demon. And then Ayre . . . Ayre had come to take her away. But she wasn't in a tree.

Kicking off the blanket, Dantzel sat up to take in her surroundings, her muscles tensing as she prepared to run or fight. When the familiar sight of Anton's home met her eyes, she leaned against the wall with a sigh of relief that drew Cabel's attention from the pot he was stirring. He leaped over to her and practically dragged her into a chair, his freckled face crinkled with concern.

"Are you all right?" he asked. Dantzel's tiredness and worry lifted a little at his good heart, still boyish and innocent in spite of its taller frame.

"I think so. What happened?"

"A man carried you in last night," Cabel said, scurrying back over to the pot before the contents could burn. "He said you were just asleep, but you were so still. You didn't move at all. We had to keep watching you breathe to be sure you were alive." Cabel stirred the pot vigorously, sneaking a glance over at her. "His eyebrows were all pointed, and he was shorter than I am. Was he a tuath?"

The word made Dantzel's stomach clench, and she

nodded. At least she hadn't woken up in the forest. "Did he say where he was going?"

"He just said he was going after Rustav. He told me to tell you not to worry, that they would both be back soon." Cabel snuck an anxious glance in Dantzel's direction. "What happened? Did the king get Rustav?"

"No," Dantzel said. "Something took him. I don't know what it was exactly, but . . ." Her voice trailed off as she paused, reluctant to voice her suspicion.

"What?"

"I think—I think there are islanders inside the castle," Dantzel said, the spoken words filling her with the fear she had tried so hard to repress. "I think it was one of the island demons that took him."

Silence filled the small room as Cabel paused his stirring, turning to look at her with dread written across his face. "But—no," Cabel said. "That can't happen. Why are there islanders in the castle? He told me they wouldn't come."

"What? Who told you?"

Cabel bit his lip. "Rustav. Before you went into the forest. I overheard him talking to Anton about the king and the islanders. He said Elanokiev was going to let the islanders come in and take over. I told Rustav I wanted to go with him through the woods, but he said the islanders wouldn't really come. And now . . ."

"He knew?" Dantzel gritted her teeth. "No wonder he tried so hard to leave me behind! He should've just told me. He's got to learn sometime that he can't do this on his own. He has to start accepting that people are here to help him."

Cabel cast her an uncharacteristically dark glare. "Tell me about it."

The spoon clanged as Cabel stirred a little harder, his young face much harder than Dantzel had ever seen it. A guilty remorse drove Dantzel's anger to the back of her mind, and she watched her young friend speechlessly for a moment before she found her voice. "Cabel, we were just trying to keep you safe."

Cabel picked up a bowl and spooned porridge into it with excessive force. "Look, I know you missed two years, but I didn't. I'm not twelve anymore. I've lost as much as anyone to the king, and I want to do something about it. Anyhow, he's not supposed to be king anyway, right? Rustav is. And Rustav would be a better king. He knows what it's like to get kicked around. I want him to be king, and I want to help him get there. Even if he did make me stay here with Anton. Twice."

"Where is Anton?" Dantzel asked, and Cabel jerked his head up the hill, his mutinous expression softening slightly.

"Up with Father Lute. He's been going every morning to pray for you and Rustav." Cabel plopped a bowl in front of Dantzel and took a seat across from her. Dantzel fiddled with the porridge absently for several minutes before she sat up straight, slapping the table.

"Listen, Cabel," she said, fired with a new determination. "You're not getting left out of this anymore, and neither am I. We're going to help that dumb, stubborn prince of Courei whether he likes it or not. Ayre will get him back from the island, and when he does, we'll have a whole country up in arms, just waiting for him to lead them into battle."

"We will?" Cabel asked, surprise registering in his wide eyes. Dantzel nodded, abandoning her porridge to gather together some dried fruit.

"There are plenty of people who would risk their lives to see a better king than Elanokiev on the throne, even leaving the islanders out of it. Once word gets out that Rilotorian's son is alive, I bet most of the country will come flocking to us. We'll have Rustav on the throne by harvest time."

"How?" Cabel asked, his voice muffled by the porridge he was shoveling down as fast as he could. "How will we know who's loyal to Elanokiev and who's not?"

In no mood to be put off from her newfound zeal, Dantzel began to answer that they would find a way, when a gruff voice from the doorway cut her off.

"I can help with that."

Dantzel turned, her heart leaping. Anton stood as straight as she had ever seen him, his eyes flashing with blue fire. The nobleman that he had once been shone through as he said grimly, "I've still got a few friends from the old days. It's time I reached out to them."

Chapter Sixteen

The harsh clanging of a bell startled Rustav into a sitting position. Everything around him was moving, noises of clanking metal and murmuring men only adding to the confusion. Completely disoriented, he stared blankly at the masses of people pushing their way into a line that seemed to stretch forever in both directions. They were in a long, stone building that allowed only a few cracks of light to shine into the dark interior—just enough to see the outlines of men moving and of straw sleeping mats lining the walls. If the smell was anything to go by, the straw had been molding for at least a decade, and Rustav was fairly certain he could see squirming shadows of bugs digging through the mats.

But he had no more time to observe. A strong hand gripped his upper arm, pulling him upright and into the crush of the men moving slowly toward a door at the end of the room. Someone inadvertently elbowed Rustav in the ribs, and he winced. The island demon's claws had left a ring of bruises in addition to that initial gash.

"Are we on the island?" Rustav asked the man who still

had a steadying hand on his arm. A gruff voice answered in his ear.

"Yes. You're going to the quarries. Don't fight them, and you'll make it out okay."

Rustav had serious doubts about that statement, but he allowed himself to be steered by the crowd toward the shouts streaming in from the open door. As he drew near, he could see a cluster of islanders standing just outside, menacing the prisoners with iron rods as chains were connected to rings around prisoners' necks, wrists, and ankles. Rustav reached up to his own neck and felt around his limbs. He had been fitted with similar rings while unconscious.

But when it came time for him to be attached to the chain, the islanders paused and drew back, casting each other uncertain glances. Rustav knew an opportunity when he saw one. In a flash, he leaped away from the crowd of islanders, anxious to be anywhere but in their grasp. Unfortunately, not all of the islanders were so slow. One of them, the burliest islander Rustav had ever seen among the short and scrawny race, stepped directly in his path and stopped him with a solid body check. As Rustav lay blinking on the ground, chains clinked all around him, attaching him to a line of prisoners who were watching curiously.

The large islander pressed a knee into Rustav's back, pinning him to the ground, while two others grabbed his left arm and twisted it as far outward as it would go without snapping. With his face pressed in the dirt, Rustav couldn't see what was happening. All he could see were two heavy-booted feet approaching. Without warning, a sharp pain seared his forearm, followed closely by the smell of burning flesh. Rustav tried to jerk away, but the islanders held him fast until the branding was finished.

The islanders scattered to a safe distance, and Rustav rose warily. He was bound to the chain by all four limbs and his neck; there was no chance for retaliation, even though the islanders seemed to fear it. Setting his teeth, Rustav glanced at the vivid, throbbing pair of triangles now pointing down toward his wrist. The men on his line moved forward, the chain pulling at Rustav until he had no choice but to stumble forward.

The bitter smell of sweat and rust rose from the iron chain, the weight of which pulled the iron ring against Rustav's neck. The movement of others in line jerked against his natural pace, but he eventually settled into a rhythm that minimized the painful jostling. Though the sun hadn't yet risen, enough light emanated from the gray-clouded sky to illuminate the surroundings. The nine other men on Rustav's line ranged from hulking creatures with bulging muscles to frail old men who hardly looked strong enough to walk. Their surroundings were rocky and bare of grass or any other form of plant life. The ground sloped upward ever more steeply, but the men at the very front were beginning to disappear over the edge of a rise. When Rustav approached the top of the rise, he found a ladder descending down into a wide quarry, where men were already cutting, hauling, and carting away stone.

I've been here before, Rustav realized as he awkwardly adjusted the chain to climb down the ladder. When he had traveled to the island with Karstafel, he had been poking around and came across this great pit in the earth filled with men that moved ceaselessly. Prisoners hauled rock and broke rock apart, all the while enduring the shouts and whips of the islanders guarding them. The scene had fascinated Rustav, and he had lain on the ground and peered over the edge to find out what was going on. The islanders had found him lying there and accused him of spying; thankfully, one of them recognized him as part of the group from the peninsula. When they dragged Rustav back to Karstafel and demanded an explanation and an apology, he had simply dismissed them with a wave of his hand and told the islanders to sacrifice Rustav if it would appease their demons. It was only luck and quick footwork that had gotten him out of that one.

At the bottom of the ladder, Rustav found himself surrounded by gray, unremarkable stone. He looked uncertainly at the man behind him, the man who had lifted him off the sleeping mat. His stubbly hair was gray, and his face was lined and leathery, though Rustav suspected that the wrinkles and gray hair came more from a life of hard work than age. His nose was long and straight, his brown eyes set deep under a heavy brow. He was crouching next to a block of stone that looked too impossibly large to lift. As Rustav stood watching, a crack and a fiery pain announced the fall of a whip across his back. It surprised him, and Rustav cried out, arching his back.

"Get to work!" snarled an islander, bringing the whip down across Rustav's shoulders again. This time, Rustav mastered himself enough not to make a sound—something he had once been well practiced at. With his ego and back still smarting, Rustav bent over and gathered a rock into his arms, hefting it with a little difficulty. The other men in the line were already starting to move, and Rustav had to hurry to catch up before the chain began dragging him. Carts were lined up to take away the stone, and Rustav dumped his load into the nearest one before heading back to the pile of shattered stone.

At first, Rustav counted the trips back and forth, looking for something to occupy his mind outside of his stinging back and straining muscles. After about sixty-seven, he decided it required too much effort to keep track and simply focused on one thought: Ayre was coming, and Ayre would get him out of there.

Though Rustav couldn't see it behind the heavy clouds, the sun must have been high in the sky by the time a piercing whistle called for a break. His line finished the trip to the carts, dropping one last load of stone before gathering in a cluster around a nearby islander passing out chunks of stale bread. Rustav took his and dropped to the ground next to the stern-faced old man chained beside him.

"Where did you come from?" the man said in a low voice, tossing a wearily curious glance in Rustav's direction. "The regular shipment of slaves isn't due for at least another week."

For a moment, Rustav was tempted to tell the whole truth just for the sake of seeing the man's reaction, but he decided against marking himself as completely insane. "I'm from the peninsula."

The man huffed. "Of course you are. Who else would be sending slaves to a country as weak as Burrihim? What did you do to merit an express trip to the island demons?"

Rustav gnawed at the bread as he contemplated how best to answer. It was like chewing on someone's sleeve. "The king took me for a threat. He had to get me out of the country as quickly as possible."

The old man's eyes lit with interest, and he stuck out

his hand. "My name's Jocham. Pleased to make your acquaintance."

Rustav shook the rough, callused hand with slight trepidation. "Rustav. Don't be too pleased. It won't ingratiate you to any of the islanders here."

"A real troublemaker, hm? Don't worry, you've got plenty of friends among the men here. We watch out for each other. We have to, in a hellhole like this. There are a few of the islanders' stoolies sprinkled in the mix, but they don't cause much trouble. They're too afraid of retaliation—and rightly so."

"How long have you been here?" Rustav asked, anxious to turn the conversation away from himself. Immediately, Jocham's eyes clouded over, staring up at the slate-gray skies.

"Six years. I was a slave in the king's court for close to eight years before that. I hated it then, of course. But some days, I think I would spend the rest of my life shoveling the king's stables if only I could be back where the sun showed her face now and again."

Six years. Was that how long Rustav was destined to be there? Suddenly, two years in the forest seemed like the blink of an eye. But at least Dantzel was still walking free—he hoped. Rustav stared down at the stale crust in his hand, worry twisting his stomach. Would Ayre really take Dantzel back to the safety of her home? Was she already back in the forest, oblivious to the world around her?

Was he already forgotten?

"You weren't kidding about the islanders, were you?" Jocham murmured, fixing his gaze on his dusty gray feet. Rustav didn't answer. He had already seen the circle of islanders closing in around him, and he was busy preparing himself for the first blow.

It came in the form of a firm nudge in the small of his back, an islander's foot digging into the already sore muscles. "Enjoying your feast, Your Majesty?"

Refusing to rise, Rustav gnawed off another piece of rock-hard bread. No point in any response; he was in chains, and there were five island guards surrounding him. Besides, it would escalate without his help. No point in speeding the process.

Another blow, harder and on his shoulder. The circle was closing in, restricting Rustav's movements even more than the chains had. If he'd had any hope of defending himself, it was long gone.

"Think you're something special?"

"We heard about you marching into the castle. You're as stupid as you are weak."

"Look at how soft he is! One good slice would bleed him dry."

"He'll be screaming for home this time tomorrow."

The blows were coming from all directions now, knocking Rustav between the islanders like a rubber ball in a stone box. He shielded his head the best he could, but the islanders took that as a particular challenge. A sharp rap above his ear made his eyes water, and Rustav lashed out instinctively, sweeping the legs out from the islander that had struck him.

The other islanders descended with vicious fury. A foot struck him squarely in the chest, sending him sprawling back on the rocks, chains tangling around his limbs. One of them yanked his neck chain upward until he had to either get up or choke to death. Stumbling to his feet and spluttering for breath, Rustav tried to raise his hands to defend himself. An iron rod came whistling out of nowhere and landed across his cheek and forehead, sending him crashing back to the ground with stars blinking in his blackened vision. He landed face-down in the dirt, barely conscious enough to feel the boot stepping on his shoulder. A voice rang out, its coldness carrying across the quarry.

"People of Courei! See the fate of your great and glorious prince, the legendary son of Rilotorian! Licking up the dust, his royal blood mixing with the dirt. We have beaten him, ground the entire royal family into less than the dust that covers your foul hides. Your country is ours."

One by one, the islanders took their final kicks and dispersed. Rustav wanted nothing more than to remain where he lay. Of all the blows he had received, the worst had been that final cry, the announcement of a heritage he neither wanted nor fully believed. But the chain was pulling at him, and Jocham had a hand on his arm. Reluctantly, Rustav allowed Jocham to help him to his feet, spitting a mouthful of blood onto the rocks before he raised his head to look defiantly at the prisoners surrounding him.

In every direction, as chained men stood, faces turned to look at Rustav. Some were confused; some were angry; the despair in some eyes was too much for Rustav. But the worst were the few who looked at him with hope, with the dream that he might be able to save them from the horror they had lived for weeks and months and years.

A whip cut across Rustav's back, and he gritted his teeth without making a sound. Averting his gaze from the hundreds of eyes fastened on him, Rustav picked up a rock and began walking. Let them think what they would. They would see the truth soon enough. No one could mistake him for a prince after a few beatings like that.

ALL THROUGH THE LONG AFTERNOON, THE monotony of the work was broken only by the crack of whips and the shouts of islanders. At some point, Rustav ceased to think about anything beyond his next step, willing himself to pick up just one more rock. The sun was going down when, on one of his line's endless trips to the carts, a frail old man, chained about five people down from Rustav, stumbled and dropped his load, pulling his neighbors down with him as he fell to the ground. In a flash, three islanders flocked to him, crowding around him and dragging him to his feet. Rustav stared openly as they released the man from the chain and dragged him away on his knees.

"No!" he screamed, kicking desperately. "Please, no! I can work, I can—"

One of the islanders clubbed him, and the old man fell silent. The others in the line were taking advantage of the break, some bent over with hands on knees, looking anywhere but at the old man and the islanders. The man's blood-chilling scream rang hauntingly in Rustav's ears long after it had ceased.

"Where are they taking him?" Rustav asked, scooting as close to Jocham as possible. The man looked down at the ground and shook his head.

"To the nest," he whispered, almost inaudibly. Rustav looked to the northwest, and burning sick rose in his throat. In the distance—though not distant enough by any means— he could see black shapes circling in the sky, high above the outline of a ruined castle.

CHAPTER SEVENTEEN

IT WAS DUSK WHEN THE ISLANDERS FINALLY BEGAN herding the prisoners back to their sleeping quarters. Jocham stood close to Rustav's shoulder; the other prisoners hung back, but their eyes darted repeatedly to Rustav's face. He did his best to ignore them all, focusing instead on staying upright until his battered body could collapse on a moldy, bug-infested sleeping mat.

As the men filed into the bland, gray building that served as their shelter, whispers began to fill the air. Men parted to fill the sleeping mats but propped themselves up on their elbows to watch Rustav's progress down the room. Too exhausted to care, Rustav fell onto the first open mat he saw, wincing at the pain that shot through his injured body.

Once all of the prisoners were inside, several islanders entered, shouting and kicking at anyone who was still staring or whispering. Though Rustav lay flat and silent, three islanders went out of their way to kick and jostle him as they passed. Rustav accepted the abuse, unwilling to give them the chance to unleash their wrath again and too tired to react anyway.

In spite of the hunger and anger gnawing at his belly, Rustav was asleep before the islanders left the room.

The next thing he knew, somebody was shaking his shoulder. Blindly, Rustav sat up, unable to open his tired eyes, but a hand pushed him back against the mat. With a great effort, Rustav managed to pry his eyes open and saw Jocham staring at him intently from the next mat over. The older man was up on one elbow, holding a finger to his lips, then beckoning for Rustav to follow him. Still mostly asleep, Rustav dragged himself onto his hands and knees and crawled behind Jocham between the rows of men, realizing too late that Jocham had brought along his sleeping mat and wondering if he should have done the same.

Most men remained asleep, too worn out by their labor for even such a night as this, but now and again a head would pop up to stare. Even less often, a man would join them, moving silently toward the far end of the room. By the time Jocham stopped, four men had joined them, each carrying his sleeping mat on his back. Everyone seemed to know what was going on except for Rustav. The lengthy crawl had woken Rustav up a little more. He was about to demand an explanation when Jocham reached out and shook the foot of a sleeping man. After a moment, the man rolled over and sat up, his face a dark blur in the black of the windowless structure. The four men and Jocham swiftly built up a tent of sorts with their sleeping mats, a tenuous structure that seemed likely to collapse as soon as someone breathed wrong.

Leaving the others to hold up the mats, Jocham fished around on the ground for a moment and struck a flint, sparking an instant flame on a small pile of cloth and straw. The light dazzled Rustav's eyes for a moment, and he squinted. But then he saw the face of the man who had just awoken—much older and gaunter than he had last seen it, but recognizable.

"Ollie?" Rustav breathed, unable to believe his eyes. The old man's eyes filled with tears, and he reached out to touch Rustav's face as the short-lived flame flickered and died.

"It's him."

The others let out a collective breath, and the shaky tent came down. Though Rustav's eyes were blind once more, he reached up and gripped the gnarled hand that still rested on his cheek. It had been over a decade since the old bookseller had taught him to decipher letters on a page. Rustav could hardly believe he was reunited with the only man who had ever been kind to him as a child. A sudden suspicion gripped Rustav as he considered the old man's words, and he whispered, "Your name isn't Ollie, is it?"

"No, my lord. I was once known as Bartholomew."

"Did you know who I was? Is that why you were so kind to me?"

"I suspected. And I hoped. I heard whispers of a pendant much like yours marking King Rilotorian's son. And there were other hints." Bartholomew's hand felt its way up Rustav's face until the thumb pressed against the scar cutting through Rustav's left eyebrow. "This scar—you split your eyebrow while trying to climb up on a dresser to get a toy your mother had taken away. You managed to interrupt trade negotiations with Allanna with your squalling; your father went running out of the meeting so fast, it's a miracle the Allannan ambassador didn't storm off back to the mainland in an offended huff."

Rustav was embarrassed to learn that his favorite roguish

scar had been the result of climbing after a toy, but Jocham quickly moved on to more urgent topics.

"We need to get you out of here, Your Majesty," he said. "We hear them talk all the time about the usurper, that Elanokiev is as good as handing them the throne. The sooner you're back on the peninsula, the better."

"Don't worry about me," Rustav said quickly. The last thing he wanted was to feel indebted to these men. If they saved his life for the express purpose of saving the country, he wouldn't be able to run from it any longer. "Someone is coming for me. I'll be fine."

Though Jocham's face was hidden in shadow, Rustav could hear the doubt in his voice. "Are you certain he'll come in time?"

Are you certain he'll even come? Rustav couldn't repress the thought that Ayre had kept him imprisoned for two full years. Would Ayre be just as happy to have him safely imprisoned on the island? Did he dare wait for Ayre to fulfill his promise? Would Rustav survive the days of endless labor, short rations, and frequent beatings? Still, he couldn't ask these men to risk their lives helping him when he had no intention of taking on the duty they expected of him.

One of the other men broke the silence, his whisper bordering on desperation. "We've tried to plan breakouts before. If the plan is risky, no one is willing to take it; if the plan has promise, it dissolves in a squabble about whether the one who escapes will really come back to help the others. We can never get enough men unified to make it work. We've all been slaves for so long that we don't even trust the people we know we can trust. But you—we've been waiting for someone like you ever since your father died, clouds buoy up his soul. If we can't believe in you, what's left to believe in?"

A sharp stick seemed to be lodged in Rustav's throat, rendering him even more unable to speak than he had been before. The prisoner, faceless in the dark, had sparked a memory of a far different scene, one that took place in the free, clear sunshine of the mountains. Rustav winced as Dantzel's voice pierced through his memory: *We have hope for better days.*

Misery flooded his heart, and Rustav longed for those simple summer days so powerfully that his chest ached, the pain of his battered ribs dimmed by the pain in his heart. *Why me?* he demanded silently. *Why do I have to be the hope these people have hung on to for so long? Why am I responsible for the hearts of a country I never wanted to belong to anyway?*

"Please," Jocham said. "We've been stuck here for years, some of us, with no way to fight the islanders except to steal a little food and water now and again. Let us help you. If your friend comes before we get you out, great. But if we can free you, it will make all the sweat and suffering worth it."

The weight settling on Rustav's shoulders was greater than sum of the rocks he had hauled all day. He had been pinned down, kept in one place for too long, and he was caught. There was no more running away. Shoulders slumping in defeat, he said, "Did you have any ideas in mind?"

Just the slightest glint of light reflected in Jocham's eyes as they flicked around the circle of men. "We'll have to be careful about discussing our plans. There are men among the slaves who would sell their souls for an extra helping of stale bread. We six here have to depend on each other implicitly. Do I have your word?"

One by one, the men swore quietly but firmly to die

before betraying their king. Each word bent Rustav's shoulders a little more. When they had finished, every gaze turned on Rustav, who, at a loss as to what was expected of him, looked pleadingly at Jocham for help. Thankfully, Jocham took charge once more, drawing the expectant eyes away from Rustav.

"We'll take a day or two to do some scouting," he said, his voice even lower than before as he cast a wary glance over his shoulder. "Keep an eye out for any snakes in the grass. We won't be lenient on this one."

With that ominous threat hanging in the air, the men began to drift back to their empty spaces. Bartholomew still had a tight hold on Rustav's hand. The old man spoke in the choking whisper of one whose eyes streamed with tears. "May the clouds bless you, my boy. My king. I prayed every day in Markuum that, no matter who you were, fate would one day show you a kinder hand than that of Karstafel. I hope that may still someday be the case, though the present outlook would suggest otherwise."

That was . . . encouraging. Rustav slipped his hand out of the old man's grasp and followed Jocham back to the gap where they had slept, every shadow looking more threatening than it had before.

By the end of three weeks, Rustav had long since overcome the crippling soreness that had plagued him during his first few days on the island, but he couldn't help thinking that the longer he was trapped in the quarry, the less strength he would have to escape. The islanders regularly withheld the second "meal" of hard bread from Rustav and the prisoners on his chain, which led to not only a continuously shrinking stomach, but also to increasing unease concerning the fellow prisoners. Rustav had noticed a silent, subtle struggle beginning in the mornings, men who did their best not to get stuck on a line with him. Hunger was enough to wear down even the greatest loyalties, and Rustav had at best a tenuous claim on these men's devotion. If he didn't do something soon, he feared that not even his legendary status would keep him from being pummeled by a starved fellow prisoner.

He had been trying to escape, of course, aided by his six trusted companions. The first escape tunnel had been blocked three feet down by an impenetrable rock barrier. They had wasted five days trying to dig around it before giving it up and searching for a better spot. The second tunnel had been spotted by a known snoop, and they had been forced to fill it in, finishing just before the islanders came to inspect. The islanders had found nothing out of the ordinary; the snoop had not been seen since. Rustav wasn't sure whether the islanders or the slaves had taken care of him, nor did he particularly want to know.

The final blow was Ayre's continued absence. The thought of it never failed to give Rustav enough angry strength to throw his load down with particular force, even on this the twenty-third day since Rustav had awoken on the island. The rock cracked against the rocks already piled in the carts, and Rustav turned away with resentment burning in every muscle. He had been a fool to trust Ayre, an even greater fool to trust Dantzel to Ayre's care. Now Rustav would die a slave on the island, and Dantzel would live a slave among the trees.

"Don't lose hope," came a low, raspy whisper. Jocham had

come as near to Rustav as he dared while they walked back for another load. "There is always a way."

Rustav looked down at the ground, barely moving his lips as he responded. "You've risked enough for me. Let me find my own way."

The answer came back swift and certain. "I will not abandon you. Not now, not ever."

Then they were back at the rocks, clearing away the rubble that other men had chipped away. Rustav hoisted a rock into his arms, his frustration with Jocham's stubborn loyalty ready to spill over. Ever since that first day, Jocham had never left Rustav's side, even when Rustav had told him to go on another line to get the second meal for a few days.

Rustav couldn't understand what would possess a man to make such a sacrifice for someone he had only just met. He couldn't understand why any of these men had put such trust in him, when they themselves admitted their ability to trust was severely impaired. But it didn't matter, not now, not while the endless march from one end of the quarry to the other continued. All that mattered was that Rustav put one foot ahead of the other.

Seven more trips. The other lines paused for a break and a second ration of rock bread, but Rustav's line was driven on with whips and rods. They managed two more trips from one end to the other and were just picking up a third load when the islanders began shouting for the other men to get back to work. In the midst of the disorganized return to forced labor, a harsh yank on the chain pulled Rustav off balance, sending his load of rocks clattering to the ground. Mouth dry with dread, he turned to see what he feared had happened.

Jocham lay sprawled across the gray rock, his body

hunched unnaturally over the rocks he had carried. His face was down, his breathing shallow. Anguish tearing through his chest, Rustav fell to his knees at the man's side and began shaking his shoulders. "Get up, Jocham," he commanded in a low voice, praying that by some miracle they could avoid being seen by the islanders. "Stand up, now. You can't let them take you. You have to stay with me."

Jocham's eyes remained closed, but his lips moved in a single, final plea. "Stay close."

Footsteps pounded against the rock; the islanders had seen their latest prey. Hands grasped at Rustav's shoulders, but Rustav fought with all his might, desperate to at least fulfill Jocham's last request. Jocham offered no opposition as his manacles were loosed from the chain, but the moment he was hoisted upright, his head snapped up, his eyes sharp and blazing.

Catching the front of Rustav's shirt, Jocham pulled Rustav to his side and began fending off the islanders one-handed. Rustav helped the best he could, but the chains hampered his movements, and more islanders just kept coming. It was all he could do to keep his balance when Jocham shoved him away unexpectedly and went limp once more. The islanders shoved Rustav the rest of the way to the ground and gathered around Jocham's still body.

"Get him out of here before he has another dying fit!" barked one of the islanders, nudging Jocham with his toe.

"What about this one?" another demanded, giving Rustav a solid whack with his rod. "He was trying to help him escape, after all."

The first islander had the second by the throat in an instant. "We kick him, we hit him, we starve him. But we don't take him to the castle. The next person who suggests it will die as surely as this pathetic worm will."

With a final kick at Jocham, the islander turned his back and strode away, followed closely by a screeching and slavering bunch of islanders gathered closely around Jocham. Rustav remained where he had fallen, held in place as much by his own shock as by the menacing whips and clubs surrounding him.

Jocham's expression hung clearly in the air before his eyes. Rustav could see the brightness, the strength, the unmistakable purpose in Jocham's face just before Jocham had shoved him aside. That wasn't the face of a broken man. Jocham hadn't collapsed from exhaustion. Why would he sentence himself to death? What could he possibly hope to accomplish? Had he simply given up hope in the end? Surely not, not so soon after encouraging Rustav to keep pressing forward.

"Get up, little prince," an islander snarled, punctuating the words with a sharp crack of his whip across Rustav's back. Rustav hardly flinched, too wrapped up in Jocham's sudden death sentence to feel his own pain. Still, the islanders were not to be ignored. Slowly, he pushed himself to his feet and paused again, his heart starting to thump uncomfortably hard against his chest.

"Pick up your filthy rocks!" the islander shouted, thankfully too angry over being left out of the sacrificial party to notice the startled realization that leaped into Rustav's eyes. "And get your lazy friend's pile while you're at it!"

Rustav responded automatically, piling the rocks into his arms, barely achieving a tenuous balance with the oversized load. He was grateful for the pressure of the rocks balanced against his body. They would hide any sign of the key that pushed into the hard muscles of his stomach, resting safely inside his shirt where it tucked into his ragged trousers.

Jocham must have gotten it from one of the island guards. They all carried a key to the chain, so any one of them could descend on a fallen prisoner. That was why Jocham had told Rustav to stay close. Rustav hadn't felt the key drop into his shirt, but it had to have been when Jocham yanked him near. Jocham had sentenced himself to death at the claws of the demons in order for Rustav to have a chance at freedom.

Rustav's stomach churned as he dropped his load into the carts to be hauled away. That was far too much. Jocham couldn't sacrifice his own life for Rustav's freedom; Rustav couldn't bear to pay such a high price.

The trek back to the rock debris was agonizingly slow. Rustav wanted nothing more than to bolt across the quarry, but chained as he was, he was forced to plod along with the rest of his line. The timing would have to be just perfect. He would have to cross paths with one of the sorters, the men who picked through the rubble looking for anything of value that the rock cutters had missed.

But the line moved with agonizing slowness. Rustav watched helplessly as the line of sorters passed by one by one, the last slipping away while Rustav was still twenty feet away. He sucked in a few deep breaths as he picked up a fresh load, glancing anxiously at the sky. The castle was at least another mile or two beyond the quarries. He had time to catch up before Jocham reached it. He would catch them on the next pass.

It was a fight not to pull at the chain in an effort to move his fellow prisoners along quicker. Anything out of the ordinary would draw unwelcome attention from the islanders, and he couldn't afford that, now more than ever. And so he kept his head ducked, his step heavy and dragging. It was only when they were thirty feet from the rock shards that he dared glance up.

His heart sank. The sorters were going to be yards away by the time he reached the piles. He would miss them again, and he wasn't sure he'd have enough time to save Jocham if he had to wait another round.

But then, as if he had felt Rustav's desperate gaze, the man on the end looked up and saw Rustav watching him. Glancing back down at the rocks, the man called out to his companions and kneeled at the rocks, digging into the pile as if he had spotted something. Rustav's heart leaped into his mouth, and he offered a silent prayer of gratitude to the clouds above.

The man was still kneeling when Rustav drew near. To avoid arousing suspicion, the sorter hoisted up a sizable rock and held it out for Rustav to take. Rustav bent over to whisper as he took the rock. "Start a fight when we reach the other side of the quarry. Draw the islanders to you."

The man didn't so much as twitch, his expression so blank that Rustav wondered if he had heard. But there was no time to repeat the message; the line was already heading back. Rustav adjusted the weight of the rock in his arms and walked away. He rested the rock firmly against the key, reassuring himself that it was really there and that it would really all work—as long as the sorter was willing to help him.

CHAPTER EIGHTEEN

IT WAS TORTUROUS NOT TO LOOK BACK DURING the long walk to the carts. Instead, Rustav eyed the wall just ahead of him. There were no ladders; the islanders took those up once all the prisoners were inside to prevent any easy way out. But the wall was chipped and gouged from years of haphazard cutting. Rustav would be able to climb out, he was certain. The question was whether he would make it to the top before the islanders threw a spear into his back.

But the one islander—he had made it very clear that they weren't to take Rustav to the castle. Was his life being spared for some more vile fate? Were they under strict orders not to kill him before some predetermined torture had been prepared? He would find out one way or another soon enough.

Rustav didn't draw a breath for the final ten feet to the carts, his ears straining for any sound that broke clear of the ordinary rumble of labor. He drew even with the carts—dropped his load—hesitated—

Shouts rang out across the quarry, and an islander standing guard over the carts swore and began running. After a quick glance to ensure that all of the nearby guards were sufficiently distracted, Rustav pulled his shirt loose and let the key drop into his hand. He had feared that his hands would be shaking too much to get the key into the small locks, but when the moment of action arrived, his movements were swift and sure. The chains fell away, and Rustav backed his way to the quarry wall. Most of the prisoners were so focused on the fight that they didn't see him. The few that did looked away quickly, careful not to draw attention. The jagged rock wall pressed into his spine, and Rustav threw all subtlety to the wind.

Leaping up, he caught hold of a protruding rock and began scampering up the wall as quickly as possible. The rocks were not as forgiving as branches: there was nothing to catch him if his grip failed, and his palms were bloody from the sharp edges by the time he was a quarter of the way up. Though his progress seemed painfully slow to his own eyes, he had made it nearly halfway to the top before he heard islanders below shouting at him.

Without slowing his movements, Rustav braced himself for the sharp and fatal pain of a spear in his back. It never came. Instead, after wasting five minutes shouting and blaming each other, the islanders hurled fist-sized rocks after him. The rocks clattered all around, two or three pelting Rustav's body. He forged on, desperate to reach the top before the noise of his escape reached the islanders back in the city.

Two feet from safety, a rock smashed into Rustav's right hand. The shock of pain loosened his grip, and the sudden shift in weight was too much. The rock gave way under his feet, and then Rustav was hanging, grasping onto life with three fingers of his left hand. An audible gasp rose from underneath him, and Rustav squeezed his eyes shut. He wasn't sure if the bones in his hand had broken, but whether they had or not, that hand would have to hold his weight a little longer.

The islanders, no doubt encouraged by his tenuous position, released a new barrage of stones. Rustav was far enough up that many of them fell short, but enough of them left new bruises on his back and legs to encourage him onward. He swung his right arm upward, catching a sizeable crack in the rock face. Hot pain stabbed through his hand, but he didn't let go, concentrating on getting his feet back into solid holds. Reach, step, reach, step—the islanders had given up throwing rocks now and were screeching and howling for their compatriots to come from the city above—Rustav got one hand up over the ledge—

And then he was rolling out, lying on firm ground, with the nearest islanders just starting to come out of the buildings half a mile away. Exhausted, bruised, and bloody as he was, Rustav couldn't withhold a triumphant laugh as he jumped to his feet. The cheers of the prisoners below quickly faded as he lowered his head and sprinted with all the strength he had left. There was nothing now between him and the castle, nothing but rocky outcroppings and thorny bushes, and the islanders would never be able to catch up to him. He had done the impossible once, and he would do it again. He would rescue Jocham, and they would get away from this demons' pit. And afterward . . .

Well, that was enough to be thinking about at one time.

The first few minutes of running across the rocky, thorny space were intoxicating. With no chains to weigh down his limbs and no whips or rods knocking him around, Rustav felt almost as if he could leave the ground and fly free, never coming within reach of the islanders again. But as the castle loomed on the horizon and the black, twisted shapes of demons began circling in the air not too far off, reality bit into the joy of freedom.

Although he was wary of taking his eyes off the demons, no matter how far away they were, Rustav forced himself to scan the ground for any sign of Jocham and his captors. Was he too late? It seemed impossible that they could have dragged Jocham that far in such a short time, but the hard rock and unforgiving vegetation left no hint of anyone having passed recently.

A shard of rock jutted up several feet out of the ground just ahead and to the right. Rustav veered toward it, anxious for a better view of the ground between him and the castle. He leaped up onto the side, casting a nervous glance upward before scanning the gray terrain.

There—not far from the castle ruins, a group struggled forward, half-hidden by the overgrown bushes and vines surrounding the castle. From the looks of it, Jocham was holding his own against the six islanders that were pulling at him, slowing their progress to almost a crawl.

"Keep fighting, Jocham," Rustav muttered as he hopped back to the ground and began running again, a spurt of grim energy propelling him forward. It would be close. Jocham would have to keep fighting to the very end if Rustav were to reach them before they entered the castle.

But whether Jocham stopped fighting or Rustav's speed was sapped by weeks of malnutrition, Rustav broke through the wall of wild hedges around the castle just in time to see the last of the islanders disappearing into the black darkness of the castle's main entrance.

Rustav hesitated briefly. Somewhere in the back of his mind, he had accepted the possibility that he would have to follow Jocham into the demons' nest itself. But he hadn't anticipated the feeling that swept over him as he stood there, not ten feet from the castle's entrance—the gut-wrenching, stabbing darkness that wrung the neck of every ounce of goodness that Rustav possessed.

He forced one foot forward, then the other. The castle wasn't just terrifying; it objected to his very being, threatening to unmake him, to burn him from the bones outward if he dared set foot inside. But he had to go inside. He couldn't sacrifice Jocham to his own fear.

Rustav didn't remember crossing the final few feet, but all at once he was standing in the shadow of the castle entrance, a shadow that chased away light as vigorously as a shark chased a wounded sea lion. Somehow, even the dull gray light that streamed in through holes in the ceiling was dark and biting.

As he adjusted to the dark interior, Rustav could see the beasts sitting on rafters, even larger than the ragged, mangy demon that had brought him to the island. They were watching curiously, but not attacking—not yet. Rustav tore his eyes away from the demons above and found Jocham standing alone, crouched in a defensive stance, clutching an islander's rod in one hand and staring straight ahead with rigid horror written in his wide eyes.

"Jocham, come on!" Rustav shouted, leaping to the old man's side and pulling at his arm. "Let's go before they—"

His throat closed in a gag as his eyes fell on the islanders that had brought Jocham to the castle. The holes in the roof let in just enough light to glint off their lengthening teeth, which were sharpening into deadly fangs. The islanders were growing, mutating grotesquely, their grinning pale faces turning to grinning black faces, eerily reminiscent of their human form, but so animal that it was impossible to tell that they had ever been anything else.

The islanders don't just worship the demons. They are the demons.

In less time than it had taken for him to realize the truth, Rustav saw in his mind's eye the hundreds of his countrymen who had died at the hands of these foul creatures. He saw the islanders in the Courei castle, transforming and befouling first the castle, then the valley, then the entire peninsula. He saw the castle decaying and rotting until it was as wretched as this one, as vile as the creatures that filled it.

Rage roared through Rustav's ears like the crashing of ocean breakers, drowning out the screeching and flapping that surrounded him. The anger burned through him like rivers of boiling water that brought new strength to his weary body. The iron rings that still circled his limbs and neck seemed to recoil from his fury, bursting open and clattering to the ground. The islanders that stood in front of him shrank back, now fully in bestial form but somehow less intimidating with hot, angry blood rushing through Rustav's limbs. Rustav tried to take a step toward them, but his legs moved awkwardly, and he stumbled. When he threw out his arms to catch himself, a gust of wind swept him back up before he ever touched the ground.

He had wings.

Leathery wings ending in pointed claws, just like the demons', only his were thicker, stronger, longer. He was looking down on the very same demons he had craned his neck upward to see only minutes before. His face was changed, lengthened into a short muzzle, mouth filled with teeth made to tear. His fur—for fur he had—was thick and smooth. The ruins no longer seemed so suffocatingly dark, an unseen source throwing light against the black creatures that were beginning to circle in fierce curiosity.

But there was no more time for wondering. The silence that had fallen over the horde of demons was broken with one challenging screech, followed by dozens more. A cluster of demons left their perches and hurtled downward. Rustav launched himself into the air, climbing clumsily at first, but quickly gaining control. Although there were fifty or sixty demons flapping through the castle ruins, Rustav's signifi-cant advantage in size and strength kept him in the air. There was a lot of tearing, a lot of flapping, a lot of shrieking. Rustav tasted foul demon fur, hot blood, leathery skin—all sensa-tions he later shuddered to remember.

At some point in the heat of the battle, Rustav heard a cry from below, far different from the cries that had been ring-ing ceaselessly in his sharp ears. Through the mass of black shapes crowding around, Rustav spotted a human, weak and frail-looking in his small, fleshy body, fighting desperately to fend off a few demons who had gone looking for easier prey than Rustav.

Jocham.

He wielded well a whip and a rod that had been dropped on the floor, but he wasn't going to last much longer. Screeching angrily, Rustav dove through the masses of demons toward Jocham's attackers. He pinned one to the ground and felt bones give way beneath his claws. The other two were soon dead as well, swift, violent deaths that

Rustav knew would haunt his dreams for years to come. The remaining demons had followed him to the ground, and Jocham was doing his best to drive them away. They had to get out of there.

One powerful beat of his wings swept Rustav off the ground, and he wrapped a claw around Jocham's torso, careful not to squeeze too hard. Then he shot upward, battling his way through the remaining demons with his teeth and the claws at the end of his wings. Rustav bashed one demon away with his wing and saw bleak light streaming in from a hole in the roof. The hole was too small, but it didn't take much to break through the rotting ceiling—and then he was in the clear, clutching Jocham, fleeing from the castle with the greatest speed he could coax out of his unpracticed wings. A few demons gave chase, but Rustav's wingspan extended at least ten feet beyond theirs. There was no way they were going to catch up in the open air, and they soon turned back.

One thought dominated Rustav's mind: Get to the peninsula. He had to get off the island, get Jocham somewhere safe. The adrenaline from the battle was starting to wear off, and Rustav was becoming aware that, strong as he had become, he was far from invulnerable. His fur—golden, not black, he could see now in the light of day—was drenched with dark blood on one side, just in front of his right wing. His left wing was torn, and he could feel the pain of bite punctures all over. Exhaustion started to creep over him as he soared above the water, and it was a battle to keep going. The coast of the peninsula was right there. He just had to make it a little farther. A little farther.

It was with relief that Rustav began sinking lower, judging land to be no more than five minutes away. There was a nice, open spot where he could set down and rest. At the thought, Rustav dipped a little lower, anxious to let his wings be still. As he swooped down, now mere feet above solid ground, he released Jocham, unsure if he could land without squashing the man.

Unfortunately, Rustav hadn't considered the possibility that the nearby humans might not take kindly to an enormous, bloodstained demon swooping down beside them. Something went whistling by his abnormally large left ear. An arrow! There was another one flying toward him, ripping cleanly through his wing before he could do anything. Pain jolted energy into Rustav's tired limbs, and he flapped harder, lifting himself up and over the coastal town.

Far off in the distance, mountains rose up to the sky, the upper slopes coated in a sea of green. For a brief moment, Rustav thought that if he could only make it to those trees, the tuatha could put it all right. They could end this nightmare. Maybe he could even forget it ever happened.

Then he caught a glimpse of the steady drip of blood soaring downward from his wing and side. He would never make it that far. Already, he was dipping lower, unable to keep up his altitude. But if his last encounter was anything to go by, he would be dead before he landed.

Scanning the land below, Rustav saw a wide expanse of domestic trees to the northeast. It wouldn't be nearly as safe as the old forest, but at least he wouldn't be completely exposed. Veering toward it, he focused on keeping his burning muscles working, sinking a little lower with every downward stroke. Somewhere in the middle of the trees, he folded in his wings, allowing gravity to work out the landing. The trees were much more fragile than the solid trunks in the old forest, and Rustav tore several up by the roots before rolling to a stop.

A small part of his mind warned that people were surely already heading into the forest with pitchforks and axes, but the rest of his aching and exhausted body reasoned that he had time for at least a few minutes of rest. Closing his eyes, Rustav gave in to his weariness, seeking temporary refuge from this never-ending nightmare.

CHAPTER NINETEEN

WHEN RUSTAV CAME TO, HIS LIMBS FELT WEAK and frail. He flexed his fingers, running his thumb along the soft tips and feeling the smallness of his hands. Whatever he was lying on was a good deal more comfortable than the forest floor he had landed on. The smell of wood reached his nose, and a part of him hoped desperately that he was in Anton's small home, surrounded by the familiar sights and smells of the village.

But he knew it was a futile hope, even before he opened his eyes and was engulfed in a flood of memories. Someone had lifted him from the ground to the branches of the trees, and judging by the way the branches crossed in a perfect hammock weave, it had been a tuath. His clothes were ragged, shredded and stained around his wounds, as if they had merged with his fur and retained the marks when they changed back. Below him stretched the damage where he had landed as a much larger creature. Trees lay snapped and uprooted in all directions, and a furrow of freshly turned dirt cut through the undergrowth.

Grimacing, Rustav raised himself to a sitting position. His wooden pendant slid down from his shoulder to rest on a bandage that had been hastily wrapped around his chest. The pendant hadn't snapped off with the iron collar; Rustav wished it had. That was where all this trouble had started. Rustav probed his injured side, wincing as he found the gash that had soaked his golden fur red.

Fur, he thought, shaking his head. Rustav could almost believe that it had been a dream, but for the pain and wreckage that remained. As he looked down at his arms, he thought how pasty and brittle they were, nothing like the powerful wings that had swept over the ocean. Once, he had thought himself strong, but now he knew what strength was. For a fleeting moment, he wished to have it back. To have claws longer than fingers, wings wider than a man was tall, a grip that could crush bone—no one would dare to cross him then. No measly human—or tuath, for that matter—would stand a chance.

But the moment passed, and a shiver shook him clear into his belly. Was he no better than the bullies of Markuum, that he leaped at the power to hurt others?

"How are you feeling?"

Rustav started, then winced and pressed a hand against his side. Ayre sat just a few branches away, his face somber. He must have been the one to tie the bandage around Rustav's wound. "I've been better," Rustav said, scowling. "Probably would've been much worse, though, if I'd waited any longer for you to come along."

"I apologize for my delay," Ayre said, his apology taking on a tone of sympathetic condolence. "Dantzel was reluctant to stay behind. It took me longer than expected to situate her safely, and in my haste to reach you, I made an unfortunate mistake resulting in my imprisonment on the island. As you might imagine, a Burrihim prison is not an easy escape. By the time I freed myself and found you, you were already on your way into the castle ruins. I would have followed you in, but by then, it was too late."

A prickle of fear rose up in Rustav's gut at the sorrowful pity in Ayre's eyes. Shaking his head to dispel the irrational anxiety, Rustav said, "What do you mean, too late? I got away fine, and I saved Jocham besides."

Ayre leaned back against the trunk, raising his eyes to look off into the distance. "Do you know the history of the inhabitants of Burrihim? How they became what you humans, in your simplicity, call the island demons?"

Rustav shook his head slowly, a heavy dread pressing down on his chest. From the way Ayre was talking, Rustav began to suspect that turning into a giant, winged beast had been just about the only option worse than being torn to shreds by the demons.

"The islanders were tuatha once. They lived in the trees, in a settlement to the north. Long ago, when the island of Burrihim was a part of the peninsula, a dragon awoke from a volcano beneath the sea, a few miles off the tip. It demolished the castle that now lies in ruins on the island, which was once the home of your ancestors. The human king called upon the tuatha to help drive the dragon back into its fiery home. Most came willingly, for those were the days before the humans sided with the dirt-dwellers and offended the bond of the Union."

A dragon . . . Rustav had seen too many strange things to disbelieve that a dragon could emerge from an underwater volcano. But the reference to "dirt-dwellers" puzzled him. Then, as the old tales came back to him, he leaned forward in interest. "You mean kobolds? Were there really cities of tunnels under the ground? Are they still living there? What did they do to offend the Union?"

"One story at a time," Ayre said, holding up a hand and keeping his gaze trained on the branches high above Rustav's head. "While most of the tuatha responded willingly to the human king's call for help, those who became the islanders cared more for their lives than their honor. They resorted to the greatest lengths to avoid battle." Here, Ayre's gaze took on a burning scorn, his mouth twisting slightly as if the words tasted sour. "Each tuath carries within himself a base, animal form that we call the fleyder. It lacks logic and reason, acting on pure instinct with nothing but brute force. These tuatha allowed their fear and their cowardice to take over, wiping away all rationality in their desperation to flee. They transformed into these hideous beasts and sought to escape."

Rustav's mouth was dry as that horrible moment in the castle ruins replayed in his head. Was that what had happened? Had he simply been so frightened that his terror stripped away all humanity, transforming him into a mindless monster?

"Before they got far, a fierce wind sprang up, blowing them back to the tip of the peninsula, where they were forced to fight the dragon alone. Though they were able to drive the dragon back to his lair, their punishment was not yet fulfilled. You see, their offense was so egregious that they were expelled from the tuatha. Their precious long lives, the lives they had sacrificed their honor to preserve, were drastically shortened, spanning hardly any longer than a human life. The inhabitants of Burrihim were no longer welcome among the fair tuatha, and so the tip of the peninsula was cut away, forming the island as you now know it. They have been bound to the island by their own lust for power. Their one link to the tuatha, their one hint that they had once been a greater people, was their ability to take on the form of the fleyder. They craved the brute strength that came with that transformation. However, while they retained the ability to transform, that power was tethered to the ruined castle."

The words hung heavily in the air around Rustav's head, stifling his mind. He knew now why Ayre was so somber. Rustav may have saved Jocham, but in doing so, Rustav had disgraced himself in the highest degree. All the tuathan strength he had inherited, and he still didn't have the strength to control his fear, his cowardice. He had failed to live up to his heritage as a prince, as a brother of the tuatha. What had ever convinced him that he could be something more than the sweepings of the street?

With his last scrapings of hope, he said, "But I wasn't like them. I was bigger, and I wasn't black. They were falling to bits, and I was just fine."

A painful spasm crossed Ayre's face, followed by a sad smile. "This was only your first time. They have decayed through the years."

Revulsion swelled up inside of Rustav, threatening to choke off his breathing. Was that his fate? To become a rotted-out hulk? Increasingly desperate, he said, "I didn't choose to change. It just happened. I couldn't help it."

With a grave sigh, Ayre finally brought his eyes down to meet Rustav's gaze. In that moment, enveloped in the certainty of Ayre's wide brown eyes, Rustav knew that there was nothing left for him, that he had successfully botched any good he had once sought to achieve. Ayre's words only confirmed it. "It is a dangerous man who cannot control his emotion, who lets fear and force govern in place of a sound mind. He puts the lives of all around him at risk, losing his reason in moments when it is most precious."

Rustav sat speechless, unable to defend himself from his own hatred and disgust boiling up inside of him. Numbly, silently, he pulled his knees up to his chest, curling into a miserable ball and wishing Ayre would look away again. After several minutes, he said, "I have to leave here."

Ayre rested his hand on Rustav's shoulder, his voice growing more gentle. "I am sorry, Rustav. This is a terrible fate to have befallen you. I could try to help you, teach you control. Perhaps, in time, you would not be such a danger to your friends."

A horrible image swept across Rustav's vision, a scene of him surrounded by the people he sought to govern, of him transforming into a murderous beast and killing his own followers the same gruesome way he had killed the islanders. Rustav squeezed his eyes shut and shook his head. "I can't risk it. If I slipped once, changed again . . . I have to leave before I do any more harm to this country."

"Where will you go?"

With a shrug, Rustav said, "Out. Away. Anywhere but here."

Ayre nodded, somber approval in his eyes as he handed over the sword the islanders had taken from Rustav in the castle. "I kept it safe for you, as promised. I hope it will prove useful on your journey."

Rustav nodded, keeping a tenuous hold on his expression as he touched the hilt, unable to meet Ayre's eyes.

Softly, reluctantly, Rustav said, "Look out for Dantzel for me. Tell her—" Rustav stopped and dropped his eyes to the ground. "Don't tell her anything. Just—make sure she's safe and happy."

ALTHOUGH AYRE HAD PROMISED TO RETURN with food and more supplies, Rustav waited only a few minutes before starting the excruciating climb down. He was dizzy with fatigue, and he slipped more than once. Every patch of bark gouged his already-shredded palms, and his wounded side screamed in protest. Rustav could already see splotches of blood seeping through the bandage. As soon as the ground was a reasonable distance away, Rustav released his hold on the branches, falling gladly onto the cushion of leaves.

He remained crumpled at the foot of the tree for several minutes, contemplating his next move. Now, he was grateful that he hadn't made it all the way to the old forest. The tuatha would never allow him back among their homes, not after what he had done. From what he could remember of his last fuzzy moments before he had crashed, these trees were only a few miles from the northern coast. He could easily sneak aboard a ship bound for the mainland. Once it landed, he could join a caravan in the Ravian Desert, where no one would care who he was or what he had done. He could raise camels. Maybe he could even make a living carving wood.

"Rustav?"

Fear sent a shock of energy to Rustav's limbs, and Rustav leaped to his feet. Pak was approaching cautiously, his hands raised as if to calm a startled horse. When Rustav didn't respond, Pak continued on in a steady stream of Tuathan.

"It was you, wasn't it? The golden fleyder. You must come back with me. The Council is in an uproar."

Rustav shook his head mutely, mouth dry with fear. Pak had already tried to kill him once, and that was just for being a prince, a child of the Union. Rustav could only imagine what Pak planned to do now. "Stay away, Pak. I'm leaving."

Pak stopped. "Leaving where?"

"It doesn't matter. You got your wish. The Union will die with me, and you won't have to dirty your hands."

Pak's face scrunched with confusion. "Rustav, I told you. I want the Union to survive. Whatever Ayre has told you is a lie. You can't leave, not now."

Yes, Pak had claimed to believe in the Union. But hadn't he also set Rustav up to be killed in the castle? Had Ayre lied about that? Did it matter? Rustav answered, his voice cracking with the strain. "I don't care anymore who's lying, if it's Ayre or you or everyone in the world. I have to go."

Ayre's voice cut in from the edge of the trees. "What are you doing here, Pak?"

Rustav's eyes flicked over to where Ayre stood, but Pak ignored him resolutely. "Rustav, come with me. You need to know the truth."

"I've already told you the truth!" Ayre said. "He only wants to see the punishment. Listen to me, Rustav: if you ever valued your life, go now."

"You must hear what I have to say!" Pak took a step forward, reaching a hand out toward Rustav. It was like releasing a spring: adrenaline flooded Rustav's veins, and Rustav sprang away, desperate to outrun his own shame. He expected Pak to chase him down, but Pak's shouts, punctuated by Ayre's, soon faded into the distance. Rustav kept running long after leaving the tuatha behind, too afraid that his mistakes would catch up to him if he dared slow to a walk.

THE PORT OF LANTRIS ROSE UP IN FRONT OF Rustav before he ended his sprint, swallowing huge gulps of salt-seared air to combat the shaking in his legs and the spinning of his head. As he bent over, hands on his knees, and surveyed the ships lined up before him, doubt began to assail the firm plan that had sustained him during his long run. Faces intruded on his memory—Dantzel and Anton and Cabel, Jocham and a hundred other men covered in rock dust. The words of a fellow slave came back to ring in his ears: *If we can't believe in you, what's left to believe in?*

Rustav shook his head. How could he ask people to believe in him, after all he knew and all he had done? He felt as though a mark had been set on him, as noticeable and ugly as the brand that now stood on his arm. Even if he had once fooled himself into thinking that he could lead these people, it was obvious now that he wasn't fit for the role. He would never escape the threat of the demon lurking in his heart.

Pushing away any thought of remaining on the peninsula, Rustav plunged into the early-morning bustle of the docks, eyeing the ships for one that was on its way out. But his attention was soon drawn away from the line of vessels by the amount of red cloaks spotting the crowd. Although Rustav was well-practiced at keeping his head down and blending in, he was all too aware that his light hair stood out like a lighthouse beacon among the dark heads of the coastal city. There were a few valley folk there to argue and haggle with merchants, but not nearly enough to keep him from being conspicuous.

"It's a dangerous time for a hay-hair like you to be wandering outside of the valley."

Heart pounding, Rustav turned to see a bear of a man standing beside him, sea-worn face covered with a grizzled gray beard. The man looked out over the ocean, his eyes as distant as if he were talking to the waves instead of Rustav. "What do you mean?" Rustav asked.

"Well, wild rumors have been flying. Elanokiev denies it all, of course, but the Guards have been looking awful hard the past couple of days for a blond kid with a piece of wood around his neck." The old sailor finally glanced sideways at Rustav with a raised eyebrow, his eyes flicking down to the leather string around Rustav's neck. "Seems to me you might need a place to avoid trouble."

Could he trust the man? Was there any choice? Every passing moment increased Rustav's chances of being spotted, and if this man was telling the truth, the danger of being recognized was higher than ever. Rustav wasn't certain what rumors the old sailor was referring to, but he had a bad feeling that it wouldn't be as easy to slip quietly out of the country as he had hoped. Still, better to be trapped with people who might be willing to help him than with people he knew were trying to kill him.

Almost afraid to speak in case his voice drew attention, Rustav nodded. Taking Rustav by the elbow, the sailor began walking briskly through the crowd, ducking and weaving around the Guards with practiced ease.

"This way, lad. *The Arrow* is about to leave port. Slouch

down, and I'll try to screen you as much as I can going up the gangplank. By the clouds, you're a tall one, aren't you?"

Rustav held his breath as he hurried up the gangplank, keeping his eyes down and ears pricked for the sound of a Guard's shout. Then he was on the rolling deck of a ship, jostled by sailors rushing to and fro in preparation for casting off. The grizzled sailor steered him into the captain's cabin and stepped back out. "I'll return as soon as we're off," he said. "Shouldn't be long now."

The door snapped shut, and Rustav found himself unable to sit still in spite of his exhaustion. He wandered the small cabin, eyeing the maps, books, and curious instruments that lined the walls as he pondered his next move. This man seemed to know who he was. Would he obey if Rustav ordered him to sail around the mountains to the mainland? Once there, Rustav could easily make a run for it.

As if in protest of another sprint, Rustav's side gave a sharp stab of pain. The few miles' run had inflamed the wound, and it burned as if freshly opened. Setting his teeth, Rustav began to pull away the bandages for a closer look but quickly covered it as the door opened again.

"I apologize for the delay," the sailor said once the door was shut tightly behind him. "Captain Hayden, at your service."

Rustav hadn't decided what exactly he meant to say to this brawny captain, so he held up a scrap of parchment he had been puzzling over, a sketch he could only guess to be a rough map of a chain of islands. "What's this?"

The captain took it with a broad grin. "That is the work of my youngest daughter. I believe it's supposed to be a whale spouting water from its blowhole." He rubbed the parchment fondly with his thumb for a moment, then his attention strayed back to Rustav's face. "It really is you, isn't it?" he murmured. "You look so like him."

"Like who?"

"The king. Rilotorian, of course, not the usurper."

Rustav swayed unsteadily, not from the rolling of the ship, but from the sudden dizziness that swept over him. In an instant, Hayden was at his side, guiding him into a chair. "You—you knew him?" Rustav asked, fighting the urge to squeeze his head between his knees.

"Not closely," Hayden said, his brow furrowed with concern as he laid a rough hand on Rustav's forehead. "I used to make special runs for the court. I have a few hidden cargo spaces for important merchandise, shipments that pirates and islanders would have loved to get their hands on. I mostly just saw him in trade meetings and such, but I had the grand opportunity of speaking with him once or twice. He was a great man, your father, a king who loved his people. And he loved you, he did indeed. I've never seen a man shine so brightly as he did when he announced your birth."

A hard lump lodged itself in Rustav's throat, and he had to look away, blinking. All his life, he had been told that his mother was a vagrant and that his father likely didn't know he existed. But now, to know that his father had been kind and caring—that he had been a great king, respected and loved by his people—it made the burning shame all the more painful. *Why couldn't I have inherited some of that goodness?*

Rustav was so caught up in his own thoughts that he hardly noticed Hayden laying two fingers across his wrist to check his pulse. At least, not until Hayden pulled Rustav's sleeve up a little more and leaned in for a closer look. Rustav pulled his arm back self-consciously, but not before Hayden had gotten a good look at the brand on his skin.

"You were on the island?" Hayden asked, his bushy eyebrows drawing together. "How did you escape?"

Rustav shook his head and instantly regretted it. The movement sent the world spinning even faster around him. Giving up any shred of dignity, Rustav hunched over with his head down, but instantly straightened again with a groan, holding his side. Hayden pulled Rustav's hand away, and Rustav was distantly surprised to see blood covering his palm.

"It's nothing," he mumbled, even though Hayden was already ripping Rustav's shirt open to get a better look. "Just a little scratch. Might've torn a little while I was running. A tuath bandaged it already."

Hayden gave him a sharp look, then guided Rustav over to the bed. "Tuath, huh? Well, you've done a good job of soaking the bandages. Let me get my ship's doctor to see if we can clean you up a little."

Although Rustav was determined to stay alert enough to explain it all to the doctor, lying on the bed proved too much for him. He blinked and couldn't get his eyes to open again. Halfway through thinking, *Maybe I'll rest a minute*, Rustav slipped into the blissful unawareness of sleep.

CHAPTER TWENTY

DANTZEL BREATHED A SIGH OF RELIEF AS SHE AND Cabel left behind the port of Elling. They had stopped in several towns along the southern coast of Courei, but she still couldn't get used to them. Not only were the rows of fish-hawkers obnoxiously loud, the sight and smell of hundreds of dead fish and mounds of fish guts left Dantzel longing for the sweetness of a spring meadow. Crude dockhands walked the streets, more than one of them giving her a leering grin and a wink before they saw the bow and quiver of arrows strapped to her back and steered off for a less thorny target.

Still, there were moments when a breeze brought in the salty freshness of the sea, when Dantzel heard the distant crashing of waves, that she understood Rustav's longing for the open ocean. The reflection inevitably brought on a bout of homesickness and loneliness. She missed those days by the stream, and she wished more than anything that Rustav were here to help on her absurdly overwhelming mission to organize a rebellion. He would come back. He had to come back.

"Are you sure this is a good idea?" Cabel asked, shifting his pack higher on his shoulders as they left the road and began to cut across a field of prickly weeds. "I'm not sure Anton meant for us to go chasing gypsies."

"Anton told us to round up all the support we could find," Dantzel said, wishing not for the first time that the old carpenter had come with them instead of just sending them off with a handful of names and a passphrase. It had taken him only a few minutes of limping around gathering supplies to realize that he would only slow them down. "Besides," Dantzel continued, "they're not gypsies."

"Okay, highwaymen," Cabel said. "Just because they rob and plunder the king's men doesn't make them any less robbers and plunderers. What's to keep them from gutting us and taking everything we have?"

"What would they take?" Dantzel laughed, gesturing to their meager packs. "Our stale bread and mushy apples? Come on, Cabel, where's your sense of adventure?"

"It took a hard hit when I almost lost you in Tarom," he said seriously. "Can you imagine what Rustav would have done to me if he came back and found you in the castle dungeons?"

Dantzel took a long look at her companion, her eyes resting on the vivid bruise under his right eye. They'd had a narrow scrape with the Guards a couple of days earlier, and she wouldn't have made it out if Cabel hadn't come bulling through the crowd for her. Sometimes, she still found it hard to believe that the small, perpetually moving, perpetually grinning boy she had known all her life had transformed into this young man capable of such solemnity.

"Roddin said that Skandar has strong ties to the Loyalist

movement," Dantzel reasoned. Then, hoping to tease out one of Cabel's boyish grins, she added, "Besides, weren't you the one who used to hold up carts coming into town on market day? I remember having to pay a handful of berries more than once to a little fiend in a black mask. You even had a highwayman name, something about—"

"All right, that's enough," Cabel interrupted with a sheepish smile. "You have to admit, though, I was a pretty terrifying rogue for being all of seven years old. And I got a nice stash of treats before Pa found out what I was up to."

"Sounds like the type of fellow we could use."

Dantzel and Cabel whirled around. The man who had spoken had to be a specter, Dantzel thought, heart pounding. Though there was nothing out of the ordinary about his red-brown hair, tanned skin, and confident smirk, he had appeared out of empty air. Dantzel had checked over her shoulder only moments ago and seen nothing.

"Are you Skandar?" Cabel asked, taking a step forward with his fists clenched aggressively. The man tilted his head back to look at them through half-closed eyes.

"I think you'd better tell me who you are first."

Dantzel repeated the introduction that Anton had taught her weeks before, the almost monastic words that had gotten them safely in contact with Loyalists throughout the country. "I am Dant, a humble servant of truth and ideals."

"Indeed," said the man, throwing his arms wide as he completed the scripted exchange. "The servant of such a commendable master is always welcome in my house. I am, as you said, Skandar, chief of the noble highwaymen. Might I assume that you are Dantzel and Cabel, the true king's loyal companions?"

"You've heard of us?" Cabel asked in surprise, and Skandar laughed.

"Who hasn't among the Loyalists these days? You're the thread sewing the ragged patches of rebellion into a smart military uniform. It's an honor to have you among us."

Cabel's chest puffed out proudly, and Dantzel couldn't help smiling. They had been sneaking around and hiding for so long that hearing Skandar acknowledge the work they were doing was a welcome reward for their labor.

"Come along," Skandar said, wrapping an arm around both of their shoulders. "My brothers and I will escort you somewhere where we can have a good talk over a good meal. We have much to discuss, I think."

Brothers? Dantzel couldn't believe it when she turned to see four other men circled around them. They had sprouted up unnoticed, as if they were a part of the weedy field itself. But before she could express her astonishment, Skandar was steering her forward, taking them over a rise and down into a surprisingly vibrant camp, fully hidden from the road. Colorful tents clustered together with men standing guard, women gathered around bubbling pots of stew, and even children chasing each other through the camp.

"I can see how we might be mistaken for gypsies," Skandar said with a wink at Cabel. "It is useful for a cluster of outlaws to avoid the appearance of outlaws."

As they walked through the camp, nearly everyone they saw called out a greeting to Skandar. Some hardly noticed Dantzel and Cabel, while others pointed and stared openly. It was a relief when Skandar told them to take a seat on a circle of stones and offered two steaming bowls of stew.

"Tell me," Skandar said, leaning against a boulder as

Dantzel and Cabel gratefully devoured the first hot meal they had touched in days. "Why is the country suddenly swarming with Guards?"

"We heard some of them talking to a merchant in Elling," Dantzel said. "They were looking for a valley boy with a wooden pendant around his neck. They called him a rabble-rouser, but the people are no fools. Elanokiev has as good as admitted that his nephew is alive and well."

"But we can't figure out why now, of all times," Cabel said, swallowing the last of his stew and setting down the empty bowl. "People have been speculating for years about Rilotorian's son, and Elanokiev has only ever said that the boy died with his parents. Why the sudden panicked search for someone he claims doesn't exist?"

"The flying beast," Skandar murmured. "It must have scared him half out of his wits."

Dantzel sat up a little straighter, a chill seeping into her flesh as she remembered the last flying beast she had encountered, the black demon carrying Rustav away from the castle grounds. "What beast?" she asked.

"Haven't you heard?" Skandar leaned forward, his eyes alight. "Four days ago, an enormous creature flew over the valley. They say the body was as big as a draft horse, with wings strong enough to send it soaring through the air. Fur of pure gold, full and fine as the king's cats. No one knows what it was."

"One of the island demons?" Cabel asked, casting an anxious look at Dantzel. She shook her head, baffled.

"No. Not unless it's a completely new breed. They aren't nearly that big, and the few patches of fur they have left are blacker than a night storm."

"That's what we've heard from the sailors," Skandar said. "We thought for a time it was a stunt from the king to scare off all the folks you've been recruiting. But the way he's acting, sending the Guards out in force, I bet he thinks it's a secret weapon that Marustavian has got up his sleeve." He looked from Dantzel to Cabel, as if hoping they would confirm that the beast was on their side. But Dantzel could only shake her head, at a complete loss for an explanation.

"This is the first we've heard of it," she said.

"Ah," Skandar said, rubbing his jaw regretfully. "Well, that brings me to another point of concern. What have you heard of late from Prince Marustavian? Is he well?"

Fear began to burn in the pit of Dantzel's stomach. She and Cabel had avoided sharing any details of what had happened to Rustav, stating only that they were limited in their contact with him in order to minimize his chance of discovery by Elanokiev. "Last I heard, he was healthy and making preparations for war. Why?"

Skandar glanced briefly at one of his comrades and jerked his head ever so slightly. The man stepped away as Skandar spoke. "We came across a rumormonger just yesterday. His words could prove most damaging to the cause, so we took him and have held him here until we could either verify or disprove his claims."

"What did he say?" Dantzel asked, eyebrows contracting. Skandar's eyes flicked over her shoulder.

"He can tell you himself."

Dantzel felt him before she saw him; the air grew heavy, reluctant to be drawn into her lungs. Dread pooled in her heart as she turned to see Ayre being marched toward them. Beside her, Cabel clenched his fists, his face suddenly white.

"What are you doing here, Ayre?" Dantzel asked as the tuath reached the group. "Where is he?"

"You know this man?" Skandar asked. Ayre tutted impatiently, and the men around him snickered. Skandar smirked. "Forgive me. This tuath."

"Yes," Dantzel said, her ears burning, "and you should keep your skepticism to yourself until you understand what you're dealing with."

One man laughed, as if she had only taken the joke a little further, but the rest glanced at each other uncertainly. Dantzel took advantage of the silence to pull Ayre a few steps to the side, Cabel following on their heels. "What's this they're talking about, Ayre? What have you been telling people?"

"Only as much as I thought necessary for them to guide me to you," Ayre said, bowing his head somberly. "I fear the news is not the good tidings you have awaited."

"What do you mean?" Dantzel demanded in a low voice, all too aware of the surrounding men and women who strained to hear every word.

"Rustav left."

The words didn't mean anything to Dantzel. Puzzled, she looked at Cabel, who asked, "Left where? Left the island? Is he back on the peninsula?"

"He left," Ayre repeated insistently. "He managed to escape the island without my assistance, but I spoke with him three days ago. He was . . . badly shaken by his experiences on the island and overwhelmed by the magnitude of his responsibility. I tried to reason with him, but in the end, my efforts were in vain. He departed aboard a ship bound for the mainland."

For a brief moment, Dantzel hung motionless in a state of shock, the words spinning through her mind over and over.

Gone? Was it possible? Had Rustav finally gotten his wish of escape?

"I know it's difficult to face after all you've done for him," Ayre said gently, placing a hand on Dantzel's shoulder. "But we won't let your work go to waste. Rustav may be gone, but we still have a country on the edge of war. We can lead the people to victory."

Dantzel had been stretched taut between her faith in Rustav and her fear that Ayre was telling the truth, her nerves as tight as her bowstring. Ayre's words pulled her just a little too far; she snapped away from them, hard anger banishing any credibility she might have given to Ayre's story. She knocked Ayre's hand away from her shoulder, and Ayre stepped back, eyes widening. "I don't believe it," she said, her tone approaching a bobcat's snarl. "He wouldn't just leave, not when we all need him so badly."

"Wouldn't he?" Ayre asked cuttingly, the warm persuasion of his voice lost in its sudden aggression. "All he's ever wanted to do is run. You know that. He left you in the forest. He left you in the castle. He's left you now, and he's not coming back. Face it, Dantzel. Your legendary hero is a coward who cares only about saving his own skin."

"You're wrong!" Dantzel snapped, a beam of light suddenly cutting through the fog that always hovered around Ayre's words. "You took him away in the forest. He came back for me. The islanders took him away in the castle. He made it back—no thanks to you, I'd bet. If he has left, he's got a reason, and he'll be back."

Ayre's face twisted, its usual soft glow replaced with harsh darkness. "You're a fool to place your hopes on someone so unstable. His rashness could prove ruinous for the entire country."

"And who would you suggest as a replacement?" Dantzel asked, pouring as much scorn into her words as possible. "You? You would lie and flatter the people into false security. The country would be so wrapped up in placid hobbies that anybody could march in and take over."

Fierce rage flashed through Ayre's eyes, and Ayre raised a hand as if to strike. In an instant, Cabel leaped in front of Dantzel, grabbing Ayre's upraised hand and holding a knife against the tuath's narrow chest. Skandar and his men, who had stood a respectful distance away during the exchange, circled around with weapons drawn.

"You should have listened to me," Ayre said, his calm voice at odds with the hatred burning in his eyes. In one swift movement, he freed his arm and knocked Cabel's knife to the ground. Skandar's men grabbed at him as he pushed out of the circle, but it was like watching a river flow through a pile of rocks.

"After him!" Skandar shouted at his dumbfounded men, but Ayre was already slipping over the hill, vanishing from sight. A few ran after him, but Dantzel knew they would never get close. Skandar turned and gave her a long, appraising look. "And? What do you say to his claims?"

Dantzel couldn't answer. The argument had drained her, left her as weak and shaky as the night she had left the forest. The war was mutating, growing and shifting out of control. It was one thing to rise up against Elanokiev, even supported as he might be by the islanders. But if Ayre and the tuatha were looking for an opportunity to take control of the throne . . . and then there was the mysterious demon-that-was-not-a-demon. For a brief moment, Dantzel thought that she could hardly blame Rustav if he had run away.

The bright colors of the tents, the clanging of cooking pots, the shouting of children were all pressing in on Dantzel. She had to get away from it all, if only for a few minutes. But she couldn't, not while all eyes were watching for her reaction. Drawing in every ounce of self-control she had left, Dantzel looked Skandar in the eye and spoke as authoritatively as she knew how. "Ayre is a word-weaver, a trickster, and a liar. He can be persuasive, but his words are hollow. Prince Marustavian is as dedicated to the cause as he has ever been."

Even as she spoke, the words snagged on a tiny but needle-sharp point of doubt in her mind. How dedicated had Rustav been? He had never accepted aloud that he was a born ruler, a future king. Dantzel knew he could do it, knew that he was the hope she had waited for since the day her father was taken, but what good was her confidence if Rustav had none of his own?

Thankfully, Skandar showed no hint of suspecting her uncertainty as he bowed slightly. "I am relieved to hear it. What would you have us do?"

"Cabel will talk to you about your skills and supplies," Dantzel said, glancing over at Cabel, who nodded. "I need some time alone to decide what to do about Ayre."

Chapter Twenty-One

Dantzel breathed a sigh of relief as she left the borders of the camp. The setting sun was sending streaks of gold across the sky, and Dantzel drank in the beauty of it, desperate to think about anything that wasn't war or betrayal. *How many more times will the sun set before I see Rustav again?* she wondered. Although she refused to believe that Rustav had left for good, she feared that Ayre had a grain of truth in his words. What had he said? That Rustav had been "badly shaken" by what had happened on the island. A shiver shook Dantzel's shoulders. What had they done to him there?

"Dantzel?"

The voice, shaky and breathless, came from just behind her. Startled, Dantzel turned, reaching surreptitiously for her bow. An old man stood gazing up at her with eyes too energetic, too strong for his frail frame. At first glance, he seemed so thin that a good breeze would sweep him away; but he stood tall and steady, with none of the bending or trembling that usually accompanied age.

"That's me," Dantzel said cautiously. The man closed the

rest of the distance between them, never taking his eyes from her face. As he drew nearer, she could see the shine of unshed tears in his eyes. Anxious to escape his intense gaze, Dantzel pulled her eyes away, catching sight of a pair of triangles blackened into his forearm. Before she could ask about it, the man's rough, knobby hand covered it self-consciously.

"I didn't catch your name," Dantzel said, wishing he would stop looking at her so intensely. The man blinked, passing a hand over his eyes and clearing his throat.

"I am Jocham," he said, and Dantzel stiffened, pulling in a sharp breath. He stepped forward, reaching as if to take her shoulders, then hesitating. "It is you, isn't it?" he said hoarsely. "You look so much like your mother."

Dantzel's vision blurred with unexpected moisture. She blinked furiously, desperate to get a closer look at the haggard face. The hair was gray, the eyes lined, the body so very thin. But the face drew out a memory—a feeling more than a memory, a cloudy sense of awe and laughter. Dantzel lifted a hand, touching the wrinkled cheek just as it flooded with tears.

"Papa?" she whispered. With a shout of laughter, Jocham leaped forward and swept her up in an iron hug, swinging her around with surprising strength. She nearly stumbled when he set her down, too stunned to bother about her balance.

"Look at you!" Jocham held Dantzel at arm's length, his beaming smile wiping some of the age from his face and bringing him closer to the joyous stonecutter that lived in Dantzel's earliest memories. "You're so grown-up and beautiful. I knew you would be, from the moment you were born. How could you not be, with a mother like yours? Where is she? Where's my Anna?"

A lump swelled in Dantzel's throat as her father looked around, as if expecting to see his wife sprout up out of the weeds. "The Guards took her, Papa," Dantzel said, the name shaping strangely in her mouth. "She's been a slave in the castle for two years. Haven't you seen her there?"

Some of the light faded from Jocham's face. "I haven't been in the castle for six years," he said bleakly, staring into the distance over Dantzel's shoulder. "I was one of the first to be shipped to the island. It was only a few days ago that I managed to escape, and I stumbled across this band only a few hours before you did."

"You escaped the island?" Dantzel asked, her breath catching. Was it possible? "How? Did . . . did anyone else make it off the island with you?"

Jocham leaned forward, his voice dropping to a conspiratorial whisper. "You'll never believe it, Dantzel. Have you heard the rumors flying, that the son of Rilotorian survived, that he's returned to take the throne from his uncle?"

"Yes, of course," Dantzel said, a laugh bubbling up inside of her as hope sprang into her chest.

"I've met him. He was on the island with me. He's the only reason I'm alive, and it was his courage that freed us both."

Tears sprang into Dantzel's eyes, and Dantzel had to bury her face in her father's shoulder as she fought to control both sobs and laughter. When she had reined in her emotions enough to speak, she pulled back and took Jocham's rough hands, squeezing all her excitement into them. "I knew it! I knew those foul islanders couldn't keep him there. Was he badly hurt? Where is he, Papa?"

"I—I'm afraid I don't know," Jocham said, his eyes

flickering to the ground and back to her face. "We were separated as soon as we reached the peninsula."

"But he's back," Dantzel said firmly, refusing to let go of the bubble of joy she had needed so badly. "And you're back! Leave it to Rustav to find my father out of all the prisoners on the island and bring him home. How did you escape?"

Jocham pulled his hands out of hers and rubbed them together, his eyes suddenly anxious. With a prickle of fear cutting through her elation, Dantzel asked, "He is all right, isn't he, Papa? The Guards didn't take him, did they?"

"No, no. Last I saw of him, he was getting away free and clear. I'm just surprised, I suppose. You talk like you know him."

"Oh," Dantzel said, waving a hand dismissively even as she fought the blush rising in her cheeks. "He lived in the village for a few months, back before he knew who he was. You know Mother. She took him in like a little lost duckling, and so we spent some time together. Well—quite a bit of time, actually." She didn't even try to explain their time together in the forest; where would she begin?

"Well," Jocham said, his head rearing back slightly. "You know him quite well, then?" Dantzel shrugged and nodded, and Jocham proceeded haltingly. "Then you know . . . that is, he would have told you of his . . . well, his unique . . ."

Dantzel drew her eyebrows together, trying to parse what Jocham was asking. Taking her best guess, she asked, "You mean that he's half tuath?"

Jocham stopped wringing his hands abruptly. "He's half what?"

Thankfully, Cabel chose that moment to come jogging up the hill toward them, taking up a protective stance at Dantzel's side. "Who's this?" he asked, eyeing Jocham suspiciously.

"Relax, soldier," Dantzel said with a grin. "This is my father. He escaped from the island just a few days ago. Guess who helped him?"

Cabel's eyes lit up. "Rustav? Where is he?"

"They were separated, but he can't be far," Dantzel said. A cloud crossed over Cabel's brow.

"You don't think Ayre could have . . ."

"I don't think Ayre would have gotten so angry if he weren't afraid we were right," Dantzel said firmly. "Rustav is here, and we're going to find him before Ayre raises any more trouble."

"Who is Ayre?" Jocham asked. "And who are you?"

Dantzel exchanged a glance with Cabel, and then decided to tackle the least confusing introduction first. "Papa, this is Cabel," she said. "Bryson's son."

"No," Jocham breathed, grabbing Cabel's hand and pumping it vigorously. "It's an honor to meet you, lad. You were still a month from life when I was taken. If you're anything like your father, I'd believe you were a fit young man to be looking after my daughter. Are you . . . ?" He looked from Cabel to Dantzel questioningly. Immediately, both Cabel and Dantzel shook their heads.

"Not me, sir," Cabel said with a mischievous grin. "But you'd be amazed to know how often your garden back home was weeded by royalty a few summers back."

"Cabel, stop it," Dantzel said, hoping her face wasn't burning as brightly as it felt. "That was a long time ago, before all of this happened."

"Right," Cabel said with mock seriousness. "Before he

saved you from the tuatha. Before he broke into the castle for your mother. Before he helped your father escape from the island."

"I thought you were supposed to be talking with Skandar."

"I did," Cabel said, drawing himself up importantly. "They're by far the best-prepared group we've come across. Skandar has been leading raids on the troops of Guards and on several of the king's merchants. They know how to maximize disruption and minimize danger of being caught. In fact, they're planning a raid tomorrow on a shipment of weapons headed to the Guards in the castle. Skandar says they could use a couple of experienced fighters if we have the time to spare."

Dantzel laughed, trying to ignore her father's wide-eyed stare. "Nice of him to include us, but that's not what we're here for. We're heading out in the morning."

To her surprise, Cabel deflated visibly. "What do you mean, that's not what we're here for? Aren't we doing everything we can to fight Elanokiev?"

"Well, yes," Dantzel said, watching Cabel curiously. "But we're already doing that. Skandar said it. We're the organizers, the ones getting everyone to pull together."

"Yeah, but this is our chance to do something more," Cabel said, looking down at his feet. "We don't have to just talk. We can fight."

"What happened to all your disapproval of highwaymen and robbers?" Dantzel asked lightly, hoping to tease him out of his sudden earnestness.

Cabel just shook his head. "Forget I said anything. I'll go tell Skandar we're leaving in the morning."

As he slouched back down the hill, Dantzel was tempted

to call after him, to find out what had suddenly possessed him to go rushing headlong into a fight. But it was surely just a passing impulse, she thought. Cabel was happy to be doing what they were doing. Right?

"If we're going to leave early tomorrow, we should gather some supplies," Jocham suggested. Dantzel turned, her worries swept aside by Jocham's words.

"You'll come with us?" she asked, and Jocham smiled.

"You didn't think you could just leave me behind, did you? Besides," he said with a wink, "I want to see my warrior daughter in action."

THE SUN WAS LONG GONE BY THE TIME DANTZEL laid out her bedroll, privately wondering how she was going to sleep at all surrounded by garish tents on all sides. But as she lay there, staring up at the stars and listening to her father's light breathing, she realized that her surroundings were the least of her obstacles to sleep. She had been burning all night to know more of Rustav, how he had fared on the island, how they had escaped, but Jocham had steadfastly avoided the topic, steering conversation either to their preparations or to their home in Gebir. Dantzel feared to imagine what it was he didn't want to tell her.

Although she told herself it was absurd, his refusal to tell her all he knew rankled. Couldn't he see what she had become? Why wouldn't he trust her? Childish as it was, Dantzel refrained from explaining to her father about Ayre and the tuatha partially in retaliation. If he didn't think she was mature enough to hear the truth, she wasn't going to risk him thinking she was taken in by old fairy tales.

And then there was Cabel. Dantzel hadn't seen the boy since he had stormed off back to camp. A few of the camp women had assured her that he was with Skandar and the scouts, but that did nothing to ease her anxiety. What if he had been serious about wanting to stay and fight with Skandar? Surely he wasn't so eager to risk putting his short life to an end.

A faint rustling alerted her to someone's approach. Dantzel quickly closed her eyes most of the way, peering through the smallest crack in the lids to see who was coming. She repressed a sigh of relief when she saw Cabel walking through the tents toward them. For a moment, Dantzel considered sitting up to ask what he had discussed with Skandar for so long, but he eyed them so furtively that she remained still, feigning sleep in hopes of discovering what had him slinking toward them like a coyote sneaking up on a chicken. No such luck. He burrowed under his blankets and was motionless, though his body was so tense that Dantzel doubted he was any more asleep than she was.

Dantzel couldn't say how long her mind spun exhaustively into the night before she fell asleep, but as the first rays of dawn turned the black sky golden, her eyes flew open, her muscles already bunched to spring out of bed. Unable to lie there any longer, she rolled her blankets together and checked on the food they had received the night before. In her preparations, she tried to make enough noise to rouse Cabel and Jocham without waking the wanderers sleeping all around them. Jocham stirred almost immediately, but Dantzel finally had to nudge Cabel with her foot.

"Already?" Cabel groaned sleepily, pulling the blanket over his head. "Can't we wait until after breakfast?"

"We'll have it on the road. Up, already!"

"You are an early riser, aren't you?" Skandar said, appearing from behind a nearby tent.

Dantzel clenched her jaw. She wished he would stop doing that, popping out of thin air to startle them at every turn. "We wanted to get an early start. The prince is nearby, and we're eager to report what we've accomplished."

"Of course," Skandar said. "I wish you every success. Pray tell the prince when you find him that Skandar and his clan are ready and waiting for his orders."

"I will," Dantzel said, relieved that he hadn't pressed them to stay. "Thank you for all you've done. He'll be grateful to have such loyal and capable men and women at his back." She turned back to find Cabel still sitting on his bedroll with his knees pulled up to his chest. "Cabel, come on! We're waiting on you."

Cabel tucked his chin into his knees. "I'm not going."

Both Dantzel and Jocham halted; Skandar faded away without a word, leaving them alone. Fear clutched at Dantzel's throat. Was this what Rustav had felt when she had refused to leave the forest? Dantzel shook her head, shaking away the chill of terror. These weren't tuatha. Nobody was forgetting anything. Cabel had proved himself both sensible and capable in the past three weeks. He had to have a reason. Swallowing the urge to drag him up by the ear, Dantzel said with as much calmness as she could muster, "Why not?"

"I talked with Skandar last night," Cabel said, talking very fast. "He says the train of Guards and weapons will pass by here early this afternoon. One of his men was hurt in the last raid, and they could use another man to fill in for him." He looked up, finally meeting Dantzel's eye with a plea for understanding. "We set out to fight Elanokiev, didn't we? And this is our first chance to do something more than just talk. They want me to stay and help. They don't care that I'm young. All they care about is that I can fight. And I can fight," he added defiantly. "Not even Rustav believed that."

The words stung, inflaming Dantzel's misgivings. Skandar and Rustav were supposed to be on the same side. Why did it seem that Cabel was choosing Skandar over Rustav? Dantzel didn't know how to respond, and so her words came out sounding flimsy in her own ears. "Rustav never said you couldn't fight. He only ever wanted to keep you safe."

"I can keep myself safe," Cabel muttered, glaring at a tent stake near his feet. Before Dantzel could protest further, a hand rested on her arm.

"Let the boy fight," said Jocham, his voice gravelly and his face somber. "His heart is in it."

Dantzel nearly responded that she didn't care where his heart was, only that it wasn't in danger of being run through with a sword, but she caught herself before the words escaped her. Wasn't she the one who had pulled him into all of this in the first place? She knew the pull of a good cause strongly believed in. Who was she to tell Cabel how and where his efforts were best spent?

Letting out a slow breath, Dantzel nodded. "I know you can take care of yourself. Just don't get hurt, okay?"

In an instant, the heavy scowl lifted from Cabel's face, and Cabel looked up with relief in his eyes. "I won't," he promised, eagerness replacing his indignation. "It's the Guards who'd better watch out."

Biting her lip, Dantzel threw her arms around Cabel and squeezed the breath out of him. One more person she loved being torn out of her life. *But just for a while*, she thought, releasing Cabel and swallowing hard against the lump in her throat.

"I didn't mean that about Rustav," Cabel said, ducking his head. "You know that. I'm on his side to the end, and this is all for him. I'll come find you both as soon as I'm done here. Try to keep him from disappearing again before I get there, okay?"

Dantzel laughed, her heart lightening ever so slightly. "I'll do my best."

Cabel turned to Jocham, who had stood quietly to the side after his intervention. "It was an honor to meet you, sir," Cabel said. "I wouldn't leave her if I didn't know you were here to watch out for her."

"The way she totes around that bow, I get the feeling she's the one who will be looking after me," Jocham said, smiling fondly at his daughter. "Go on, son. Fight your war and come back safe."

Chapter Twenty-Two

Words floated around Rustav's head, buoyed up on the heavy fog that was surrounding him. The voices were urgent, but so far away that they hardly brushed his consciousness.

"You can't move him like this. If he starts bleeding again—"

"The Guards won't care if he's bleeding or not. Can't you stitch him up in the hold?"

"With what light? I'll do more damage than good! He wouldn't survive that sort of crack surgery!"

Were they talking about him? Rustav tried to tell whoever it was that he didn't need surgery, but his mouth wouldn't open wide enough to let the words out. The voices fell silent for a moment, but then resumed with more intensity. "Take him under and keep him quiet. You'll just have to do what you can."

A cup pressed against Rustav's lips. The taste of warm, bitter liquid made Rustav grimace and turn his head away, but someone held him in place, holding his nose and pouring the rest of the liquid in. Spitting it out would take too much energy. Reluctantly, Rustav swallowed and drifted back into a heavy sleep.

Though Rustav knew perfectly well that he was on a ship, he felt no surprise upon finding himself deep in an unfamiliar forest. It was similar, in some respects, to the old forest on the mountain, but light streamed through the branches, illuminating the forest floor in a golden glow that was nothing like the oppressive darkness of the old forest. He walked through the trees, reaching out to brush his fingers along the strangely smooth bark. Melancholy still pressed against his chest, but the light surrounding him penetrated deep, pulling the pain out of his wounds and his heart.

How long he wandered through the trees, he was never certain; but after some time, a voice, rich and vibrant, washed over him like a wave of heat.

"Marustavian."

Rustav paused, then turned slowly. A tall man stood just behind him, with golden hair reflecting the glowing light and eyes that were the brightest blue Rustav had ever seen. His robes, though simple, were a deep royal purple. As the man smiled, Rustav's throat closed, cutting off his breath. Rustav had to try several times before he could get his mouth around the unfamiliar word.

"Father?"

"My son," the man said, opening his arms. Rustav collapsed into the man's embrace, filled simultaneously with the greatest joy and the greatest grief he had ever felt.

"I'm sorry, Father," Rustav choked, burying his face in his father's shoulder like a child.

Taking hold of Rustav's shoulders, Rilotorian held his son out to see his face clearly. Rustav bowed his head, unable to look his father in the eye as he asked, "For what?"

"I'm a failure. I'm nothing more than a scoundrel off the streets of Markuum. Everyone expects me to be some legendary king come to save the country, but I'm not. I'm just a boy with a piece of wood."

Rilotorian tilted Rustav's chin upward until the boy was looking into his father's eyes. "You are no more *just* a boy than this is *just* a piece of wood. You are the first child of the Union in centuries to understand what that means. You have reestablished a bond with the tuatha. You have escaped Burrihim and know the true nature of the islanders. You have lived among the people and know their sorrows. And you are my son." Rilotorian held up the Crest that hung around Rustav's neck. "This was once no more than a piece of fine wood. But it has since been shaped for a very specific purpose. As have you, my son."

The words brought a flicker of hope into Rustav's heart, but it wasn't yet enough to dispel the gloom completely. Rustav spoke his next words in a rush, pushing them out as fast as possible in order to minimize the pain of speaking them. "But how can I dare claim I'd be a better leader than the islanders when I've proved that I'm as bad as they are?"

Forehead furrowing, his father said, "Why would you think so little of yourself?"

Rustav bowed his head once more in shame. "On the island, I did something awful. I—I changed. I turned into a monster. Ayre told me that doing that was enough for the tuatha to disown me."

A stormy gray hue entered Rilotorian's eyes. "You saved a

man's life and returned to the peninsula to fulfill your duties. If tuathan traditions call that evil, then perhaps you should look elsewhere for allies."

"Who?" Rustav asked, unable to keep the frustration from his voice. "The mainlanders? If they managed to get over the demons, they'd just as soon make us a colony."

"The tuatha are not the only creatures of legend you have encountered," Rilotorian replied, his voice beginning to echo strangely. "Though you were only a child, the link of friendship may be strong enough for a beginning."

"What? I don't—I never—what do you mean?" With a strange twist in his stomach, Rustav asked, "Have you been watching me?"

"Of course. Did you think your mother and I could bear to leave you alone after we had gone? As painful as it has been to see you suffer, we have looked on proudly as you have risen above your circumstances."

"How come I've never seen you before? And why can't I see Mother now?" Rustav asked, looking around hopefully as if she might melt out of the trees. Rilotorian shook his head, his face beginning to blur as the light among the trees faded.

"The mysteries of death are beyond even the dead. But we are always with you, my son, and always will be. Go forward with our love in your heart."

Rustav blinked, finding himself in a very different place as his eyes adjusted to the darkness. The air was close and cramped, and the world around him swayed ceaselessly. A human shape hovered over him, and Rustav forced his mouth to move, finding it much harder than it had been only seconds ago. "Father?"

"Hush," said the figure, placing a cold hand on Rustav's

mouth. "Most of the Guards have left, but there are a few still on board. Captain Hayden will let us out when they are well on their way."

Slowly, Rustav remembered—standing on the docks, the Guards in the crowd, an old seadog approaching him. Rustav could only vaguely remember anything that had happened on the ship, most of it lost in a haze of pain. He felt after the gash in his side. It had been freshly bandaged, along with several other wounds, and Rustav already felt stronger. Still, he was glad of the opportunity to lie still and ponder what he had dreamed.

Was there any meaning in it, or was it just the effect of blood loss mixed with the herbs that had been forced on him? It had been so clear, so detailed, and so full of hope that Rustav was reluctant to dismiss it. Even now, in the dark confines of the hold, he could almost feel the rays of sunlight, his father's hands on his shoulders.

But the claim that Rustav had met other mythical creatures as a child—that had to be nothing more than wishful thinking, a desperate search for something to fall back on. Rustav had met plenty of strange people on the docks, but they had all been very much human.

And as for friendship—that was as far of a stretch as the mythical creatures. Ollie, or Bartholomew, was the closest thing to a friend Rustav had ever experienced in Markuum, and he was as human as the rest. Rustav couldn't recall even imagining desert sprites or any other sort of legendary being on his travels with Karstafel. Just the demons.

What were the possibilities? The trees, perhaps, but Rustav had no contact with them as a child. Ayre had mentioned kobolds in passing, and Rustav recalled reading about them here and there in the tuathan library, but he would remember meeting a kobold. The gray skin and glowing eyes would give it away. Besides, according to the tales, they hardly ever ventured into direct sunlight. The only way to run into one would be to sit right on top of one of the entrances to their tunnels.

Rustav bolted upright, hardly noticing the pain in his side. In an instant, his companion was beside him, pushing at his shoulders; but Rustav refused to lie back down, possessed by a ridiculous idea, an impossible idea. "I'm fine," he whispered sharply, trying to brush the man away.

"You are not fine! Lie down this instant before you tear through all of my blindly sewn stitches and bleed to death! I will not be responsible for the death of the king!"

"I'm not king yet," Rustav grumbled, only half-paying attention to the doctor. He stared hard into the darkness, probing and stretching his memory as far as it would go. Those early days, when he had first discovered his cave in the cliffs—had there really been someone there, or had it been a child's imagination? It was a gamble—he had only been four years old, and it had only been a few days. Did he really dare rest the fate of the country on such fuzzy memories?

Light spilled into the hold, impossibly bright after the long darkness. Rustav squinted upward, and the doctor took advantage of his distraction to force him back down.

"Glad to see you two are getting along down there," came Hayden's gruff voice. The doctor straightened, hands on his hips.

"Would you get us out of here so I can give him proper medical attention? I can hardly believe he's alive, much less awake, after what he's been through."

"I'm fine," Rustav repeated, ignoring the pain and dizziness that was far less important than what he had realized. He tried to sit up again, but the doctor had a firm hold on him now.

"Sit back and relax, Your Majesty," Hayden said with a deep chuckle. "Doctor Mortimer here won't let you up until he's satisfied. Hold tight and we'll lift you out."

Two ropes dropped into the hold, and Mortimer tied them securely to either end of the makeshift bed Rustav was lying on. Hayden took one rope, a burly sailor the other, and they hauled Rustav upward. As soon as he was out of the doctor's reach, Rustav sat up again.

"Take it easy, sire," Hayden said as they guided the bed out to rest on the floor. "You were in pretty hard shape. We wouldn't have stuck you down there, but the Guards were about to board us. Someone back at port claimed to have seen you coming aboard, and they searched the ship for hours."

Mortimer hoisted himself out of the hole, striding over to Rustav with a stern expression. "It's a miracle that hold didn't turn into your tomb," he said brusquely, pushing Rustav back down. "Let me see what damage I did trying to fix you up in the dark."

"Does your crew know I'm here?" Rustav asked, his eyes flicking warily to the sailor who had helped pull him up.

"If they don't yet, they soon will," Hayden said, watching closely as Mortimer unwrapped the bandages. "You ever tried keeping a secret on the open sea? Everything floats to the top sooner or later. I don't know what you were worried about, Mortimer. Those look a good deal neater than the last time you had to stitch me up."

"He was at least holding still," Mortimer grumbled, eyeing his work with restrained satisfaction.

"Can your men be trusted?" Rustav asked. Hayden snorted.

"If they couldn't, I'd've been strung up ten years ago. I'm afraid you've fallen among pirates, milord. We've attacked too many of the king's vessels to count."

Rustav raised an eyebrow. "Then why did the Guards bother searching for me? Why didn't they just arrest you and take the ship?"

"Well, we don't look like this when we're pirating, do we? We've gotten good at dressing up the ship and ourselves for our raids. To the Guards, we're nothing more than an honest merchant vessel off to the mainland for trade."

For an instant, Rustav was caught on the mention of the mainland. They would take him there if he asked, he was sure of it. He could make up any number of reasons why he needed to go there.

If he disappeared to the mainland, would Courei be able to rid itself of the island plague and defend itself from the tuatha? Possibly. There would be others who might step up to lead the country to victory.

But if it didn't—if Courei fell—would Rustav spend the rest of his life wondering if he could have made a difference? Would he forever be haunted by the people he had left to be slaughtered by the islanders?

Voices filled Rustav's mind, voices of Dantzel and Cabel and Jocham and Anton, of the island slaves and the castle slaves. *I don't want the islanders to get me. . . . Your place is here, defending your people. . . . We have hope for better days. . . . If we can free you, it will make all the sweat and suffering worth it. . . . If we can't believe in you, what's left to believe in?*

Rustav had done nothing to deserve the hope and trust that so many people had already placed in him. But that didn't mean he couldn't start working for it.

"We can't go to the mainland," Rustav said, clamping down on the last traces of his desire to run. Hayden nodded.

"We'll take you wherever you need to go, Your Majesty. Where are we headed?"

The words stuck in Rustav's throat for a moment, reluctance holding them back. But in the end, certainty won out, certainty that it was the only way to salvage a war effort he had already sabotaged with his foolish mistakes.

"Take me to Markuum."

Acknowledgments

There are so many people who helped this story leave my head and land on the pages of a real-life, published book, and I can't express enough gratitude for the support they have all shown me.

The team at Cedar Fort turned my dream into reality. Many, many thanks to Alissa Voss, who saw something of worth in my manuscript and used her editorial wisdom to make it even stronger; to Melissa Caldwell, who worked her magic in the finishing touches of the book; to Kelly Martinez, who answered questions, encouraged, and guided me through the world of marketing; and to Kristen Reeves, who created a spectacular cover.

And of course there are my fellow Norns, Carin and Kessia, who read draft after draft and always found something to praise. *Demon's Heart* would never have gotten where it is now without the Fates reminding me to slow down and describe things.

Every teacher I've had has touched my life, but two in

particular deserve mention for this book. Ron Woods clued me in to some important aspects of character motivation, among other things, and has gone far beyond his duty in offering advice and feedback long after my freshman days in his creative writing class. And Janet Aurre—I don't think you knew the fire you lit with the "Joby's Journal" assignment back in eighth grade. It was your class that cemented my need to become an author.

My family has always been supportive, even when I was far too insecure to let them read anything I wrote. I owe a lot of gratitude to my parents, my brothers, and my sisters (in-laws included) for their enthusiasm and for keeping me from taking myself too seriously. Thanks in particular to Peter for drawing a map without Charizard on it.

Most of all, I am grateful to my husband, Nathan, for his patience with my plot overhauls, with my demands to read a fourteenth version of the first chapter, with the days when the real world took a backseat to a bolt of inspiration. I'm even grateful for the days he goes all Freudian in interpreting my stories.

And finally, I'm grateful for my sweet little Rose, who constantly inspires me by soaring beyond expectations with a grin and a giggle.

Glossary

Book of the Trees: a written history of unknown origin, allegedly written by the trees.

Burrihim: the island off the tip of the peninsula. The castle ruins on the island are said to be inhabited by demons.

Courei: Rustav's home country. A small, peninsular country whose main economy revolves around sea trade and artisanship.

Eldest: the oldest of the tuatha, and the leader of the tuathan Council.

Fleyder: the bestial form of the tuatha.

Gebir: a village in the foothills of Courei; Dantzel's home.

Kobolds: mythical creatures said to live in tunnels beneath the ground.

Markuum: a port city on the western tip of the Courei peninsula.

Tuatha (tuatha suthain): mythical creatures with long lives and a love of woodworking.

Union: the marriage of a human king and tuathan Council member. All heirs to the Union are half human, half tuath.

Union Crest: a tuathan design meant to be worn by the heirs of the Union and to signify their relation to the tuatha.

DISCUSSION QUESTIONS

1. Dantzel and Rustav distrust each other at first. Why? How do they overcome their distrust?

2. Why does Rustav choose to stay in Gebir the day of the wedding celebration? How has his motivation to stay changed from when he first arrived?

3. After Rustav rescues Dantzel from the forest, he wonders if she would have been happier if he had left her there. What do you think?

4. Why doesn't Rustav want the slaves on the island to help him escape? What changes his mind?

5. Although those who know Rustav accept him as a prince, he is unable to do so himself. Why does he doubt himself? Is he right?

About the Author

Emily H. Bates grew up in Northern California, where she spent much of her young life happily closeted away with a book. She graduated from Brigham Young University with a degree in German linguistics, married a dashing young man from her study abroad in Germany, and now writes novels in English. She currently resides in Washington with her husband and her very busy daughter.